ꓺutch Black &

The Prairie Monster

by Calvin Niblack

Prologue

My name is Butch Black. I grew up in Kansas, Rock County, Kansas to be exact. Yeah I know, being from Kansas I've heard every Oz joke there is, and trust me on this one, there isn't any yellow brick road that leads to the Emerald City either. Unless you consider the color of a dirt road yellow; I've always considered it as brown, but to each his own. Although, come to think of it, we do have a few scarecrow's here and there.

I was raised in a three bedroom ranch style house on a corner where two dirt roads intersect. Growing up in Rock County, we were known as simple country folk back then, and we were proud of that fact. As a young boy we referred to the kids that grew up in town as townies. People that lived in the big city, well they were just city folk.

There were eight of us kids when I was growing up, as well as my mother, and my father. I have five sisters and two brothers. Being the oldest, my two brothers are ten and twelve years older then I am. With my brothers being that much older than me, we didn't spend very much time together when I was growing up. When I was eight, my oldest brother Leon was twenty, married, and had a child of his own. My other brother Roger was eighteen, and had been drafted into the army. He was part of the Big Red One at Fort Riley, Kansas.

As the youngest boy in our family, I spent most of my time with my best friend Berry. Although my sisters were the best sisters a boy growing up in the world could ever have, they were still just girls to a young boy growing up.

Berry and I were born on the same day, just about two hours apart from each other, in the same small hospital. We went to the same school together, rode the same school bus, and played on the same ball teams together. Berry, his brothers, and sister lived with his parents in a farm house about a mile down the dirt road from our house.

They were neighbors and like everyone else around us they would do anything, and everything they could to help out when someone was in trouble. That's just the way it is growing up in the country, neighbors helping neighbors.

When living out in the country if you drive by someone you don't know on the dirt road you would always stop and ask what they're doing, who are they looking for, or what brings them out to the country. Everybody would watch out for everybody else. That's just the way it is out on country roads in Kansas.

If you drive by someone you knew you would always smile and wave or just raise up a hand to acknowledge you saw them.
Under no circumstances did you ever address a grown up other than Mr. or Mrs.

3

The Sheriff of Rock County, Kansas, is from Chicago, Illinois. That's a long way from the plains of Kansas, but Sheriff Peter Wells is good at what he does. He's not a big man standing only about 5'6", and with a slender build he doesn't look very intimidating, but looks are deceiving. What Sheriff Wells lacks in physical appearance he more than makes up for in his intelligence. I don't know what his IQ is but it has to be up there pretty high.

Pete likes to wear a ball cap from his hometown when he's relaxing. I don't say much about that Chicago Blackhawks ball cap that he wears every now and then. To be honest I don't know what to make of it or what sport it represents.

Besides that, Pete's easy to poke fun at, so it's real entertaining to have him around.

Deputy Frank Wallace, on the other hand, causes more problems for the sheriff then he fixes. He isn't the smartest person in the world, but Deputy Wallace tries hard; it's just that his comb is missing a few teeth; I mean that if he were a computer keyboard he would have two space bars, if you get my drift.

Deputy Frank Wallace is just one of many deputies that work for Sheriff Wells. You can't blame Pete for Deputy Wallace. Frank was a deputy when Pete was made Sheriff. I have known Frank all of my life. He is the same age as Berry and I, and he went to the same school as Berry and I did.

Deputy Wallace has had family in these parts for many generations. His ancestors were some of the first settlers to come to Rock County, Kansas. I know that if I ever needed Frank's help on anything he would be there. He might be late, but Frank would be there.

Then there's Mr. Shawn Murphy. He is an old cattle rancher that has been farming and ranching around here all of his life. Mr. Murphy has lost more cattle to the *Prairie Monster* than anyone else. He has seen a lot in his life, but the one thing he hasn't seen is whatever is killing off his cattle.

Mr. Murphy is in his eighties now and is as active as he was when he was in his fifties. Standing about 6'2", and without an ounce of fat on him Mr. Murphy is still an imposing figure of a man even with his grey hair and clean shaven face. I hope I can do the things that he does when I get to be in my eighties.

I'm about to tell you the most amazing story. It's about how some fairytales are real. Believe it, or don't believe it, it's up to you, but it will make you think twice about going camping on the great plains of Kansas.

When I was a young boy I had been told every bedtime story and fairytale there was to be told. I was even told the story about Cinderella, but with a twist. It was a young boy instead of a girl and it was called Cinderfella.

5

Instead of a glass slipper it was a cowboy hat that was left behind at the cattleman's ball.

I suppose that was the way they did things back when I was a kid. Take a popular bedtime story and put a country twist to it.

I am now forty-seven years old with thinning hair, and a thickening waist. My black hair has started turning grey, and I need reading glasses for my brown eyes to be able to read small print. I'm married, and have nine kids of my own. Two of them are grown and married themselves. Three of them are attending collage, and four of my kids still live at home and go to the local school in town. It's a bit of a bus ride to school everyday, but the kids don't mind. Some things never change.

I have the best job in the world. I'm a fish and game officer for the great State of Kansas. My office is in the county courthouse right across from the sheriff's office. I see a great deal of the sheriffs' department's inner workings, and I share information with Sheriff Wells on a daily bases.

Right now I have a big problem. Actually its a rather huge problem. I have something or someone killing cattle, and it's bringing back old memories. Memories of what happened back in the summer of 1971.

I was only twelve years old when I first realized that not all fairytales were made up. That was when I almost lost my life to what most people around here call the *Prairie Monster*. Little did I know at that time, my life was going to change forever. I was never the same after that summer in 1971.

These cattle mutilation's that are starting to happen again have brought those memories of my past flooding back. Memories of when I witnessed the vicious attack and murder of my best friend Berry Decker. That's when I started believing in the *Prairie Monster*.

What? You say you're not from Kansas, and you have never heard of the *Prairie Monster*.

Well you better start believing in fairytales because this one's real. If you're not careful you just might find out how real it is.

Berry and I didn't believe all those stories we heard either. They were just stories that people around here had told over and over again. Generation after generation the stories about the *Prairie Monster* have been told.

When I was standing over Berry's grave I made a promise to him, and to myself. I swore that I would find out what attacked us, and I would see that the beast pay's for what he did to Berry. I plan to keep that promise, and I will do whatever it takes to find Berry's killer, even if I have to spend the rest of my life doing so.

It didn't take me long before I found out that I would have to do it by myself. Berry's family moved away shortly after Berry's death. I always thought it strange that Berry's parents just packed up and moved away right after Berry's funeral.

I never could figure out what possessed them to run like that. They were good people, and they deserved better then what they got while living in Rock County.

Shortly after they moved, the Decker's old house burned to the ground. Nobody ever found out how the fire started. I'm not even sure anybody investigated the fire. Everybody just acted like nothing happened.

Everybody around Rock County thought that the fire was started by Mr. Decker, but why? They weren't living there anymore. Why would he burn down his old house?

I never did see Berry's family again, but I did hear about six years later that Berry's father had passed away of alcoholism. The night I heard about Mr. Decker's death I said a prayer for him, and asked him to say hi to Berry for me.

If you ever find yourself out camping on the plains of Kansas, enjoy yourself, have fun, but be aware when the sun goes down.

Beware of the two glowing red eyes that are bright. Beware of the *Prairie Monster* that lives in the night.

Chapter 1

It's back.

It was an early Tuesday morning in mid-March; my wife Vickie was in the shower. Our four youngest kids Kevin, RaeLynn, Cheyenne, and Cody were getting ready to walk down to the school bus stop at the end of our driveway. As they were putting on jackets, all four of them hit me up for money to buy snacks at school.

My kids know that I'm a sucker for loose change. After digging into my pocket and coming up with enough change for everyone I sent them on their way. Wishing them a good day at school I told them that they didn't have time to play; the school bus would be here shortly.

It was five minutes after 7:00am, and the school bus picks up at fifteen after. Our driveway is about two hundred yards long so the kids had a long walk to get to the bus stop. I stood at the front window and watched until they boarded the school bus.

Now it was my time to sit back and read the newspaper before I head off to work. Just then the telephone rang out. As I walked over to pick the phone up and answer it, I looked at the caller I.D. and noticed that it was from the Murphy farm.

"Hello"

"Butch is that you?" Mr. Murphy inquired.

"Yes sir, Mr. Murphy it is. What can I do for you?" I have to admit I was more than curious why I was receiving a telephone call so early in the morning from Mr. Murphy.

"You need to get over here. It's back. I found one of my cows dead in the back pasture this morning."

Knowing very well what Mr. Murphy meant by "its back", I paused for a moment.

"Are you sure sir?" Not that I doubted his word, but this was important to me, very important to me.

"Yes I'm sure! You're the fish and game officer around here, do you want to take a look at this dead cow or not?" Mr. Murphy responded with anger in his voice, slightly insulted that I questioned him.

With some hesitation and a little bit of nervousness I told Mr. Murphy that I'd be right over.

"I'll be there in about fifteen or twenty minutes Mr. Murphy, please be careful."

As I hung up the telephone, Vickie was just walking into the room in her bath robe still rubbing her hair with a towel.

"Who was that on the phone?" She asked as she wrapped her hair up in the towel.

"It was Mr. Murphy. He has a problem with one of his cows and wants me to come by to take a look at it." Not wanting to worry Vickie, I decided that it would be best not to tell her that the cow was dead.

"You look a little pale this morning. Are you feeling ok?" Vickie asked as she put her hand on my forehead to check for a fever. I nodded my head up and down as I told her that I was feeling just fine.

"I'm ok. I need to gather up my things and go by the Murphy farm, so I don't have time to sit and read the newspaper this morning."

Vickie walked back towards our bedroom and into the master bedroom's bathroom. I could hear her hair dryer come on. With the kids off to school, the house was quiet.

I walked over to the den and sat down at my desk for a moment to reflect on my thoughts from the past. Sitting in my office chair I looked around. We have two desks and two small tables with computers on them in our den.

Vickie had her desk with a notebook computer sitting on it where she did her work. She would volunteer for everything that came along, from Girl Scout leader to room mother at the kid's school.

The kids would do their homework at the tables sometimes arguing over who would use the computers first. With four kids still living at home and only two computers for them to do homework on; it sometimes gets to be a problem. Times sure have changed from the time when I was a kid. When I was growing up we had to go to the library to do homework papers. Now they just log on to a computer.

Then there's my desk. It's an old roll top desk where I keep my papers. Every drawer is locked along with the roll top. Not that I need to keep it locked. I wasn't trying to hide anything, it's just that I was formulating a plan to solve a mystery that was centuries old. I have some rather graphic pictures of dead animals that the kids didn't need to see.

I was after a demon from my past that has haunted me for over thirty years. After unlocking my desk and collecting my notebook and digital camera, I stopped and picked up an old 3X5 picture on my desk. It was the last picture taken of my friend Berry and me together just weeks before his death. After taking a long look at this picture of my friend Berry smiling with his hand on my shoulder, my mind began to wander.

I sat there thinking in my mind that I sure could use your help old buddy. I put the picture back in the desk and locked it back up.

It was time to get going. I went to the master bedroom closet where I kept my gun locked up in a handgun safe, and retrieved it. Making sure that it was loaded I holstered it and went to give Vickie a kiss goodbye.

She was still in the bathroom blow drying her hair. I could see her green eyes in the mirror looking at me. In a loud voice so she could hear me over her hair dryer I said my goodbye for the day.

"I'll see you tonight Sweet Pea." My little nickname for Vickie. We both leaned in towards each other and kissed.

"I Love you. You be careful out there today." Vickie said as she looked at me in the mirror.

"I will." I told her as I turned and walked away.

I grabbed my jacket, notebook, and digital camera then I headed out the back door to my truck.

Earlier in the morning there was frost on the windshield of the truck but the morning sun had already burned it off. After starting up the truck and driving down the driveway I stopped at the end of the driveway and watched a couple of deer running in the pasture across the dirt road from me.

I love this time of the year, this is what country living is all about. Birds are everywhere, deer running in pastures, wild turkeys, clean fresh air and no traffic noise.

It is so quite at night you can hear the train running and the tracks are over five miles away. You couldn't pay me to live in the city.

After turning right out of the driveway I headed towards the Murphy farm, it wasn't a very far drive, just a few miles.

As I drove down the unpaved dirt road all I could think about was that scar I've had for years. It is on my back up on my right shoulder blade. I will never forget how it got there. It's a grim reminder of my youth and of the friend that I had lost to a fairytale early one summer morning.

When I turned into Mr. Murphy's driveway and drove up to his house Mr. Murphy was waiting for me outside. He stood there on his porch steps with a cup of coffee in his hand and an old black cowboy hat on his head. I rolled down the window on my truck and hollered out to him.

"Here we go again Mr. Murphy, spring is still a couple of weeks away and we're already having animals come up dead again." I was a little surprised this usually didn't happen until late spring or during the summer months.

"Butch I'm not going to put up with this anymore, I'm tired of finding dead cows!!!" Mr. Murphy was very upset. He had lost a couple of cows last year and was in no mood to listen to any excuses.

Mr. Murphy put his coffee cup down on the porch rail, and begin to walk towards me as I sat in my truck.

"Mr. Murphy I will do everything I can to get to the bottom of this. This kind of thing has gone on far too many years now." I wasn't telling Mr. Murphy anything he didn't already know. I was trying to be more reassuring and understanding, hoping to calm him down a little.

"Butch, this has been going on long before you were even a twinkle in your daddy's eye!" That seems to be a popular saying with the elderly people around here; I hear it a lot.

"How many times do I have to tell you to stop calling me Mr. Murphy anyhow? You can call me by my first name, Shawn." I just can't bring myself to call Mr. Murphy, Shawn. I've known and respected this man all of my life and he deserves to be called Mr. Murphy.

"Yes sir, Mr. Murphy."

"If you'll please get into the truck we'll go take a look at your dead cow and try to come up with some answers together." I like to involve the resident that lost the animal as much as possible. It lets them know that I am trying to solve the problem, and it gets the community more involved.

"I'll walk over to the gate. I'm not that damn old." Mr. Murphy said with a frown as he started walking towards the gate that led to his back pasture.

15

I thought it best to just let it lie, don't say anything and drive up to the gate which was about twenty yards away. So I drove the short distance with my mouth shut.

As Mr. Murphy walked up to his gate he unhooked the small chain that was used to latch it with. As he was swinging the gate inwards, the morning sun caught it and I noticed the red tube gate still had a bit of morning frost on it. I hadn't realized how cool it still was outside. Too much on my mind I guess.

As I pulled the truck through the gate and into the pasture I watched Mr. Murphy in my rear view mirror close the gate behind us, and latch it back.
I could see where to go without needing to ask. Most farmers and ranchers use ATV's nowadays and they leave a very easy trail to follow. Mr. Murphy had obviously been out checking on his cattle this morning; the tracks he had made where fairly obvious, and would be easy to follow.

As Mr. Murphy climbed into the truck I asked him.
"So how many animals have you lost to this over the years?"
"I've lost too many to count. My father lost several head of cattle back when he was alive, and his father before him had lost several head. That's not counting the horse's my grandfather lost too."

"Butch why do you think it stopped for all those years and then one day a few years ago it started killing again?" Mr. Murphy asked as he rolled down the window about half way. Dressed in heavy coveralls I imagine that he's a little on the warm side sitting inside my truck.

"I don't know sir but I've been preparing for the chance to find out for over thirty years now."

"It doesn't help having those UFO idiots around either. Dropping cows from a flying saucer, that's ridiculous. It's not a secretive governmental project either." I told Mr. Murphy as I continued driving slowly through his pasture following the trail that his ATV had left.

"Butch you and I both know what it is and I think it's time that you confronted it." Mr. Murphy was blunt and to the point with his statement. He knew what I was thinking it was, and I knew what he thought it was.

"Yes sir I'm trying. I still have the scars from the last time I ran across him and that was over thirty years ago." I said to Mr. Murphy as I rubbed that scar with my left hand.

"Butch you know that when you get thrown from a horse you need to get right back on." Mr. Murphy is definitely old school. He reminds me a lot of my father the way he talks.

"Yes sir, but this wasn't any kind of horse I ever saw before; he was on two legs, and his hair was very thick." I tried to explain myself to Mr. Murphy without going into too much detail.

"How do you know it was a male?" Mr. Murphy had just asked me a question that was hard to explain. I really didn't have a legitimate answer for him.

"I just do Mr. Murphy, I just do. I also know that it's not an alien. Have you seen some of those reports that they have printed in the newspaper?"

"Now I don't pretend to know what it is exactly, but one thing I do know is that it's big and it's hairy, and it's very fast too."

"The hair is almost like straw. It has very thick strands of hair, very thick. Maybe that's why it never leaves any behind." I tried to explain a little to Mr. Murphy of what I knew for sure.

As we drove through the pasture, I could see the rest of Mr. Murphy's cattle off in the distance grazing.

When we pulled closer to the dead cow's carcass laying in the field the first thing I noted was that it was out in the open, nothing else around it. No trees, no bushes, no other cows, nothing. It was just like all the others I had come upon through the years.

There was a barbed wire fence about fifty feet from where the cow laid and there were trees on the other side of the fence.

The river ran just past the barbed wire fence. The same river I fished in as a boy. The same river where I stopped being a boy, and I began being a man.

That slow moving, deep river where I got that scar on my back, and I lost my best friend.

I came to a stop about twenty feet away from the carcass lying out in the short grass that hadn't grown very high during the winter months. We just sat there staring at it, neither one of us saying a thing.

As we both stepped out of the truck, I stood there and surveyed our surroundings. I was being cautious and very much aware of the danger that we might be in out here in this pasture.

I needed to keep in mind that there was something very dangerous out here and that there was more than my life to consider, there was Mr. Murphy's life too.

"Just like all the other ones I've ever seen. All the blood has been removed and some choice organs look to be missing." I said in a nervous but curious voice, not wanting to take my eyes off of it.

"Take a look Mr. Murphy. There are no signs of a struggle, any tire tracks or footprints anywhere on the ground around the cow's carcass."

"I don't know how it can be so precise without leaving any clues on how it is able to collect what it wants." I didn't know if I wanted reassurance or confirmation from Mr. Murphy. I'm still a bit overwhelmed every time I come up on one of these dead animals.

"Hey Butch, look around and listen."

"Why aren't there any birds around?" Mr. Murphy had made a good observation.

He was right. There should have been several birds flying around the area and there wasn't anything around us.

"I don't know. That's eerie, isn't it sir?" I was more then a little uneasy at this time. All I had with me for protection was my hand gun.

"You don't suppose he's watching us right now do you?" Mr. Murphy asked. I do believe that he was feeling a bit uneasy too. I can't blame him though we really didn't know what we where up against.

"I don't think so Mr. Murphy but to be honest I couldn't tell you. Something's wrong. I can feel it."

"Would you do me a favor Mr. Murphy?"

"Could you keep this one under your hat for a few days please?" I had asked Mr. Murphy to keep this between him and me for a while because I didn't want the media to get a hold of this.

"Sure Butch. I don't have any desire to turn my life into a circus."

"I'll tell you one thing though, I'm going to start carrying a rifle with me and I will shoot anything attacking my property." Mr. Murphy was to the point that he didn't care if he shot someone or something. He was tired of losing livestock, and he was going to put an end to it one way or another.

"Just please be careful Mr. Murphy. I don't want to find you out here someday." Now I'm concerned about the well being of Mr. Murphy. These old ranchers are kind of set in their ways, and they get a I'm invincible attitude.

After noting the time that I started [7:50am] in my journal and that there were no clear signs of a struggle, no clues of any kind that I could see left behind. I began to take a few photos with a digital camera.

"Mr. Murphy, every time I see one of these mutilated carcasses I can't help but think that there must be a reason for this to be happening."

"It will just start killing again and then stop without any regularity." I said to Mr. Murphy hoping that he might have a few ideas to offer. I don't pretend to be a scientist and at this point I will take any and all help I can get.

"Butch, you know what it is. Evil!!! Pure living, breathing evil."

"You're the only one to see it up close and live to tell about it." Mr. Murphy said with a very serious look about him.

"Yes sir but no one would believe me back then. I was only twelve years old and the authorities thought that I was in shock after seeing Berry killed."

"They said that Berry and I were attacked by a pack of wild dogs."

"I know better than that. I was there."

"Berry and I were not attacked by any pack of wild dogs. It was what my grandmother used to call the *Prairie Monster*." I explained to Mr. Murphy that I didn't believe the sheriff's report back then and I don't believe it now.

"I know it had to be hard on you Butch. If it's any comfort to you, I believe you."

"I watched you change from a boy to a man after Berry's death. You can't blame yourself for what happened to your friend."

"It's not your fault that Berry died and you lived. I think that God saved you for a reason. You're the one that's going to put an end to all of this." Mr. Murphy was being very understanding but I don't remember him stepping up when all this happened to Berry and I back when I was twelve.

"Thank you Mr. Murphy I do appreciate the support." I thanked Mr. Murphy for his thoughtful comments. He means well.

"I can see it in your eyes Butch; you have a determined look about you."

"I'm eighty-two years old now. When I was a young boy growing up, my great-grandfather would tell me stories about the *Prairie Monster*. His father told him stories about the *Prairie Monster*. So you see it's been around for a very long time." I had the feeling that Mr. Murphy didn't share that information with everyone.

"Yes sir, I've been doing research on this for several years now. If you will give me a few minutes to finish taking pictures and notes I will tell you what I have found out up to now." Of course I didn't have time to go into everything right now but I didn't mind sharing some of my information with Mr. Murphy.

"Butch I know this is very close to your heart, but keep in mind that you have a wife and kids who depend on you. Don't do anything stupid." Mr. Murphy was well aware of my intentions of hunting down and finding the creature that attacked Berry and I.

"Yes sir, I'm not going to be caught off guard again."
"When I go hunting for this thing Mr. Murphy, I plan to be a lot better armed than I was when I was twelve years old. I only had a fishing pole with me at the time when Berry and I were attacked thirty some years ago. We had just gone down to the river for some early morning fishing."

I walked over to the truck putting the digital camera on the hood of the truck and picking up my notebook again. As I began to write in my notebook Mr. Murphy told me that I had help if I wanted it.
"If you need anything Butch, anything at all, there are a lot of farmers around here that would do anything for you." Mr. Murphy wanted to make sure that I knew that I wasn't alone this time.

I continued to take notes in my notebook acknowledging what Mr. Murphy had said with a nod of my head. I didn't want to miss anything so I was writing down everything I could think of.

I wrote in my notebook what the area looked like, and about what the temperature was. It was about a forty-acre pasture and I could see about twenty to twenty-five more head of cattle off in the distance grazing.

There was a small pond with a windmill beside it in the far corner of the pasture.

With the exception of a few big rocks sticking up here and there, the pasture was pretty bare, no trees or bushes.

I laid my notebook down on the hood of my truck and picked my camera back up.

As I walked around the dead cow taking photos, I would also take a few photos of the surroundings. I've seen a lot of other photos of these incidences, but very few photos of their surroundings.

I walked back to the truck and retrieved a yard stick from behind the seat. I laid it across the open wounds on the cow's carcass and snapped a couple of shots.

When I thought I had enough photos taken, I then took a couple of Mr. Murphy. He just stood there like he was frozen in time.

"What was that for?" Referring to the pictures I took of him, Mr. Murphy asked. You would have thought that I had just stolen his soul the way he asked me about taking his picture.

"It's nothing Mr. Murphy I'm just trying to document everything."

"I'm going to walk over to your fence and have a look around." I explained to Mr. Murphy. I wanted to let him know what I was doing and where I was walking off to. I was trying to keep him involved in as much of the investigation as I possibly could.

As I came closer to the fence, I stopped and took a few pictures. It was an ordinary five strand barbed wire fence with posts made out of Hedge Apple tree branches spaced about every ten feet apart. Pretty standard for this part of Kansas.

No breaks in the wire and it doesn't look like it's been pushed down anywhere either.

With a good eye you can always tell when someone pushes down on a barbed wire fence to cross it. I walked all the way up to the fence to inspect the barbs on it. I was looking for any hair that might have gotten snagged on it. No such luck.

As I stood there looking past the fence and into the trees I had an overwhelming feeling that this was my time. I was going to solve this mystery and finally put my mind to rest about the death of my best friend Berry. I started walking back over to the truck where Mr. Murphy was standing.

"I'm about through here. Are you ready to go?" I asked a silent and stoned faced Mr. Murphy. I wonder if he was upset because I took his picture.

"I'm just a spectator here Butch you're the one in charge. We can go anytime you're ready." This was a much calmer, more subdued Mr. Murphy.

"Yes sir let me note the time again. [8:33am]." I also noted that there where no obvious clues to be found in the area.

As we climbed back into the truck I began to tell Mr. Murphy about the research that I've been doing for years. Documenting everything that I could lay my hands on about animal mutilations and where they happened.

"It seems that this kind of thing, these mutilations, have been going on long before the white man even came to Kansas Mr. Murphy."

"I have documentation of eyewitness accounts from Indian tribes in this region over one hundred fifty years ago."

"I have newspaper articles from a reporter that went in search of, what he was calling in his articles, Monster of the Prairie."

"He wrote several articles about something that was killing off buffalo and taking their blood without leaving a drop of it behind."

"He wrote about stories that tribal elders had conveyed to him. About how their people lived in fear when the evil spirits would come visit their tribe and the curse that was brought upon them."

"The elders would talk about how they would find dead deer in the woods with parts missing from the carcass and no blood to be found."

"The reporter even submitted a sketch of a horse that appeared to have been operated on with precise cuts and had several organs removed. He had noted that there was no blood to be found."

"His last report said that he was going to trap the monster and bring it back to display it. No one ever heard from him again." I told Mr. Murphy more than I should have. Although I trust Mr. Murphy I really don't want the information I just told him to get out.

"That's quite a story Butch It's along the same lines as all the other stories my great grandfather told me." Mr. Murphy knew more then I thought he knew about the *Prairie Monster*.

We sat there in the cab of the truck while I continued to tell Mr. Murphy about all the information I had gathered over the years.

I've been waiting for the right time to go looking for my chance to get even, and solve this mystery that has terrorized me for over thirty years.

"I have hundreds of pictures Mr. Murphy. Pictures of mostly cattle mutilations just like that one." I said to Mr. Murphy as I was pointing at the dead cow that was lying in his pasture.

"I have a lot of written statements from farmers just like you, and not a single eyewitness account of how it happened."

"All these years Mr. Murphy, all these years, and it seems that I am the only eyewitness to the *Prairie Monster*."

"Why me, I often asked myself. Why was I allowed to survive, and continue to live on?" I said to Mr. Murphy as he sat there in the cab of my truck staring at me.

"I told you why. You're the one that's going to solve this mystery. You've been given a great opportunity to right a wrong that has haunted you for years. Butch, everyone around here knows what happened to you and the Decker kid"

"We all knew that you were telling the truth back when you were attacked"
"It's very hard for people to come forward and speak up Butch, they're afraid of being labeled. They don't want to go around town, and have people talk behind their backs about them being the town idiot."

"You know how it is Butch, you've been there, and nobody wants to go through what you went through." Even though I understood Mr. Murphy, I didn't agree with him. Not this time anyway.

"I understand Mr. Murphy, and I don't blame anybody." It was more of a patronizing; I understand I said to Mr. Murphy as I started the truck up and turned the steering wheel while I began to back up ever so slowly and carefully.

"Mr. Murphy, what ever happened to the Decker family?" I asked thinking that he might know something that I haven't heard before. There were several rumors that had gone around after they moved. As a twelve year old all I could do was wonder.

"They let it run them off Butch. Plain and simple, they let it run them off." Mr. Murphy was referring to the *Prairie Monster*.

"I don't blame them after losing their son like they did. I think that the father Ray Decker just couldn't handle the loss of one of his children. That would be a tough one to take."

"I'm surprised that you hung around." Mr. Murphy said as he gazed out the windshield, not wanting to look me in the eye.

"I have to live somewhere Mr. Murphy. This is my home and I'm not going to let it run me off."

"Besides that, I have a job to do here." I explained to Mr. Murphy as I pulled up to the gate. Mr. Murphy got out of the truck to open the gate again. He paused to look back across his pasture, and while standing there with the door of the truck half open, he talked about his desires to see all of this come to an end before he dies.

"You know Butch, I've seen a lot in my life but the one thing I want to see before they plant me six feet under is who, or what, is doing this and why in the hell are they doing it?" Mr. Murphy made what seemed to be a reasonable request.

"I know Mr. Murphy and if you'll hang in there, I promise to get to the bottom of it this time. I give you my word sir. I have a score to settle; for me and for Berry." I explained to Mr. Murphy. Hoping that he wouldn't give up on me.

As I watched Mr. Murphy open the gate again so I could pull the truck back through and out of the pasture, I thought to myself I hope I can be as active as he is when I'm eighty-two years old. He's maybe a little rough around the edges, but I think he's earned the right to be that way. Mr. Murphy has lived a long and hard life. Farming and ranching isn't easy work.

After pulling my truck over by the driveway, I stepped out to see if there was anything Mr. Murphy needed before I left.

"Mr. Murphy, I'm going to go now. Is there anything you need before I take off?" I asked not expecting Mr. Murphy to really need anything; it was more of a courtesy question.

"Got time for a cup of coffee Butch?" Mr. Murphy asked. I didn't know if it was because it's the neighborly thing to do, or if he had something that he wanted to talk to me about.

"I'm not a coffee drinker sir, I never really acquired the taste for coffee, but I do have time to talk. What's on your mind sir?" I asked as I stepped over to where Mr. Murphy was at. He had walked over to the front porch of his house.

"I don't want to get too personal Butch, but how old are you?" I could tell that Mr. Murphy was uncomfortable asking me my age.

"That's ok Mr. Murphy it doesn't bother me to tell my age. I'm forty-seven years old." I explained to a very visibly uncomfortable Mr. Murphy.

"That's what I thought." Mr. Murphy replied as he hung his head.

With some hesitation in his voice I could tell that Mr. Murphy had to get something off his conscience.

"I was your age right now when you where attacked…"

"Butch I'm ashamed to say that I didn't do anything back then. I just didn't want to get involved." I could tell that this had been bothering Mr. Murphy for quite awhile.

"You've turned out to be a fine man and I want to apologize for not doing what I could when I should have, and I want to apologize for my attitude this morning. I know you want to find out what's going on and stop it. Butch I know that this means the world to you." Mr. Murphy was being very apologetic.

"Mr. Murphy you don't have anything to apologize for. To tell you the truth when I was twelve years old I didn't believe all the stories that I had heard about the *Prairie Monster* either. I thought that they were just fairytales told to us kids to scare us."

"Berry and I would go fishing down at the river all the time and never once did we ever think that we were in danger or that we could ever be attacked while we were at our favorite place in the world."

"Mr. Murphy, Berry and I spent more time at the river during the summer than we spent at our own homes. We would camp out by the river for days at a time. We would get in trouble with our parents for not checking in and letting them know we were alright."

"The best time of my life was spending time with Berry down by the river. Unfortunately it was also the worst time of my life."

"I hang on to the good memories and I don't forget the bad one. I owe that to my best friend."

"I will never forget sir, not as long as I live. I will never forget what happened that night." I told Mr. Murphy there was no need for him to worry about the past.

With sadness in his eyes and with a somber tone to his voice Mr. Murphy spoke of regret.

"It just should have never happened to you two boys." Mr. Murphy was starting to tear up as he spoke.

"Nobody saw this coming Mr. Murphy. I think we were just at the wrong place at the wrong time. It was just bad luck on our part." I tried to make it sound a little better than what it was.

"Butch I will not make the same mistake twice, all you need to do is holler at me and I'll be there!!!" Mr. Murphy said with great passion, and I felt a bit of commitment on his part.

"I will do that sir. When it's time."

With a hand shake we said our goodbyes and then I walked over to my truck climbed in it and started to drive down the driveway towards the dirt road, waving to Mr. Murphy as I drove off.

Chapter 2

Lunch with the Sheriff.

I didn't know what my next move was going to be. I guess I needed to get with the sheriffs department and let Sheriff Wells know what had happened. He's not from around here, and he's not going to be happy that Mr. Murphy called me first.

Sheriff Wells and I don't see eye to eye on very many things. I'm more forgiving of minor law infractions than he is. Like fishing without a license I will usually just give a warning, Sheriff Wells is of the opinion if you break the law you should be punished. If he catches you speeding you will get a ticket. I believe he would arrest his own mother for speeding if given the opportunity.

Don't get me wrong, Sheriff Wells has a very tough job to do and he is a good person. He is just a little gun-ho when it comes to executing his duties as sheriff of Rock County, Kansas.

Besides that I enjoy poking fun at him every chance I get. I think he enjoys poking fun at me too. He's just not very good at it. My office is right across the hall from the sheriff's department in the county courthouse.

We even go to lunch together a couple times a week. He can't help it that he grew up in the city. I guess we all can't be privileged and grow up living the country life.

It was about [9:15am] when I pulled into the parking garage of the county courthouse. The sheriff's car wasn't in his parking space. That was unusual; he is normally here by now. There was just the sign that said Sheriff Peter Wells. I thought about swapping out his sign for a handicap sign but I don't think he would see the humor in it. I walked through the employee's entrance and down the hallway to where the offices are.

I could see Doris the receptionist for the sheriff's department through the glass door. Doris has been the receptionist for the sheriff's department for about forty years. She goes a little heavy on the makeup, and her hair color changes regularly but she's as nice as can be. Doris also has the bluest eyes I have ever seen. Her eyes are by far the first thing you notice when you meet her for the first time.

"Good morning Butch." Doris said as I walked into the outer offices of the sheriff's department.

"Good morning Doris. Where's Barney Fife at this morning?" Jokingly I was referring to the sheriff as I leaned over the counter and asked Doris.

"He's on his way in right now. He should be here in about ten minutes." Doris replied while looking at me over the top of her glasses.

"Of course you're not going to tell him I called him Barney Fife."

"Are you?" I asked Doris with a wink of my eye and a little tilt of my head.

"Of course not. I want to keep my job." Doris said with a big smile on her face. Of course that's why I called the sheriff Barney Fife to begin with, to get a smile out of Doris and brighten her morning just a bit.

"I need to talk to him. I'll wait for him in his office. Ok Doris?" I wasn't really asking as I started walking towards the sheriff's office.

"Butch! Now you know that he hates it when you do that." Doris said hoping that I would stay out of the sheriff's office.

"Yeah I know. That's why I do it Doris." I replied as I walked into the sheriff's office.

I closed the door behind me and sat down on the sheriff's couch that is against the wall. His couch sits under a row of windows that leads out to the other offices where the sheriff can see his deputies making out their daily reports.

Sitting there waiting on the sheriff, I picked up one of his magazines from off the coffee table. Guns & Ammo; that figures.

Just then I heard the sheriff come into the front offices.

"Good morning Doris." The sheriff said as he stopped and picked up his messages sitting on Doris's desk.

"Good morning Sheriff. How's your day going so far today? I trust you slept well last night?" Doris said to the sheriff, giving herself away, that she had something to hide.

With a bit of a suspicious tone in his voice the sheriff asked.

"Ok Doris, what's going on?"

"What's going on sir???" Doris acting like she didn't know that I was in his office and he was going to be upset about it.

Just then the sheriff looks through the windows and see's me in his office.

"Never mind Doris I see him sitting in my office again."

"What does he want this time?" The Sheriff asked as he stared at the back of my head through the windows, sitting on his couch in his office.

"I don't know Sheriff." Doris whispered.

"Don't worry Doris I'll take care of this." The sheriff said with a stern tone to his voice as he walked over to his office door and opened it.

"What are you doing in my office Butch!!!?" The sheriff said loud enough for everyone in the offices to hear.

"Oh come on Sheriff, I thought you told me that you have an open door policy in your department."

37

"Matter of fact you told me that you were proud of that open door policy." I said to the Sheriff knowing that he meant his deputies could come in and talk with him, not me.

"I do have an open door policy for the people that work for me. At least they have enough respect to wait until I'm here to come into my office." The sheriff said as he shut the door and walked over to his desk and sat down.

"What happened to you this morning Pete? Did you have a hard time dragging your butt out of bed?"

"It's shameful for the sheriff to come to work this late when the best part of morning is already gone." I couldn't help myself; I was already poking fun at the Sheriff.

"I was up at [5:30am] this morning Butch. Not that it's any of your business."

"I went out on patrol with one of my deputies this morning. I do that every now and then to evaluate their performance."

"Don't you have an opossum to catch or something?" The sheriff said, trying to get back at me for coming into his office when he wasn't here.

As I stood up and walked over to the chair sitting in front of the sheriff's desk I sat down and began to tell the sheriff about Mr. Murphy's phone call this morning.

"Pete I need to tell you about a telephone call I received this morning."

"This sounds serious." The sheriff said as he realized that I wasn't joking.

"Mr. Murphy called me at about [7:30am] this morning. He had been out checking on his cattle and he came across one that had been killed. Just like the two that he lost last year."

"I went by his place and took some pictures with my digital camera and I took some notes."

"It's him Pete; I know it is." I explained to the sheriff that I thought the _Prairie Monster_ was back.

"Why didn't he call my office?" Pete asked as he reached for a pad of paper and started writing some notes down on it.

"I think Mr. Murphy wants to help me get to the bottom of this Pete, and he doesn't want any of this to get out." I said to the sheriff while gesturing with my hands.

"Next thing you know he would have a bunch of UFO nuts out there on his farm." I tried to explain to the sheriff as he continued writing.

"Butch will you do me a favor and send me a copy of your notes and a copy of the pictures you took."

"I'm going to keep this off the record for now Butch. I can understand Mr. Murphy's reasoning for not calling my office." The sheriff said without even looking up from his notepad as he continued to write.

"Thanks Pete I owe you one. I was surprised you took it so well." I replied to the sheriff as I stood up thinking that I needed to leave while I was still ahead.

"Butch I know what this means to you. I may not agree with the way it was reported, but you did bring me into the loop and I appreciate it." Pete was almost trying to thank me in his own way.

"Do you have time for lunch today Pete? I'm buying." I asked Pete, it was the least I could do.

"How can I pass that up Butch? Just give me a call about thirty minutes before your ready to go eat lunch." I'm almost surprised the sheriff didn't take my invitation to lunch as a bribe.

As I walked towards the door, I stopped and thanked the sheriff once again.

"Thanks again Pete, I do appreciate your help."

"Sure Butch, try to remember we're all on the same team here. I'm not the enemy"

"Oh yeah, by the way, stay out of my office when I'm not here." Pete told me as I was almost out of his office.

"You bet Sheriff." I said with a wink and a salute as I backed out of Pete's office and closed the door behind me.

When I walked past Doris I whispered.
"See it wasn't that bad."
Doris just smiled.

I went across the hallway to my office then unlocked and opened the door leaving it open. I turned the lights on and walked over to my desk which sits behind a counter. It's about twelve feet back from the counter and faces the front.

I have posters of wildlife around on the walls and pictures of my wife and kids on the desk next to the computer. I turned on the computer and then checked the answering machine.

No messages. That's no surprise. Everyone around here knows me and if they need something they just call me at home or on my cell phone.

Just as I got started logging in all my notes from this morning on my computer, Deputy Frank Wallace stepped into my office.

"Hey Butch I saw you out in old man Murphy's pasture this morning. What were you doing out there? Looking for Big Foot again?" Frank has been teasing me about Big Foot ever since we were kids. That's ok though, I've been teasing Frank about that birthmark on his forehead for almost as long as he has been teasing me.

Frank has a birthmark right in the middle of his forehead that looks like the number sign. Everyone has played tic-tac-toe, at one time or another in their lives. I would tease Frank about his parents being the tic-tac-toe champs and Frank was their prize. Sometimes I would call Frank, Tic, and I would ask him where's his brothers Tac, and Toe.

"First of all Frank, its Mr. Murphy, not old man Murphy. Second of all, it's not Big Foot I'm after; it's something much more intelligent. Finally Frank, if Mr. Murphy wanted you to know about his two headed cow he would have called you." I said to Frank knowing that he couldn't leave that comment alone.

"Wow!!! Does Old man Murphy really have a two headed cow?" I can't believe Frank actually fell for that. He's always been good for a laugh or two.

"No you idiot. You'll never change will you? Mr. Murphy is having problems with something spooking his cattle at night."

"You wouldn't be hanging around his pasture at night would you Frank?" I asked a bewildered and upset Deputy Wallace.

"You know what Butch, you weren't funny back in high school and you still aren't." Deputy Wallace replied back to my sarcasm.

"I'm sorry Frank, it's just been one of those days. Mr. Murphy's problem with his cattle is more than likely just dogs." Not wanting to tell Frank what I suspected. I thought it best to lead him on a bit.

Besides that I had asked Mr. Murphy to keep this quiet for a few days, I think he expected that I would do the same.

"I think I'm going to need to spend a couple of nights over there watching his cattle." I told Frank just in case I needed his help later.

"Butch if you want me to I'll drive by his pasture and keep an eye out on his cattle when I'm out on patrol. Besides, I get bored just sitting along the road waiting for someone to speed by." Frank was offering to help out.

"If you would Frank, I would appreciate it. I'll clear it with Sheriff Wells."

"Please don't let Mr. Murphy know what you are doing. He thinks he's still a young man and can handle anything, if you know what I mean." I asked Frank, knowing that Mr. Murphy didn't like Frank, and wouldn't want him around.

"Yeah I know what you mean Butch. His wife passed away about twenty years ago and you just don't see him around very much anymore after she died."

"He used to hire a bunch of us when we were teenagers to put up hay and do chores around his farm. Ever since his wife passed away he tries to do everything himself. The old guy is going to end up hurting himself one of these days." Deputy Wallace told me, but if I was him I wouldn't talk like that around Mr. Murphy.

"Thanks Frank. If you see anything would you please give me a call, no matter what time it is?" I knew that Deputy Wallace worked nights and I wanted him to know it was ok for him to call me in the middle of the night.

"I would be more than happy to call you in the middle of the night and wake you up Butch. I'll just think of it as one of the perks of the job." Frank said with a smile. I do believe he is actually looking forward to calling me in the middle of the night.

"I'll remember that the next time I catch you out on the lake in your boat without a permit or with an open can of beer sitting beside you Frank." I had to remind Deputy Wallace that I had let him go on more then one occasion when I had caught him on the lake with an open beer.

Frank knows that I catch violators looking through a pair of binoculars before I approach them in their boat.

"Bottle of beer Butch, bottle. I don't drink beer out of a can and at least I don't throw it into the lake when you pull up in your patrol boat like everyone else." Deputy Wallace was right; most people usually drop their beer over the edge of the boat when they see me coming, but by then it's already too late.

"I know Frank, and that's why I never cite you for it, that and just professional courtesy." I explained to Deputy Wallace as he stood there yawned, and stretched his arms upwards.

"I would love to stand here and chat with you Butch but I'm tired and it's been a long night I'm going to go home and get some sleep. I will see you later." Frank was visibly tired as he turned and started to walk away.

"Ok Frank, bye. You be careful driving home." I hollered out to Frank as he walked out of my office. He waved back at me acknowledging that he had heard me.

After Frank left I went back to putting my notes into the computer from this morning. When I was finished with my notes I downloaded the pictures off of the digital camera onto the computer. I put everything into a folder on the computer I had named, Mr. Murphy March 2006.

Then I went ahead and I emailed it to Sheriff Wells like he asked.

When I was through studying the pictures I put that folder into my *Prairie Monster* folder that I kept on the computer. It was clearly the biggest folder on my computer and I would download it onto a backup disk every now and then.

I hadn't realized how much time had went by, sitting there staring at those pictures. By now it was getting close to noon and I had forgotten to call Sheriff Wells about lunch thirty minutes in advance. So it looks like I'll be eating lunch a little late. Just then the sheriff walked over to my office.

"Hey Butch, did you forget about lunch today?" The sheriff asked as he stuck his head through the doorway of my office.

"No I was just about to call you. Did you get my report on Mr. Murphy's dead cow?" I asked as I stalled for more time to close out my files on the computer.

"Yes I did. I want to talk to you about it at lunch today." The sheriff sounded eager to discuss it with me. I hope that he can put all that investigating knowledge to work, and help me solve this nightmare.

"I'm ready anytime you are Sheriff." I told Pete even though I wasn't quite ready. I was still closing down my computer.

"Then let's go I'll drive today Butch."

"Just let me shut down my computer and I'll be right there Pete." As the computer was shutting down I stood up and started walking over to the Sheriff standing in the doorway.

"Let's go Sheriff." I turned off the light and closed the door behind us.

"Where are we going for lunch today, Butch?" The sheriff asked as we got into his patrol cruiser.

"How about barbeque today Pete?" I asked the sheriff. I knew that barbeque was one of the sheriff's favorite.

"That sounds just fine with me Butch." Pete replied, but I don't think that he really cared where we ate just as long as I was buying.

The sheriff turned left as we pulled out of the parking garage. It wasn't a very far drive to the barbeque place. About three minutes down the street.

As we pulled into the parking lot of the restaurant, Sheriff Wells noticed that there was a car parked in a handicapped parking space and it didn't have a handicapped tag or a handicapped placard on the rear view mirror. I knew that Pete couldn't let it go. I'll bet that if he ever forgot to put on his seatbelt he would write himself a ticket.

"Just a minute Butch I need to write a ticket before we go eat." The sheriff said while pulling out his ticket book.

"Put your ticket book away Pete that car belongs to Mrs. Smith she is elderly and walks with a walker, I'm sure she just forgot to hang her handicapped placard on the rear view mirror." I tried to explain to the Sheriff while shaking my head back and forth.

"I'll put my ticket book away if you go in and have a talk with her Butch." The sheriff asked as we stepped out of his patrol cruiser.

"Don't worry I promise to talk to her and if she doesn't comply you can slap the handcuffs on her, and on her walker." I said with a smile as we started walking towards the restaurant.

"Very funny Butch, but its people like Mrs. Smith I'm trying to protect." The sheriff was right, and I knew that he was right.

"I know Pete I'm just having fun with you." I admitted to the sheriff. He needs to relax a little.

We walked into the restaurant and sat down at a table. The waitress came over and gave us a couple of menus and took our drink order.

Iced tea for both of us, no lemon in one which would be mine, I never have cared for lemon.

I told Pete just to order me today's lunch special. I see Mrs. Smith over there with her walker getting ready to leave.

As I stood up and walked over to Mrs. Smith, I could see the waitress coming back to our table to take our order. I smiled at her as we passed each other, and softly whispered that the sheriff knows my order. She nodded her head up and down in acknowledgment. I walked up to Mrs. Smith as she was just starting to stand up.

"Hi Mrs. Smith, here let me help you."

"Hello Butch, you're such a nice man, thank you."

After helping Mrs. Smith out to her car I asked her about her handicapped placard not being on her rear view mirror.

"Where's your handicapped placard at Mrs. Smith?"

"It's in the glove box Butch, I have a hard time reaching it over there so I just leave it in there most of the time." Mrs. Smith explained.

"I rode over here with the sheriff Mrs. Smith and he doesn't know your car so I told him who you were and that you had a handicapped placard so he wouldn't write you a ticket."

"I also told him that you would start putting your placard up when you park in a handicapped parking space. Maybe if you start keeping it in your ashtray it would be easier for you to get to. After all you don't smoke." I suggested to Mrs. Smith, trying to resolve this issue before someone got mad.

"I don't like that sheriff Butch; he's not from around here. I think I heard that he's from Chicago." Mrs. Smith said with a frown on her face.

"Yeah I know Mrs. Smith, but I've got to know him and he's a pretty good guy. After all he's just trying to do his job." I tried to explain that the sheriff had her best interest at heart.

"Alright Butch I'll do it for you but you tell that sheriff I'm keeping my eye on him." Mrs. Smith said while shaking her finger at me.

"Yes ma'am I will do that. You have a good day Mrs. Smith."

I walked back inside the restaurant and sat down at the table. Our food had just arrived and the sheriff was about to add some barbeque sauce to his sandwich.

"What did your Mrs. Smith have to say?" The sheriff asked as he was pouring way too much barbeque sauce on his sandwich.

"She thanked me for reminding her to put her handicapped placard on the rear view mirror."

"She told me to tell you that you're very observant and we are lucky to have you as our Sheriff." I tried to sugar coat what Mrs. Smith had to say about the sheriff.

"You are so full of it Butch." Pete wasn't buying any of it.

"Come on Sheriff. Would I lie to you?" I asked a very suspicious Sheriff Peter Wells while he pushed down on his sandwich like it was going to hold all that barbeque sauce that he had just put on.

"In a heart beat and you know it." The sheriff replied as he dripped barbeque sauce all over the table, trying to eat his sandwich.

"Well she wasn't very happy Pete. Mrs. Smith thinks that you should know everyone that lives in Rock County."

"If you ever want to get re-elected you better start being a little friendlier and take the time to stop and talk to the citizens around here." I tried to give Pete a little advice.

"I know Butch. It's just that I'm not really a politician. Maybe you can help me get to know people around here?" The sheriff was actually asking for my help for a change.

"Ok Pete, anytime you want to; only after I get to the bottom of this cattle mutilation thing going on right now." I told Pete as I reached for my iced tea to take a drink.

"That's what I wanted to talk to you about Butch. I was wondering if you would tell me what happened that night that you where attacked and that boy was killed."

"It's the only open death case on the books that I can find."

"Pete you're the Sheriff I'm sure that you have all the paper work on what happened to Berry and me that night." I said to the sheriff with a curious look on my face, wondering what I could tell him that he hasn't already read.

"Your right. I do have all the written accounts of what other people thought happened. But I would like to hear everything that led up to what happened and I would like to hear it from an eyewitness."

"I would understand Butch if you don't want to talk about it. I mean no disrespect, to you or to your friend that died." Pete was being courteous and respectful, but he still had a job to do.

"Berry" I said to the sheriff.

"I'm sorry?" The sheriff said in a not understanding what I was saying kind of way.

"His name was Berry Decker and he was my best friend." I told the sheriff in a very somber way as I could feel my eyes begin to water a little.

"Butch I'm just trying to help. I don't want to cause you any grief." Pete was being compassionate.

"I know Pete and when we get back to the office I will do what I can to explain what happened to Berry and I."

"I know it's hard on you Butch, but sometimes when someone looks at an old case with a fresh pair of eye's they see things that went unnoticed before." The sheriff said as we sat there and continued eating our lunch. I have to admit Pete was making sense.

"Thanks Pete I know that you will do everything you can to help me, and I'm glad you're here in our county as our Sheriff." I told my friend, the sheriff.

We didn't talk much the rest of the time we were at the restaurant eating lunch, we just sat there eating and when we where through, I picked up the check to go pay.

"I'll get the tip." The sheriff said as he threw a five dollar bill down on the table.

I thought to myself well he just got the waitress's vote in the next election.

It was a short drive back to the courthouse but it seemed to take a long time. We had just pulled into the courthouse parking garage when the sheriff's patrol car radio came on asking if he was back from lunch yet?

51

"10-4" The sheriff replied.

The dispatcher told the sheriff that there was a wreck out on old Thunder Road and 55th.

"I'm sorry Butch I'm going to need to let you out and go check on this accident."

"That's ok Pete, just look me up later and I'll tell you what happened to Berry and I back then." I told the sheriff as I undid my seatbelt.

As I stepped out of the sheriff's patrol cruiser, he backed up and drove out of the parking garage.

No emergency lights and siren, that's a good sign it means that no one was hurt.

I had a lot on my mind as I walked back to my office, I don't even know if I passed anyone along the way. Again I left my office door open as I turned on the lights, walked over to my desk and sat down.

I sat there and thought to myself, it's time. It's time to end this mystery that's haunted this area forever, time to bring closure to a nightmare that's plagued me for over thirty years.

I'm scared, not of dying but of living. Living with the idea that I might be able to stop this and not having the courage to do anything. I must put my fears behind me and move forward, like I said, it's time.

I started looking over all the materiel I had on the computer. I know the answer is here somewhere; I just need to find it.

I've seen all these notes and pictures a hundred times but maybe it will come to me this time. All I could do is study them again and hope I catch a break, and see something that I missed before. This wasn't going to be easy either. I've spent a lifetime going over all this information. I know the answers are right here in front of me, why can't I see them? Sometimes I think all of this is going to drive me crazy.

After a couple of hours had passed staring at my computer screen I leaned back in my chair and while rubbing my eyes I said to myself out loud.

"I could use some help here Berry."

Just then I heard Sheriff Wells speak.

"Talking to the dead now, are you?"

Not realizing the sheriff had walked up to the open door to my office I was a little embarrassed, I tried to explain to him.

"Sorry Sheriff I didn't see you standing there."

"Butch are you going to be alright or am I going to need to put you in a cell?" The sheriff was joking. Or at least I hope he was joking.

"Come on in Pete I'm ok. I'm just getting frustrated." I told the sheriff about being discouraged over my inability to solve this nightmare that has haunted me most of my life.

"Yeah I know how it is sometimes." The sheriff said as he was walking into my office.

"See how this works, you invited me into your office and I came in. You didn't come in and find me sitting in here did you?" Pete was referring to how I'm always going into his office without him being there. It was his turn to get his little digs in.

"Maybe you can teach me how to do that some time?" I told the sheriff, I couldn't let him get the last word in.

As Sheriff Wells came around the counter and sat in the chair on the other side of my desk, I just remembered that I had asked Deputy Frank Wallace to keep an eye out on Mr. Murphy's pasture.

"Pete I had a talk with Deputy Wallace earlier this morning." I was trying to explain to the sheriff, but before I could, Pete interrupted me jumping to conclusions.

"What's he done now?" The Sheriff asked.

"Nothing Pete, nothing that I know of anyway. I asked Frank If he would drive by Mr. Murphy's pasture every now and then while he was out on patrol at night and give me a call if he sees anything."

"I told Frank that I would talk to you about it and make sure that it would be alright with you for him to drive by a couple times a night." I was hoping the sheriff wouldn't get too mad with me.

"I will take care of it Butch. I'll have a talk with Deputy Wallace and instruct him to put it on his drive-by and inspect report sheet that he fills out every night."

"I will also instruct him to give you a call if he sees anything out of the ordinary, right after he calls me first." The sheriff said with a little attitude. I don't think he liked me asking his deputies to do something before getting with him first.

"I understand Sheriff and any help I can get is appreciated." I was trying to smooth things over.

"Ok Butch, are you going to show me your famous *Prairie Monster* file?"

"Like I said Pete any help I get is appreciated. Do you want to look at it here or do you want me to copy it and send it to you?"

"If you don't mind Butch just copy it onto a jump drive and I will take it with me."

"I don't mind Pete, but please keep in mind that I've been working on this for most of my life and I don't want all my work to get out."

"You can trust me Butch I'm not going to share it with anybody else."

"I know Pete. I just don't want other people to see it and think that I'm crazy."

"I think everybody already pretty much thinks your crazy Butch, but I won't add to the problem."

"Believe it or not Butch, I do my job very well, and it's not that I don't believe you. I try not to form an opinion until I know all the facts." Pete said with a slight grin on his face.

"Pete it's going to take a few minutes to download the file to a memory stick; there are a lot of pictures in it, and my computer isn't the most efficient piece of equipment that I have in this office."

"Pete I know that you do your job very well. You're the most anal sheriff that I've ever met, and I mean that with no disrespect."

"No offense taken. Butch, I told my second in command that I was going to be busy the rest of the day, so you have my full attention."

"Pete I don't want to be nosey, but just how did you get to be Sheriff of Rock County, Kansas? I don't just mean that the county commissioners appointed you after Sheriff Moore had his heart attack and resigned two months after winning re-election."

"Butch, I can tell you that five years ago I would have never thought that I would ever settle down in a small town in the middle of Kansas. I was offered the Sheriff's job and I thought why not give it a try. Who knows, I might like it."

"Pete, everyone knows that you're from Chicago, and that you used to be some kind of teacher, but it's a huge leap from the big city life to a small county sheriff in Kansas."

"Butch, I was more of a training officer than a teacher. I don't like to use the word teacher in front of the people that I'm training."

56

"Most of the men and women I train feel that they know their jobs and don't need to be taught, but they don't mind learning new training skills. I know its six of one and half a dozen of another, but it's all in how you word it."

"I trained law enforcement officers in proper investigational skills and what to look for at crime scenes. It's always the little things that will get criminals caught."

"About two and a half years ago before Sheriff Moore won re-election, he had told all the voters that if he was re-elected he would work to turn the Rock County Sheriff's department into a new modern law enforcement agency that the rest of the counties across the United States would be envious over."

"That's when he called me up and hired me to come down here to Kansas and help him modernize everything and train his deputies."

"Sheriff Moore liked what I was showing him and his deputies, and when he had his heart attack and resigned he recommended me as his replacement."

"I know that it surprised a lot of people but I was just as surprised as everyone else. I would have guessed that Sheriff Moore was going to recommend one of his own deputies before he would have recommended an outsider."

"So Pete, why do you go out on accident calls? Why don't you let your deputies handle it? It looks like you don't trust your own deputies." I asked the sheriff.

I wasn't trying to be rude to the sheriff; I was trying to be up front and honest with him.

"It's not that I go out on all accident calls. I have dispatch call me if it requires a tow truck to be called in. Remember I'm an instructor so I take these opportunities to train my deputies. Keep in mind that insurance companies are scrutinizing our every move on both sides of an accident scene."

"My involvement has paid off too. All my deputies are getting to where they're good at investigating an accident now."

"I'm thinking that it's about time for me to start letting my deputies handle accident calls by themselves." The sheriff explained to me with pride.

"So what does your family think about you moving to Kansas, Pete?"

"I don't have any family Butch. I grew up in an orphanage where I was abandoned at the door when I was an infant."

"When I was seventeen I did a ride-along with a Chicago police officer. It changed my life forever. I was hooked on the intricacies of law enforcement."

"I got a job as a night watchman while I attended college. It was the perfect job for me. I had all night to study my criminal justice books and I got paid for it.

"I ended up graduating at the top of my class."

"While I was in college, I found out that I have a knack for spotting things that other people overlook."

"After I graduated, I began to instruct other law enforcement agencies on how to be more observant at crime scenes." Pete continued to tell me about his road to Rock County, Kansas. From the windy city of Chicago, to the windy plains of Kansas, that's a big leap for a city boy.

"I had been an instructor for about twenty years when Sheriff Moore hired me to come down here and help him modernize the Sheriff's department."

"That's when I first showed up here, and you talk about a culture shock when I first came here. The only thing that was like Chicago around here is the wind and the cold."

"Well Pete, I hope all that knowledge can help me. I don't think it'll hurt. I'm glad that you're here, even if you're a city boy."

"Butch the reason I accepted the job of Sheriff was because of the people. The people around here are so friendly I can't believe it. I'm still learning how to react to it all."

"I've been in big cities all over the United States and I can't believe how friendly and peaceful it is out here in the middle of nowhere."

"What I have always wondered Pete, is why do so many people want to live in the big cities?"

"I think Butch that they just don't know how it really is out here in the country. Of course if most of them lived out here it wouldn't be as friendly."

"I guess your right Pete, but they don't know what they're missing."

"Ok Butch that's enough about me what about you and your friend Berry? I'd like to hear everything you can remember leading up to that morning that you and he were attacked down by the river."

"I want to hear your version, in your own words about what happened when you were being attacked."

"Pete all I ask is that you keep an open mind on my story. I know that it's hard to believe but it's the truth." I told the sheriff before I started to tell my story.

Chapter 3

Berry's death.

I sat back in my chair and put my feet up on my desk. Looking up at the ceiling I slowly closed my eyes and began to remember back to when Berry and I went fishing. I could visualize myself in my mind walking towards Berry's house back when I was twelve years old.

A small grin came across my face, I remembered the good times. There were a lot of good times before there was the one bad one.

I guess it's best to start at the beginning. I started telling the sheriff my story, still leaned back in my chair with my feet up on my desk and my eyes closed.

"It was in 1971 when Berry and I were attacked. It was around the middle of August. I had gone over to Berry's house the night before to eat dinner and spend the night with him and his family. Berry and I were going to go fishing the next day."

"Berry's mother made the best mashed potatoes. My mouth is starting to water right now just thinking about them. She would add lots of extra butter and I always considered it a treat for me to eat dinner at their house."

"I could smell the chicken frying as I came up to the back door. I had my fishing gear with me, and I sat it down against the side of the back porch."

"As I knocked on the back door, I peered through the window and I could see Berry's mother frying chicken, making gravy, and stirring potatoes boiling in a big old pot on the stove."

"People talk about multitasking these days, mothers back when I was growing up did it all the time, everyday of their life."

"Berry's mother waved for me to come in. She was a thin very attractive dark haired lady who always wore red lipstick. I can remember it like it was yesterday, she had on a light blue apron that looped around her neck and tied at her waist. It was a homemade apron. Nobody back then bought aprons they just made them as they needed them."

I sat there in my chair with my eyes closed, remembering back in time. I could smell everything as if I were there right now. I can remember greeting Mrs. Decker like it was yesterday.

"Hi Mrs. Decker! It sure does smell good in here."

"Thank you Butch. Are you talking about the chicken frying in the skillet or the peach cobbler in the oven?"

"It all smells good to me Mrs. Decker."

"Wow it sure is hot in here." I said while wiping the sweat from my brow.

"That's what happens when you cook silly. Someday when you get married maybe you'll appreciate your wife a little more after she cooks dinner for you." Mrs. Decker said with a smile as she stood there at the stove in her apron cooking dinner.

"Berry's out front somewhere. I want you boys to be careful tomorrow down at that river."

"Yes ma'am we will, and I want to thank you for letting me eat dinner over here."

"Butch you know you're always welcome to eat over here anytime you want to. By the way, we're having liver and onions tomorrow for dinner. Would you like to join us for dinner tomorrow too?"

"No ma'am, but thank you for asking."

Not that I would ever hurt Mrs. Decker's feelings but I hate liver and onions, and so does Berry. I've got a feeling that Berry will be eating over at my house tomorrow.

As I walked through the kitchen and past the dinning room, I could see Berry standing in the living room looking out the front door. We looked so much alike we could have been brothers. Both of us had burr haircuts back then.

"Hey Berry what are you looking at?"

"Nothing I was just waiting for you."

"Hey Berry do you want to run down to the river for a few minutes and get some firewood for in the morning, before dinner?"

"No we better not. My mom would get mad if we were late for supper. Let's just go up to my room and wait until she calls us to dinner."

Berry's room was upstairs. He shared a bedroom with his eight year old little brother Mike.

"Where's Mike at?" I asked as we entered their bedroom and noticed that he wasn't around.

"Mike and Mary went to my grandparent's house to spend the week with them, and to help them clean out their garage." Mary was Berry's ten year old sister.

"That's good to hear Berry. That means Mike won't be bugging us to take him along when we go fishing tomorrow. Your little brother can be a pain in the butt sometimes."

"Yeah I know what you mean Butch, but sometimes it's nice to have him there to pick up firewood and get the fishing net ready when we catch something. After all, isn't that what little brothers are for?"

"Butch my mom is fixing mashed potatoes tonight for dinner instead of fried potatoes, just because you bragged about them the last time you were over here."

"I can't help it, Berry they're good."

"By the way Butch it's my turn to do dishes tonight so you know what that means don't you."

"Yeah it means that it's my turn too."

Berry and I spent the next half hour just sitting around in his room talking. That was good times back then.

Berry's mother called us down to dinner with the rest of his brothers and his father.

After everybody ate dinner and the dishes were cleared, the peach cobbler was dished out with cream. Not that canned stuff either, real cream.

It was the best peach cobbler that I have ever eaten in my life.

"Mrs. Decker, why is it that your cobblers taste so much better than everyone else's?"

"Now Butch you keep talking like that and I might just have to keep you as one of mine own."

"As long as you keep cooking like that I'll stay as long as you'll let me ma'am."

After each one of Berry's brother's finished eating, one by one they got up and went over to their mother and kissed her on the cheek and said good supper mom, and then went on their way.

When Mr. Decker was finished he wiped his chin, stood up and said.

"Good supper mama, now you boy's take care of those dishes don't leave them for your mother to do Berry."

"Ok dad."

"Ok Mr. Decker." I replied as I was finishing up my peach cobbler.

It didn't take us long to do the dishes. Neither one of us liked doing dishes, so when we had to do them we didn't mess around.

Besides that we were going fishing in the morning and we wanted to get in bed early.

After sitting around and listening to the radio for a couple of hours and talking about how many fish we where going to catch we called it a day and went to bed. I slept in Mike's bed.

Berry set his alarm to wake us up at [3:00am], although neither one of us really needed an alarm clock to wake up. We both had what my grandfather used to call an internal clock.

This meant that we would wake up on our own just before we wanted up. I don't know how it works; all I know is that I always wake up early.

At about [2:55am] I woke up and opened my eye's I just laid there waiting for Berry's alarm to go off. About two minutes later, before the alarm had a chance to go off, Berry said in a soft voice.

"Hey Butch are you awake yet?"

"Just laying here waiting on you buddy."

"How did you sleep Butch?"

"On my back. Why?" I've always been sort of a comedian, never giving a straight answer when I think I can get a laugh.

"No I meant did you sleep well?"

"Yeah I slept great Berry. It took me about one minute to fall asleep and I slept until about two minutes ago."

"How did you sleep Berry?"

"On my back." Berry said with a snicker.

"I suppose I deserved that." I replied with a laugh.

After we both got out of bed and got dressed, we very quietly walked downstairs to go out the back door. Berry took some of his moms beef liver out of the refrigerator to use as bait.

"Berry what are you doing? Catfish like chicken livers not beef livers."

"Hey I don't care just as long as I don't have to eat it. Besides that, moms not going to miss a little and if I get caught I'll tell her to just consider it my share."

"Is that before or after she grounds you?" I whispered to Berry, knowing that if he gets caught he's going to be in big trouble.

Berry grabbed an empty bread sack to put the liver in and stuffed it in his back pocket.

At that point I just wanted to get out the back door without his mother finding out that Berry had taken some of her beef liver that she was going to fix for supper that night.

"What are you going to use for bait wise guy?" Berry asked as we were picking up our fishing gear that we had put on the side of the back porch.

"Don't worry about me Berry. I have a fool proof plan. I'm going to use an old family secret to fishing taught to me by an old family member."

"Oh yeah, what's that?"

"Well if I told you Berry than it wouldn't be a secret anymore now would it."

"Butch you spend more time with me then you do with your own family. Are you telling me that I'm not as much family as your own brothers?"

"Not at all Berry, I just don't want you to catch more fish than me. Don't forget my friend; whoever catches the biggest stringer of catfish doesn't have to clean any of them." I reminded Berry of our long standing fishing agreement.

"Yeah I know Butch; by the way, I noticed that you're getting real fast at cleaning fish. I guess it's because of all that practice you've been getting lately." Berry was right he had beaten me the last four or five times we went fishing.

"Don't count your fish before they're caught. I have a real good feeling that you're about to get a good look at what a real fisherman can do." I was starting to brag to Berry about how many fish I was going to catch this morning. I was feeling good about our fishing trip this morning.

"Oh give me a break Butch. The day you beat me at fishing is the day the world stops spinning. Are you going to tell me your big fishing secret?"

I thought to myself for a couple of seconds, and then decided to let my friend in on my secret.

"Ok I'll tell you Berry, but you have to promise to keep it to yourself."

"My grandfather told me that the trick to better fishing is to never buy your bait. You need to use the same bait that the fish are eating in their surroundings."

"My grandfather explained to me that if you're going to use worms then dig them up where you fish, if you're going to use minnows or crawdads catch them in the pond or river that you're fishing in." I told Berry my secret to better fishing. I would say that he was more then intrigued with the whole idea.

"You know what Butch? That actually sounds like it might work. I'll tell you what, if my way doesn't work you share your bait with me, and if your way doesn't work I'll share my beef liver with you. Is it a deal?" Berry was starting to have second thoughts about his bait, and his chances of catching more fish than me.

"You bet Berry. Those fish don't stand a chance with us today." I said with a smile and a high five to my best friend.

It was about [3:30am] when we headed out the back way of his yard being as quiet as possible.

Our fishing poles in one hand and our tackle box's in the other hand. I had a seine under my arm.

My plan was to catch my bait. Neither one of us had a flashlight. We didn't need one, the moon was almost full and both of us knew our way around the back pasture that headed down by the river.

There weren't very many trees around that slow moving river back then. A few big rocks sticking up out of the ground was all we needed to navigate our way to the river.

It really didn't matter if the moon was out or not, all we needed was to catch a glimpse of one of the big rocks sticking up and we both knew exactly where we were.

Those big rocks where like landmarks for us. We could walk the pastures around there blindfolded and never get lost. They where strangely scattered around the pastures where I grew up.

It was like a big volcano had spit them out millions of years ago and they just stuck where they landed. It was nice to sit down on one every now and then and rest. That's what we did that morning; we were almost to the river when we sat down to rest and look at the moon and stars.

"Hey Butch, don't you think it would be cool to go into outer space?" Berry asked as he gazed upwards into the starry night.

"Nah, there isn't any fish up there, and besides, I'm not much into doing dangerous stuff like having a rocket strapped to my butt, and having it lit on fire."

"Butch I'm talking about going places, and doing something with my life. You know making something of myself." Berry always seemed to have his head on straight, even at a young age.

"Berry I like it here. I don't think I'll ever move away."

"I like it here too Butch. It's just that I would like to explore other possibilities, see how other people live."

"Berry Decker the explorer." I said as I looked up and fanned my hands outwards as if I was reading it on a marquee.

"You know what Berry? That has a ring to it."

"Come on Butch, the fish are waiting on us."

"Oh no!" Berry said with a worried look on his face as he stood up.

"What's wrong Berry?"

"I forgot about the beef liver in my back pocket. It must have smashed when I sat down and broke open the plastic bag. I can feel blood from the liver all over my back pocket and on my leg."

"My mom's going to kill me if she finds out." Berry was in a pickle now. Knowing that his mother was going to be more than a little upset, Berry just stood there looking at me.

"How are you going to explain this one Berry?" I asked while shaking my head back and forth.

"Maybe I can wash it out when we get to the river."

"That's a good idea Berry and maybe the soap fairy left you some laundry detergent down by the river too."

"Come on Butch this isn't funny."

"I know it isn't funny to you Berry, but I find it easier to handle problems with humor. You should know that by now."

"Besides, you have to admit that it is kind of funny." I said to Berry trying to brighten up the moment and make the best of a bad situation.

"Yeah Butch, it would have been real funny if it had happened to someone else."

"When we get to the river Berry, you go ahead and start getting up some firewood and I'll try to catch some minnows and crawdads with the seine."

"Why should I have to get all the firewood?"

"Because you're the one that's going to be without pants on after you wash them, and there going to need to dry. Besides, how do you expect me to catch any minnows or crawdads after you've been in the river splashing around?"

"I guess your right, but it just doesn't seem fair that I have to get all the firewood." Berry said as we picked up our fishing gear and started walking towards the river again.

As we arrived at the river and put our fishing gear down, Berry started walking around picking up little twigs and small tree branches. I took the seine over to the river, stuck one of the two poles in the river mud close to the edge. I then unrolled the seine and walked about eight feet along the bank of the river with it.

I know this river well, it's only about eighty feet across but it's very deep out in the center of it. It's a slow moving river but it's deep and it's muddy.

You can always catch minnows and or crawdads along the edge of it. It's my favorite place in the world to fish at, and spend time with my best friend.

It's easier to seine with two people, but I've done it by myself several times. You just need to move a little faster when you do it alone.

I walked into the edge of the river and begin to seine across the bottom of the river bank. I made a quick half moon swipe coming out into the river about six feet and back up towards the bank.

When I walked back up to the bank of the river I jerked the seine up and out of the water very quickly so I wouldn't lose what I had caught in my seine.

Wow I hit the mother load. I hollered at Berry to bring me the minnow bucket. He was about fifty feet away. Man was he going to be surprised.

"Berry!"

"Bring the minnow bucket and come here, look at all the minnow's and crawdad's that I caught." I cried out to Berry, I had never seen this many before.

"Yeah, yeah how can you see what you caught; it's dark out?" Berry replied sarcastically, not believing that I had caught as many as I said I caught.

Those would be the last words that Berry would ever say. Just then I saw two red glowing eyes off in the distance.

"Berry what's that behind you?"

When Berry turned around and looked at it, we both just stood there frozen. It was big and hairy and stood upright on two legs. It was silent; I mean you couldn't hear anything. You couldn't hear it breathing or grunting or anything, and when it moved you couldn't hear it move either.

It was silent, silent and deadly.

Once it decided to move it was on Berry in an instant. That big hairy thing moved so quickly that I didn't even have time to blink. I had hollered at Berry to lookout but it was too late.

Berry never stood a chance; he was being attacked by this thing right in front of my eyes. I couldn't believe what I was seeing. Berry was picked up like he was nothing, tossed around like he was a rag doll. The beast just stood in one spot never moving his lower torso or feet.

I dropped the seine and ran towards them grabbing my fishing pole along the way. I thought I could use it as some sort of a weapon. As I ran towards Berry and the beast, I was trying to get its attention by hollering at it.

My plan was to try and hit it in the eye with my fishing pole somehow. It wasn't much of a plan but I was only twelve years old and didn't have much to work with. All I knew was that my best friend was being attacked and I had to do something.

As I got close enough to try and poke it in the eye with my fishing pole the beast took a swing at me with its gigantic hand.

It had four claws at the end of its fingers that cut deep into my back. That's how I ended up with that scar on my right shoulder blade.

All I remember is that I ducked and turned my body trying to escape its blow. I remember I felt it hit me, it knocked me down to the ground, and I hit my head on a rock and was knocked unconscious.

I awoke the next day in the hospital with my parents standing over me. They asked me how I was feeling and I told them that I had an awful headache.

Then the sheriff came in and asked me what I had remembered. I told him everything and he didn't believe me. He told me that Berry and I were attacked by a pack of wild dogs. He even tried to convince me of that, but I kept telling him that it was the *Prairie Monster*.

"I know I saw it and if you ask Berry he'll tell you the same thing. It was attacking him first." I tried to explain to the sheriff.

Then it got quiet the sheriff didn't say anything. He walked over to my mom and dad and they started whispering. I knew something was wrong, so I asked what was going on.

"Ok Sheriff, what's going on?"
"Mom?"
"Dad?"
"Where's Berry?"

"I want to know about Berry!" I knew something was very wrong. Just then the doctor came in and asked everyone to step out.

"Everyone out, I need to check Butch out and go over a few things with him." The doctor told everyone in the room as he flipped up my medical chart.

The sheriff, my mom, and dad all walked out of the hospital room and shut the door behind them.

"Well Butch, you've had quite the experience haven't you. Let's give that heart and lungs a listen to." The doctor took out his stethoscope and began to put it on my chest and listen to my breathing.

"Breath in…. Breath out." The doc would say.

"Breath in and hold it this time."

"Ok breathe out."

"What about Berry?" I asked.

"Shhhhh." The doc said as he continued moving his stethoscope around my back and chest.

"I want to know about Berry!" I persisted.

"Your parents will be in here after I'm through examining you and they can talk to you about your friend. Now will you please let me finish looking you over? I do have other patients I need to see." The doctor explained to me, without revealing what happened to Berry. I knew that something was wrong.

After the doctor was through listening with his stethoscope he began to unwrap the bandage on my back and poke at the wound that had been sewn shut.

"How many stitches doc?" I asked, I don't know why but everybody always wants to know how many stitches they get.

"You have thirty-seven stitches in your back. There are fourteen stitches on the inside of the wound and twenty-three on the outside of the wound."

"You had a very deep wound and we need to keep you here for a couple of days to make sure it doesn't get infected." The doctor said as he was poking around at my back where he had sewed me up.

"Is it giving you very much pain young man?" The doc asked after he had just finished poking at it.

"No. It really wasn't bothering me until you started messing with it. I mean yeah it was sore but it wasn't unbearable." I explained to the doc.

"How does your head feel Butch?"

"I have an awful headache." I explained to the doc hoping that he wasn't going to start poking around on my head next.

"I'll have the nurse give you something that will help with the pain. It will help you get some sleep too."

As the doctor stood there writing on a clipboard he would glance up at me every now and then.

"Ok Butch the nurse will be in to redress that wound on your back and give you something for the pain. Do you have any questions?"

"Yes I do, where's Berry?"

"I will let your parents talk to you about your friend." The doctor said as he was walking out of the room and writing on his clipboard.

I could see the doctor standing out in the hallway talking with a nurse; he had left the door open. Just then my parents walked up and were standing there waiting for the doctor to get through talking with the nurse.

The doctor signed something for the nurse and then turned and started talking to my parents. I couldn't hear what they where saying but every now and then I could read their lips. It looked like my mom was saying ok and yes and thank you.

After what looked like the doctor explaining what was going on to my parents, he used a lot of hand jesters while he was explaining; the doctor looked right at me. I don't know what he said but I could see that he said Berry's name.

I had a gut feeling that this wasn't going to go well, and that I wasn't being told everything.

Just then Mrs. Decker walked up to my mom and they hugged. Then I could see, what looked like my mom telling Mrs. Decker that I was going to be ok.

They both started crying and held each other. I could see my mother tell Mrs. Decker that she was so sorry.

My heart dropped. I knew that this was bad. I hollered out to Mrs. Decker because I wanted to know what was going on.

"Mrs. Decker, where's Berry?"

My father had walked away. My guess is that he didn't want me to see him emotionally upset.

My mother and Mrs. Decker just stood there looking at me, both of them with tears running down both cheeks.

"I want to know where Berry is." I hollered again.

Mrs. Decker hugged my mom and this time she was telling my mom that she was sorry.

They both kissed each other on the cheek and I could see Mrs. Decker walk away. My mom took some tissue out of her purse and wiped the tears from her face, her eyes were red and swollen from crying.

She took a deep breath and then walked into my hospital room and shut the door behind her.

My heart was pounding so much I could feel it in my chest. My mom sat down on the side of my hospital bed and reached out to hold my hands.

"Mom what is going on? I want to know."

"Where's Berry?"

"Son you need to lay back and try to relax. I'm afraid I've got some bad news for you."

"How bad is he mom?"

"I know that Berry was hurt bad."

"But he's going to be ok isn't he?" I pleaded with my mother. My mom just sat there looking at me with tears streaming down her face.

I knew she was trying to compose herself to talk with me, but she couldn't find the strength to do so at the time.

"Mom please tell me everything's going to be alright. Please."

"Mom." I pleaded.

"Son I'm sorry to have to tell you that Berry didn't make it." My mother was trying very hard to compose herself and tell me about Berry without crying. She wasn't strong enough to do so. Thinking about it now I know that I couldn't do it either.

I just sat there staring at my mother; I didn't want to believe her. I was numb I didn't know what to say or what to do.

"Butch, he was already dead when they found the both of you by the river."

"There was nothing anybody could do for him. Berry had been dead for a few hours by the time the both of you were found."

"I'm so sorry son."

"No…. It can't be. I don't believe you."

"Please!"

"Mother please no!"

"Don't let it be!"

I begin to cry. My mother reached out and hugged me, holding me tight. We both cried together. She whispered that it was going to be alright.

My heart was broken. I had just lost my best friend and my world had been turned upside down. Nobody believed me on what had happened, they all thought that I was in shock after Berry's death.

I wasn't in shock. I knew what happened and after a while my sadness had turned to anger.

Anger over what had happened to Berry, and anger over the sheriff trying to tell me what happened when he wasn't even there.

I spent the next four days in the hospital recovering. The swelling on my head took longer then they expected to go down.

When I was released from the hospital my mother came to pick me up.

I had missed Berry's funeral so I asked my mother to drive me to the graveyard so I could say my goodbyes.

It was very hard to walk over to Berry's grave but I needed to pay my respects. I had asked my mother to wait in the car; I needed to do this on my own.

I made my peace with Berry. It was hard to say goodbye, very hard and emotional. I promised Berry that I would find who or what it was that killed him. I've been looking ever since.

When I walked back to the car, I asked my mother to drive me over to Mr. and Mrs. Decker's house so I could pay my respects to them. After all they were like a second family to me.

"Can we go by Mr. and Mrs. Decker's house on the way home mom?" I asked as I put my seatbelt on.

"It wouldn't do you any good Butch, the Decker's moved right after Berry's funeral."

"You're kidding."

"No sweetie they came home from the funeral and begin to pack up there belongings that day."

"But why mom?" I asked in disbelief.

"Butch it's hard to explain but when you have a loss like they did, sometimes it's easier to move away and start new."

"Son that doesn't mean that they will forget Berry, it's just that they don't want to be reminded of how he died." My mother tried to explain but I knew what she was really trying to say was that every time they would see me they would wonder why. Why did there son have to die?

"Mom what happens now? I mean nobody believes me so how do we get Berry's killer?"

"Butch I want you to forget about how Berry died and don't worry about what killed him. The sheriff is taking care of it."

"Butch I want you to make me a promise, and I want you to promise it right now."

"What's that mom?" I asked wondering what my mother had on her mind.

"I want you to promise to me that you will never, ever, go fishing on that river again."

"Promise me Butch."

"Mom I promise to you that I will never fish that river again." I told my mother and I've kept that promise all these years.

After my mother drove home I went to my room and cried. Hiding it from her, after awhile I fell asleep. It had been another hard and emotional day for me.

About two hours later I awoke to a knock at the front door. I went to see who it was. It was the sheriff.

The sheriff and my dad where talking until I walked in the room then they stopped. My dad walked outside with the sheriff and continued talking with him when my dad came back inside I asked him what the sheriff wanted.

He told me that the sheriff had brought my fishing pole and gear back to me and that he put it out on the front porch. I went outside and sat on the front porch swing, staring at my fishing gear thinking about Berry until my mom called me to dinner.

After dinner that night I took the trash out to the burn barrels and burned it. While the trash was burning I walked around the house to the front porch and grabbed my fishing equipment.

I took a good long look at it and then I walked back around the house to where the trash was burning and threw it all in.

When I turned around, I saw my parents at the window watching me. We never talked about what happened again.

"I will not give up on trying to find out what happened, and I will not ever change my story. I told the truth then and I'm telling the truth now."

"Berry and I were attacked and Berry was killed by the *Prairie Monster*. That was fact; I know that it's hard to believe, but I was there. I will find out the truth about the *Prairie Monster*, somehow, someway.

Chapter 4

Someone that finally believes.

Sheriff Wells just leaned back in his chair and looked up at the ceiling. I could see that he was thinking about how to ask a question.

I had just told him this amazing story and I know that it had to be hard for him to believe, but it was the truth. I didn't know if he was about to ask me if I was crazy, or if I was on drugs.

The story that I just told was the truth, the whole truth, and nothing but the truth, and I wasn't on drugs ether. Berry and I were having too much fun enjoying life without messing it up by using drugs.

It was pretty much the same look that everyone else gave me when I told them the same story. I've been telling this story for over thirty years now and I have yet to find one person to believe it at face value. That's why I stopped telling people.

There the sheriff sat not saying anything; just sitting there staring off into space.

"Go ahead ask it; whatever you want you're not going to offend me. I've heard it all." I told Pete waiting for him to ridicule me and my story.

"Tell me about the liver." Pete asked as he continued to stare off into space, almost as if he was concentrating on something he was looking at.

"Liver? What liver?" I didn't realize what Pete was getting at; most people just shook their heads back and forth.

"Butch I'm talking about the beef liver in the back of Berry's pocket, where did it come from? It could have been that your *Prairie Monster* was after the beef liver in Berry's back pocket."

"Of course Pete I can't believe I've been so stupid all these years. Why didn't I think of that, the beef liver is the key to this?" I was excited to think that I might have a break in this mystery after all this time.

"Just wait a minute Butch. This, I think is a clue; it's not a key; it doesn't solve a thing right now. It's just a clue. I don't want you to get your hopes up too soon."

"I have other questions too. So let's proceed slowly." The sheriff was right, and I could see why he is so good at his job.

"Ok Pete, ask me anything you want. I'm not too proud to accept all the help that I can get. I've made promises to people that I plan to keep."

"Look Butch, it's after five so why don't we call it quits for today and pick this up tomorrow? I'll devote the whole day to you." The Sheriff said as he stood up and stretched his arms.

"Pete I've got time right now if you want to continue tonight." I was ready to solve this right now, I was more excited about solving this then I've been in years.

"Butch I know that you want to get to the bottom of this right away, but the most important thing that you need to know about investigative work is to not rush things."

"Now I've got some work to do over at my office, and then I want to read that file you have on the *Prairie Monster*, and look through all the pictures that you have."

"Remember Butch, a picture is worth a thousand words. I also have some ideas in my head that I want to write down, and some questions I want to ask you later." Pete explained as he put his hands on my desk and leaned over to look at my computer screen to see if the computer was through downloading the file.

"I'm sorry Pete, your right. I have things to do too. I still need to go by the post office before they close." I told Pete as he arched his back. Sitting in that chair while I told him my story must have gave him a bit of a back ache.

"No need to apologize Butch I'll get with you tomorrow." The sheriff said as he stuck his hand out palm up wanting the jump drive I downloaded my notes and pictures on for him

"Don't worry Butch I'll keep this safe and confidential." Pete assured me that no one else would get access to my *Prairie Monster* file.

"I know you will Pete, and thanks for not thinking I'm crazy." I thanked the sheriff with a smile and a hand shake.

"Oh I still think your crazy Butch, but just not about this." The sheriff said as he turned and walked out of my office.

I shut down my computer and walked over to the door, turned the lights out in my office, closed and locked the door. I had a lot on my mind as I headed out of the county courthouse towards my truck in the parking garage. I haven't felt this good about my chances to solve this mystery in a long time.

As I walked past the sheriff's patrol cruiser, I thought to myself, if I know Pete, he's going to spend most of the night working on what I gave him.

As I headed out of the garage, I turned the opposite direction that I needed to go to get home. I needed to go by the post office and pick up their deer reports.

We use the rural postal delivery carriers to count how many deer they see when they're out delivering mail. We compare it to what they reported over the same time in past years.

That way we can get a feel of what the deer population is. It works amazingly well.

I pulled into the parking lot of the post office and parked at the back of the building. As I was getting out of my truck, Laura Lee, one of the mail carriers came walking out of the side door of the post office. She had my reports in her hand.

Laura Lee only stood about five feet tall, but she always kept herself in great physical shape.

"We were just about to give up on you Butch." Laura Lee said with a smile. Laura Lee is always so happy and full of energy, it's always a pleasure to talk with her.

"I'm sorry Laura Lee. I got caught up talking with Sheriff Wells this afternoon and just lost track of time." I explained to little miss perky.

"That's ok Butch here's your deer reports for this quarter. I don't know if your aware of it or not but we enjoy keeping these reports for you. We take bets on who's going to be the closest to their numbers from last year." Laura Lee explained how she and the other mail carriers would break the boredom of there everyday jobs of delivering mail.

"Now Laura Lee, you know gambling is against the law, don't you?" I said to Laura Lee while smiling at her and shaking my head back and forth.

"Oh Butch it's not like we're big spenders. The winner gets a soda pop out of the vending machine from everyone else." Laura Lee explained to me about their big gambling operation.

"You mail carriers will bet on anything won't you?"

"Hey Mr. Black, you get your deer reports don't you?" Laura Lee replied in a, remember we're doing you a favor kind of a way.

"Yes Laura Lee and on behalf of the Wildlife and Parks Department we would like to thank you for the outstanding effort that each and every rural mail carrier puts into these deer reports. It is very helpful to us in keeping track of the deer population in Rock County."

"You've been practicing that speech for a while now, haven't you Butch?"

"No it's in our handbook on how to thank volunteers. It's right next to how to thank poachers for not shooting you when you're arresting them." I said to Laura Lee jokingly.

"Well just the same, I would appreciate it if you didn't say anything to the sheriff. He's kind of a butthead about stuff like that, if you know what I mean?" Laura Lee said to me as she turned and started to walk away back towards the post office.

"I know what you mean Laura Lee but he's getting better." I hollered out at her as I was getting into my truck to leave.

It was about time that I started heading home. It had been a long and interesting day to say the least, and right now I was missing my wife and kids.

As I drove towards home, I thought that I would take a drive by Mr. Murphy's place and just take a look. I really didn't know what I expected to see.

I just felt that I needed to do something. When I went by everything looked normal.

I continued driving home and pulled into my driveway and reversed back into my parking spot.

As I walked into my house, my five year old boy, Cody, hollered out that I was home as he came running up to me and gave me a hug.

"Dads home."

"How's my boy?" I asked as I hugged him tight.

"Guess what dad? I lost a tooth at school today."

"That's cool son! Where is it?" I asked as I congratulated him.

"I swallowed it at lunch." Cody explained with a toothless smile.

"Swallowed it. Why did you do that?" I asked Cody while I looked up at Vickie, as she shrugged her shoulders.

"I didn't do it on purpose. I was eating a cookie and the next thing I knew it was gone. See!" Cody showed me his smile and he was missing a front tooth.

"Cody how do you expect the tooth fairy to collect your tooth?"

Cody just smiled and shrugged his shoulders.

I said hi to everyone else and went to put my gun away. My wife Vickie followed me into the master bedroom. I put my gun away in the closet safe where I keep it locked up.

Vickie asked me how my day went.

"Did you have a good day today?"

"I had an interesting day today. How did your day go Sweet Pea?"

"I hope that it was ok, I told Kevin that he could stay after school today and help out with the play." Vickie explained why Kevin wasn't home yet. I hadn't noticed that his car wasn't here. He was picking it up today from the auto shop class at school. They had been working on it for about two weeks now.

"I don't care his grades are good, and I think every student should help out at the school when they can." I said to Vickie as I closed the closet door after locking my gun up in the safe.

"Butch we can go ahead and eat when you're ready. Kevin won't be home for dinner. The school is going to feed the kids that are helping out, pizza from the Pizza Palace. I told him to call before he drives home that way we know that he's on his way."

"I don't like him driving home that late in the afternoon or early evening, but we're going to need to start trusting his driving sooner or later." Vickie was obviously nervous about Kevin's driving ability, especially driving after dark.

"Yeah I know what you mean. He's only fifteen years old and he thinks that he should be able to drive wherever and whenever he wants to." I told Vickie knowing that it worries her every time one of the kids gets to be driving age.

That night I had a lot running through my mind so when we sat down to dinner I didn't say very much. The other kids talked about school and Vickie talked about their homework and how important it was to stay on top of it at the end of the school year. School was going to be out for the summer in about two months and we want the kids to enjoy their summer vacation. So we push them to get good grades so they don't have to attend summer school.

Just as I was finishing dinner my cell phone rang. I excused myself from the table to go into the other room to answer the call. I got a frown from Vickie, cell phones at the dinner table was like wearing a hat on your head inside the house.

I looked at the caller ID and it said withheld. That usually meant someone from the government was calling me.

"Hello." I answered my cell phone.

"Butch this is Sheriff Wells. Can you come back down to the courthouse?"

"I suppose so." I said to the sheriff in a low, quiet voice.

"Butch, you better bring your gun with you."

"What's wrong Pete? You sound serious." I asked with concern and curiosity. I wondered what was going on. Pete had never called me at home and asked me to come back down to the courthouse, and to bring my gun.

"I've been studying your pictures from your *Prairie Monster* file. I think that I might know something about how they escape." I could hear Pete over the telephone take a deep breath after he had explained to me why he wanted me back down at the courthouse.

"Pete did you say how they escape? Do you mean to tell me that you believe me?"

"Butch, something's going on and I know it's not natural whatever it is. Just get down to the office I will meet you there."

"You're not at the courthouse Pete?"

"Yeah I'm in my office right now but I need to go down to the equipment room and try to find something."

"Butch just get down here as soon as you can."

"Ok Pete I'm on my way."

"Don't forget your gun Butch. I'll see you when you get here. Bye." Pete said as he hung up the telephone.

I went to the bedroom closet to get my gun and an extra box of ammunition. Just then Vickie came up to me and asked if there was a problem.

"Butch what's going on, who was that on your cell phone?" She knew something was up.

"It was Sheriff Wells and he needs me to come down to his office Sweet Pea."

"Butch something's been wrong every since you got that phone call this morning from Mr. Murphy. I want to know what is going on."

I laid my gun and ammunition down on the dresser and reached out to hug Vickie. As I was hugging her, I told her everything was going to be alright and not for her to worry

I don't know what you call it. Whether its woman's intuition or just a wife knowing her husband but Vickie knew something was going on and she wasn't going to let me leave until I told her what it was.

"Butch I'm your wife and I deserve to know what's happening." Vickie said while she was almost in tears, she was very concerned and was starting to get upset. She knew that I wasn't telling her everything.

"Sit down please." I asked Vickie as I motioned for her to sit on the edge of the bed.

I sat down beside Vickie and looked into her eyes and told her that I didn't have time to explain everything, but I will stay in touch.

"Sweet Pea I don't have much time but I will let you know that I think Mr. Murphy's cow was killed by the _Prairie Monster_, and that Sheriff Wells has agreed to help me look into it."

"I gave the sheriff a copy of all my notes and pictures of the *Prairie Monster* file today and he has found something. I don't know what yet but he asked me to meet him at the courthouse and to bring my gun." I tried to reassure Vickie but she was clearly upset and afraid.

"Butch it's not your job. Let the sheriff take care of it. That's what he gets paid to do remember. Protect and serve." Vickie pleaded tearfully.

"I'm sorry Sweet Pea but I have to go. I owe this to myself and to Berry." I was trying to explain to Vickie when our six year old daughter Cheyenne came walking into the bedroom.

"What's wrong with mommy, daddy?" Cheyenne asked, and then here came Cody and RaeLynn into the bedroom.

"Well all we need is for Kevin to walk in then everyone will be here." I was trying to lighten the mood a little; the kids didn't need to get upset.

"What about your kids Butch? Don't you owe them a daddy?"

"I owe them a safe world to grow up in and I'm going to give it to them. I'm sorry Vickie but I have to go. I have to do this."

"I love you very much Sweet Pea, take care of my kids." I said to Vickie as I stood up and holstered my gun.

"You kids give your daddy a kiss and a hug goodbye he has to go make it safe out there for us." Vickie said tearfully to the three little ones.

After giving the kids a kiss and a hug I turned to Vickie, kissed her passionately, hugged her tightly, and winked at her.

"I'll see you later Sweet Pea, I promise."

"You better old man. I love you." Vickie replied back as she wiped away her tears.

Just before I walked out the back door and went to my truck I told the kids.

"Everyone stays inside. I don't want anybody going outside for anything. Tell Kevin when he gets home to stay inside."

"Bye." I said as I waved to everyone in the house while I was walking out to my truck.

Vickie was standing at the back door window when I looked back and gave her a little wave with my hand. I could read her lips telling me to be careful. I shook my head up and down.

Everything was happening so fast I felt like a kid on his first day of school. Wanting to go but at the same time I was scared. I'll admit I wasn't nervous; I was good old-fashioned scared. It sounded like Pete was starting to believe me, and he was willing to help.

These were my demons and I was about to confront them. I was determined to face my fears, and see this all the way to the end, no matter where it took me.

Sometimes it's a lonely drive down these dirt roads on the way into town. Especially when you have a lot on your mind.

Just then my cell phone rang; I flinched not expecting a noise in the cab of my truck. I picked it up and looked at it. The caller ID said that it was the Murphy farm. I flipped it open and answered it.

"Hello."

"Good evening Butch it's me. I hope I'm not calling at a bad time?" Mr. Murphy asked.

"No it's ok Mr. Murphy, I'm on my way into town. What can I do for you?"

"Butch I just called to thank you for what you did today."

"Oh that's alright Mr. Murphy I was just doing my job. I do appreciate that you called me this morning and gave me the chance to gather up some evidence and pictures."

"No Butch I'm not talking about this morning out at my place. I'm talking about this afternoon what you did for Mrs. Smith at Billy Bobs Bar-B-Q after lunch."

"How did you know about that Mr. Murphy?" I asked because I knew that he wasn't there.

"Butch I have dinner with Mrs. Smith every now and then. She's a widow and I'm a widower and we enjoy each others company."

"So tonight when we had dinner she told me about your talk with her this afternoon."

"Mr. Murphy I was just trying to help so there wouldn't be a problem later. The sheriff didn't mean any harm he was just looking out for people that need those handicapped parking spaces."

"I know Butch and I told her that she needed to keep her handicapped placard handy."

"I also told her if she wanted to we could go down to the D.M.V. and get her a handicapped license plate and I would change it out for her."

"That's a good idea Mr. Murphy. I should have thought of that." I replied to Mr. Murphy. I'm actually a little envious of him thinking of that idea, and not me.

"See Butch we old people still have a few good ideas every now and then. Anyway I just wanted to call and thank you for what you did, I'll let you go now." Mr. Murphy said as he hung up.

I was just then arriving at the county courthouse parking garage; my conversation with Mr. Murphy had temporarily taken my mind off being scared. I was feeling better about things.

I've always thought that what goes around comes around. So whenever I can help someone out, I try to do what I can. So who would have thought that helping out Mrs. Smith this afternoon would have come back to help me out this evening by keeping my mind off being scared. It truly is a small world after all.

I parked in my parking space and walked through the employee's entrance of the county courthouse. The lights were on, but there wasn't anybody around.

It was after five o'clock and all the offices where empty. The receptionist had gone home and all of the night deputies where out on patrol. I looked around the offices and couldn't see Sheriff Wells anywhere.

I assumed that he was still downstairs in the equipment room. I couldn't help myself. I went into the sheriff's office to wait on him.

I sat down on the sheriff's couch and looked down at his coffee table. Looking through the sheriff's magazines I thought that I really need to bring him some wildlife magazines.

I was trying to do anything I could to keep my mind off of being scared. Just then I heard someone coming. It was the sheriff.

He walked into his office with what looked like a fat pair of binoculars under his arm. As the sheriff walked past me, he asked me to come over to his desk and sit down.

He sat behind his desk and I sat down in front of his desk. He put the binoculars down on the right side of the desk, and picked up some pictures that he had laying on the left side of his desk.

"That's a fat pair of binoculars you have there Pete."

"Those are night vision binoculars Butch." Pete explained while he shuffled through those pictures he had picked up.

"Wow Pete where did you get those at?"

"It's part of bringing this department into the twentieth century. It was a promise that Sheriff Moore had made to modernize the Sheriff's department and I intend to keep that promise."

"Ok Pete enough about the night vision binoculars what did you find out about the *Prairie Monster*?"

"Well Butch I probably have more questions than I have answers but I do think I have a starting place."

"Before we get to all of that tell me about the beef liver in the back of Berry's pocket?"

"Ok Pete what do you want to know about it? It was beef liver. Beef liver is pretty much beef liver, what else is there to say?" I asked Pete, I was lost trying to figure out what the sheriff really wanted to know. What was he asking? What was he after?

"Butch I want to know as much as you can tell me about that beef liver that was in the back pocket of your friend Berry. I know that it sounds like a silly question but I'm trying to get as much information as I can get out of you." Pete was saying as he pulled out a yellow legal pad of paper and began to write.

"Alright it was beef liver that Mrs. Decker had in the refrigerator at Berry's house. She had plans to fix it the next day for dinner with onions."

"I don't know what else she was going to fix with it. The beef liver was in some sort of plastic bowl with a lid on it."

"Berry opened the lid and cut off a chunk. He put the lid back on the bowl and put it back in the refrigerator."

"Berry then put the beef liver in a plastic bread sack and stuffed it in his back pocket."

"Pete I don't understand. It looked like beef liver and it smelled like beef liver."

"Just what are you looking for?" I asked Pete, not knowing exactly where he was going with his questions, I was a little confused.

"Butch why was the beef liver in a plastic bowl and not in a store wrapper?"

"Probably because Mrs. Decker got it fresh from one of the local ranchers after they had slaughtered one of their cows."

"Pete when I was growing up we would buy beef, hogs, chickens, fresh cow's milk, and eggs, from local farmers and ranchers. It was cheaper."

"Why? What does that have to do with anything? You can buy the same thing at a grocery store all day long." I asked Pete as I explained how country folk usually bought their meats.

"Think about it Butch. The beef liver in the back of Berry's pocket was from a fresh kill. The blood that ran down his leg and got all over his clothes was fresh."

"Fresh meat has a stronger smell to it than processed meat." The sheriff explained to me as I sat there wide-eyed in amazement.

"Pete I can't believe I didn't put two and two together. I feel so stupid."

"So you see Butch, your friend Berry did this to himself. You weren't in anyway responsible for what happened to him. It was a combination of his mother buying fresh beef liver and your friend being a little careless with it, and getting it all over his leg."

"Now that we have an idea why he was killed and not you, we need to find out who, and how they are doing this." Pete said as he flipped back a few pages on his legal pad.

"Butch how much do you know about this reporter from the past? The one that wrote about the Monster of the Prairie."

"You know the one that disappeared and was never heard from again." Pete asked as he flipped some more pages on his legal pad.

"Pete what I know is what you have there in the file I gave to you. I have his newspaper stories and that he disappeared trying to trap the monster."

"In his last report he said he was going to bring the monster back and display it. That's all there is on the reporter that disappeared."

Pete just sat there looking at his notes that he had written down on his legal pad, not saying anything at first. Then with a big smile on his face, he said.

"No Butch that's not all there is."

Chapter 5

The reporter.

Pete sat back in his chair and smiled. Looking down at his notes he looked like the cat that just swallowed the canary. Pete knew something and it seemed like he was in possession of a lot more information than he was letting on. I didn't know what he knew, but I was about to find out.

Pete had put his investigating knowledge to work and he had scored some very helpful information.

"Ok Pete what's up? I know you know something about that reporter so let's hear it." I asked Pete, who could hardly contain himself.

"Butch you know what the name of the newspaper was that he worked for?"

"Yeah Pete I know, it was the Philadelphia Eagle, but you already knew that, didn't you?"

"Butch did you know that the Philadelphia Eagle is still publishing newspapers today under a different name?"

"Yes Pete I knew, it's all right there in my notes."

"Butch you'd be surprised what you can find out on the internet. The Philadelphia Star purchased the Philadelphia Eagle, about sixty years ago. And they have computerized all their data."

"The Philadelphia Star has the rights to all the data that the Philadelphia Eagle had, and that includes all the stories, reports, notes and pictures that were in the Philadelphia Eagle archives."

"In the Philadelphia Eagle archives there were a lot of employment records. The Philadelphia Eagle had kept very good records of their employees."

"That reporter that was doing a report on the monster of the prairie used a pen name. Butch do you know what his real name was?" Pete was asking as he turned another page on his yellow legal pad of paper.

"Pete all I know was the name that he used in the newspaper articles he wrote, and that was John Wall. I didn't even think of John Wall as a pen name, the thought never crossed my mind. Why would it make a difference?"

"You're not going to believe this Butch. He was born right here in Rock County, Kansas. He still has family living here."

"Butch he went to school in Philadelphia and upon graduation began to work for the Philadelphia Eagle as a cub reporter."

"When an assignment came up for a reporter to do a story on a monster that was terrorizing the prairie the editor decided to give this young cub reporter his big break."

"Butch the young reporter, who already knew the area because he was born here and he grew up here, was Jonathan Wallace"

"He was the oldest child of Mary and William Wallace. They had thirteen children all together nine boys and four girls."

"Being the oldest son, Jonathan moved away when he was sixteen years old to go to school in Philadelphia, with his parent's permission and with their blessing."

Pete began to explain how the Philadelphia Eagle made everyone they hired write a short story about their lives, and where they came from and how they got there. It was their way of doing a background check on their employees back then.

"When the editor hired Jonathan he had him write a short autobiography and asked him to come up with a pen name for himself."

"Jonathan made it easier on himself by shortening his real name and just went with John Wall. By the way Butch you went to school with Jonathan's great, great nephew."

"Would you care to guess who it is?" Pete asked with a big smile on his face.

"I already figured it out Pete. You're going to tell me that Deputy Frank Wallace is the great, great nephew of Jonathan Wallace."

"Wow Pete talk about stranger then fiction. How did you find out all of this?" I asked, because I thought that I had taken all the information there was to take off the internet.

"Butch not too many people know that most newspapers will allow law enforcement agencies access to there archives that they have on file. They give us a pass code to use when we need to access those files from time to time."

"The Philadelphia Star has all its old records on computer which I am able to access from my computer right here. Their computer has on file the last report that John Wall sent in to his publisher."

"Butch the Philadelphia Eagle chose not to publish John Wall's last report he sent in on the monster of the prairie."

"So Butch, what most people think is the last article published in the newspaper is the last report sent in by John Wall, but it's not."

"Wait a minute Pete you mean to tell me that all these years I've only had part of the story on the monster of the prairie?" I asked as I was still amazed how much more information the sheriff was able to obtain.

"There's a lot more you haven't seen Butch. John wrote about how the monster only attacks at night and that it has a fondness for fresh animal blood."

"He also wrote about how he slept during the day and hunted the monster at night. John wrote how the Indians taught him to stalk the monster, but he also wrote that the Indians had made several attempts to kill the beast, but they were unsuccessful."

"The Indians had told John that it couldn't be killed because it was already dead and it lived in the spirit world."

"Butch, John wrote that the only way to see the monster was to sit very quietly in a tree, and to stake out an animal as bait for it to kill."

"He wrote that the monster was amazingly fast and that it was very strong." Pete continued to explain what he had found out. He was talking so fast it was hard to keep up with him.

"Butch there were a couple more things that John Wall, or Jonathan Wallace, wrote about the beast. One thing was that it had glowing bright red eyes."

"Do you know what that means Butch?" Pete asked as he looked up at me from his note pad.

"No not really but I am amazed how much information you have been able to gather in such a short time. You weren't kidding when you said that you do your job very well."

"Pete tell me why the bright glowing red eyes are so important, and what is the other thing that John wrote about?" I said to Pete as he sat there behind his desk making notes on his yellow legal pad.

I was truly impressed with Sheriff Wells and his ability to conduct an investigation. Pete was without a doubt out of my league.

"Well Butch you now have someone to corroborate the statement you gave to the sheriff back when you were twelve years old. That should make you feel better about sticking to your story and not changing it under pressure from others."

"Butch you're going to need to sit back and listen to what I have to say about how the creature comes and goes without getting caught." Pete said as his face and attitude turned serious.

Just then we heard someone coming. I stood up and turned around to look. Pete leaned over to his left side to see who it was.

Deputy Frank Wallace came walking up to the sheriff's open office door and knocked on it. Pete told him to come in.

"Come on in please deputy." Pete said to Frank as he leaned back over in his chair. The sheriff started thumbing through his notes as if he was looking for something that he had made notes on that he wanted to discuss with Frank.

I went ahead and sat back down and asked Pete if I needed to step out. The sheriff just shook his head back and forth as to tell me no. Deputy Wallace walked up to the sheriff's desk and stood there with his hands on his hips.

"Hi Frank." I said to Frank as he nodded his head up, saying hi. We country folk call that hi hatting someone.

"Deputy Wallace I have a few personal questions I would like to ask you, if you don't mind? You are under no obligation to answer them if you choose not to. It will not be looked at in a negative way if you choose not to answer any of my questions."

"If you do answer them it will not be looked at in a negative way. Do you understand what I'm telling you Deputy Wallace?"

"No not really." Frank responded while he looked at me and raised his eyebrows, as if he was asking me if I knew what the Sheriff was trying to say.

"Deputy Wallace I have asked Butch to sit in on our conversation because it directly involves him. If at anytime you wish for Butch to step out just say so and I will ask him to leave." The Sheriff explained in the same cold unfriendly way.

"Pete the way you talk you have me scared to say anything. You really need to work on your people skills."

"Frank, the sheriff is going to ask you about the *Prairie Monster* and your distant relatives." I tried to ease the tension. I thought that if I asked first it may be a little easier for Frank to talk.

"Frank when we were growing up you would always tease me about the *Prairie Monster*. I can remember when you would ask me, how's big foot, or have you seen the bogeyman lately."

110

"All joking aside, Frank did your parents or grandparents ever talk to you as a kid about the *Prairie Monster*?"

"Of course I heard all those bedtime stories. The same ones everyone else did around here, but I was never into fairytales." Frank said as he stood there. Deputy Wallace couldn't believe that he was called down to the sheriff's office for this.

"Excuse me Deputy Wallace, but did any of those stories include distant family members being attacked?" The sheriff asked as he looked up at Frank from his notes.

"Yeah I suppose so. Why? What's this all about?"

"The sheriff is helping me Frank, and he has uncovered some evidence that may be beneficial to you and your family."

"What kind of evidence?" Frank asked.

Sheriff Wells and I just sat there and looked at each other. Neither one of us wanted to jump right out there and tell Deputy Wallace about his great, great uncle at this time. We would rather hear everything that Frank knew before we let him know what we know.

"Deputy Wallace, would you share your childhood stories that you heard on the *Prairie Monster* with Butch and I?" The sheriff asked Frank. I know that Frank had to have thought that we were crazy.

"Sure, but keep in mind that it was told to us kids to scare us." Frank said as he reached over to the wall to pick up a chair and put it down in front of the sheriff's desk so he could set down on it and tell his story.

Frank began to tell his story explaining that it was his grandfather that would tell all the kids about his uncle that was killed by a monster.

"I guess I was about twelve years old the last time my grandfather told me the story."

"Yeah I was twelve because Butch and Berry had just been attacked by some wild dogs. Grandpa told the story right after Berry's funeral."

"We all thought that he was trying to scare us so we wouldn't go off playing down by the river."

"Grandpa told us about an uncle that he had, that went back east to school and became some hot shot reporter for some big newspaper."

"My grandfather said that he had changed his name and became a city boy. He wasn't the same person he was when he left home and went off back east to attend school. He had forgotten his roots."

"He said that one day his uncle came back home to do a newspaper story on the monster that roamed the prairie for centuries."

"Grandpa said that his uncle went to live with the Indians for a couple of weeks and that he was learning all about evil spirits and how to deal with them."

112

"He told us to beware of the creature with glowing red eyes that are bright."

"Grandpa told us about his uncle writing stories and mailing them off to the newspaper that he worked for back east."

"He said his uncle had some big plan to capture a monster and take it back east with him."

"My grandfather told us kids that his uncle drew pictures of the animals that the monster had killed."

"It will suck the blood right out of your body without spilling a drop."

"Grandpa said that he never saw the beast for himself, but he knew it was real because he had seen the dead animals it had left behind after it had killed it, drained all the blood, and took a few of it's organs. Like the heart, liver, kidneys."

"He went on to tell us about how excited his uncle was that he had figured out where the monster lived, and he was going to pursue it the next chance he had." Deputy Wallace continued to tell the sheriff and I about his grandfathers *Prairie Monster* story.

"He was going to capture one and take it back east to Pennsylvania with him."

"Grandpa said that ropes would do no good. It didn't matter how many ropes you could get on the beast he was too strong to be held down by ropes."

"He said that one day his uncle left to go spend a couple of days in a tree so he could catch a glimpse of it, and kill the monster."

"My grandfather told us kids that his uncle had several knives on him and that he had a bow with about a dozen arrows that he planed to use to kill the monster with. His uncle said that guns were too noisy and would give him away."

"That night my grandfather rode his horse out to see his uncle. He said that his uncle was well hidden up in a tree."

"The Indians had taught his uncle how to camouflage himself in a tree, to blend in, to become one with the tree."

"Grandpa told us kids that he was the last person to see his uncle Jonathan alive."

"My grandpa told us that his uncle warned him to stay away from the stones."

"That would be the last time anyone would see or hear from his Uncle Jonathan again."

"Grandpa told us that there was a full investigation conducted and the sheriff spent weeks looking for his uncle and his uncles belongings."

"He said that nothing was ever found and that the sheriff had listed his Uncle Jonathan Wallace as missing."

"So right about there is where my grandfather would tell us to beware. Beware! Beware of the two glowing red eyes that are bright. Beware of the _Prairie Monster_ that lives in the night."

"Or something like that." Frank told quite a story to Sheriff Wells and me.

114

"Frank what stones was your grandfather talking about?" I asked Deputy Wallace about his grandfather warning to stay away from the stones.

"I don't know Butch. It was a fairytale. I didn't ask." Frank said as he shrugged his shoulders.

"Frank weren't you the least bit curious about what happened to your great, great Uncle Jonathan and his warning about staying away from the stones?" I asked with amazement that Frank wasn't curious.

"Butch even at twelve years old I didn't believe in fairytales. You should try living in the real world." Frank replied sarcastically.

"Deputy Wallace!" The Sheriff said in a stern voice. Pete didn't appreciate Frank's sarcasm.

"Yes sir." Frank responded, knowing that the sheriff was upset with him for saying what he said.

"Deputy Wallace I don't know how to tell you this but you just confirmed a story that I received from another reliable source." The sheriff explained to Frank without revealing too much.

"Oh you've got to be kidding me. All that stuff is just fairytale stories that old people have been telling kids for years." Frank said as he looked back and forth between the sheriff and me.

"No I'm afraid not Deputy Wallace. It seems that a reporter for the Philadelphia Star named John Wall came here to do a story."

"Before you say anything about the reporter's name being John Wall instead of Jonathan Wallace, he was using a pen name. John Wall, the reporter, was really Jonathan Wallace, your great, great uncle. He chose to shorten his name under the advice of his editor at the Philadelphia Star."

"John Wall was sent here to do a story about a monster terrorizing the prairie. He was sent because he was born here and he knew the area, he had family here, and he grew up here."

"Your great, great uncle wrote several articles on what he called The Monster of the Prairie, and sent them back east to be printed in the Philadelphia Star newspaper."

Frank just sat there listening to the sheriff. I know it had to be hard for Frank to believe all of this but what the sheriff was telling him was fact.

"Deputy Wallace, do you understand that the stories that your grandfather told you are probably true?" The sheriff asked a bewildered Frank.

"Yes I understand but I'm just having a hard time believing it." Frank said as he rubbed his head.

"Everything that I have told you is fact Deputy Wallace, it's a part of history and you should be proud of your heritage. Your great, great uncle was a very good reporter." The sheriff explained to Frank.

"There are just a couple of things that Butch and I would like to know. Can you remember anything that your grandfather told you that might help us find and kill the monster?"

116

"I'm sorry sheriff I just didn't pay that much attention to my grandfather's stories."

"I always considered the stories that grandpa told us as fairytales, something he used to try and scare us with."

"I want to thank you Deputy Wallace for sharing your grandfather's story about your great, great uncle with Butch and I."

"That's ok Sheriff. If I remember anything else I'll call you."

"Butch I want to apologize to you for all those years of teasing you about Big Foot. I had no idea that this thing really existed." Frank said as he stuck his hand out to shake hands with me.

"Frank nobody ever believed me so you weren't the only one to tease me." I explained to Frank as I reached out and shook his hand.

"Deputy Wallace I know I don't have to tell you this but, keep all of this to yourself. We don't need a panic on our hands."

"Yes sir Sheriff, can I go back to my patrol now, or is there anything else?" Frank asked as he stood up and put the chair back against the wall that he had grabbed earlier.

"Your dismissed Deputy Wallace, and lets keep alert out there ok."

I thanked Frank as he was walking out of the sheriff's office. He just nodded his head up and down in acknowledgement. I think that Frank was still having a hard time believing all of this.

As I sat there in a chair in front of the sheriff's desk I noticed that he was busy writing on his yellow legal pad again.

"Well Pete we learned that ropes can't hold it and that guns are too noisy. Oh yeah we should stay away from the stones." I said to Pete as he flipped a page on his note pad and wrote something else down.

"Butch we learned more than that. We learned that a reporter that grew up around here figured out where it lives and how it comes and goes."

"We learned that being off the ground could be to our advantage. We learned that one man with a bow and arrows, and several knives couldn't stop it."

"Butch it's just more clues to the mystery and it gets us closer to the answer."

"Of course if we go after this thing Butch we're going to need some bait. I don't know how the Kansas Humane Society is going to react if we stake out an animal for it to kill."

"Pete when this is over I want you to teach me how to be more observant and not to jump to conclusions too early."

"Butch you just need to slow down and look at the whole picture, and take the time to look at the little things that are right there in plain sight."

"For instance Butch, did you know that every picture that you took that's in your *Prairie Monster* file has a big rock sticking out of the ground in the background?"

118

"The clue has been there every time you looked at those pictures, but you didn't see it." Pete had just pointed out my obvious inexperience as an investigator.

"What do those big rocks have to do with anything Pete? I mean those rocks have been around here forever, and they would be too heavy for someone to move."

"Yes Butch they would be too heavy for someone like you or I. But what about something that is so strong that several ropes couldn't keep it contained?"

"Butch do you think that this creature could be strong enough to move one of those big rocks that are scattered all over?"

"I guess you could be right Pete. I had never considered that before, it just never crossed my mind."

"Like you said Pete it's been staring at me right in the face for years and years and I couldn't see it. I can't believe I never saw that." I said to the sheriff with my head hanging down.

I felt so stupid and incompetent after Pete had found out more in just a few hours then I did in thirty years of investigating.

"Butch I didn't tell you that it's been staring at you for years. I told you to let a fresh pair of eyes look at your file. Sometimes a fresh pair of eyes will see things that other's have overlooked."

"Butch you just overlooked the obvious, everybody does. It takes training to look for things like that, I'll be happy to work with you on it."

"Butch this is just good investigational skills. As a matter of fact let's just consider this your first lesson." Pete said as he was trying to boast my ego.

"Thanks Pete."

"Hey Pete I'm getting thirsty would you like a soda from the machine?"

"Sure Butch thanks."

As I stood up and walked out of the sheriff's office, all I could think about is how stupid I've been all these years.

It was a short walk to the break room where the vending machines are at. One dollar in the pop machine will buy two cans of pop. It seemed like a small price to pay for all the help so far.

It was clear to me by now that the sheriff was out of my league, he knew his job and he knew it very well. I can see now why Pete was so much in demand.

As I walked back into the sheriff's office, there Pete sits taking notes on his yellow legal pad.

"Sheriff Peter Wells you're not bad for a city boy. You could work on your bed side manner a bit, but you're pretty good at what you do, I'm impressed and I don't get impressed very often." I said to the sheriff as I handed him a can of pop.

"Wow Butch! That must have hurt for you to say that about a city boy." Pete said with a smile as he sat back in his chair and opened his can of pop.

"You don't know how much. But I give credit where credit is due." I told the sheriff as I opened my pop and sat back down in the chair that was in front of his desk.

"Butch I hope you realize and understand that some of the things that I have found out, you don't have access too as a civilian. That's the only reason that you didn't find these things out." Pete said while he continued to write notes on his yellow legal pad of paper.

"Ok Pete what do we do next?"

The sheriff didn't even look up from his notepad.

"Pete I'm thinking that we need to get a farmer or a rancher to donate a cow to us so we can stake it out by a big tree. What do you think?"

"Well Butch I would like to try and find out more about that tree that Jonathan Wallace was in when he disappeared. Who knows it might still be standing."

Of course Pete was right. There I go again putting the cart before the horse. I was just so excited about the opportunity to get to the bottom of this I was rushing things again.

"Ok then Pete how do we go about trying to find one tree out of millions? It's going to be like looking for a needle in a haystack."

"Well Butch let's use our heads, and step back and look at the whole picture. Where would you start looking first if you were working on this by yourself?" Pete asked as he sat forward in his chair tapping his pen on his note pad.

"Well Pete I guess I would start by calling the Kansas State University research and extension natural resources agent. I would ask him if he has a list of the oldest trees in this area. I could Google it and see where that would take me. What do you suggest?"

Pete leaned forward and wrote something down on his pad of paper. The sheriff then looked up at me and said with a smile.

"Butch I just wrote myself a note to call you if I ever have a question about the outdoors. I would have never thought to call Kansas State University and ask them."

"That's a very good place to start Butch. See if you just slow down and think about it you can figure this out."

"Where would you start at Pete?"

"Butch I was thinking about going onto The National Arbor Day Foundation web site and looking to see if they had a listing for the oldest trees in Rock County, Kansas."

Both ideas were good but there was one more that came to mind. I had just remembered something that Mr. Murphy had said earlier in the day about the *Prairie Monster*.

"Pete I think I might know someone who would know which tree Jonathan Wallace was in when he disappeared."

"When I was with Mr. Murphy this morning he told me that his great grandfather used to tell him stories about the *Prairie Monster*. I'm thinking that if we talk to Mr. Murphy he might have an idea about which tree it might be."

"Butch do you think we could go by his farm and ask him right now?"

Just then my cell phone started playing Conway Twitty's, "Hello Darling", that's the ring tone that I have programmed into my cell phone for when Vickie calls me.

"Excuse me Pete it's my wife calling me." I stood up and walked away from the sheriff's desk and answered my cell phone.

"Hello."

"Slow down."

"Ok I'm on my way. Take the kids back home and I'll call you when I find him."

"I will, don't worry, I will."

"Bye."

"I love you too."

"Pete I have to go."

"My son Kevin is missing."

Chapter 6

The search for Kevin.

Pete stood up and without a second of hesitation said to me.

"Butch your not going anywhere without me. We'll take my patrol cruiser and a couple of hand held police radios with us."

In just a matter of seconds the sheriff had grabbed a couple of radios and those night vision binoculars and we were out the door. On the way to the sheriff's patrol cruiser Pete asked me for the details of my conversation with Vickie.

"I don't want to be nosey Butch but I need to know about the conversation you had with your wife."

"Vickie said that Kevin called on his cell phone and told her that his car had died on his way home from play practice, and that he couldn't get it started back up."

"Kevin told Vickie that his car had died on the dirt road just past the river."

"She said that she tried to tell him that she would bring the other kids with her and come pick him up. When she was trying to tell him to stay there his cell phone went dead."

"So Vickie loaded the three little ones up and went after Kevin. When she drove to his car his emergency flashers were on but he was no where around."

"That's when she called me." I explained to Pete as we were driving out of the parking garage.

"Butch why don't you try calling your sons cell phone and see if you can get a hold of him?" Pete told me as he turned on his red lights but no siren.

I called Kevin's number and it went straight to his voice mail. I hung up and tried again, this time when I got his voice I left him a message.

"Kevin this is your father, if you get this message call me immediately, I need to know where you're at."

"Butch pull yourself together you have to stay focused. Don't start falling apart on me now." Pete said as he turned onto the dirt road that leads past the river and on down towards where I live.

"What do you mean Pete? I'm ok I'm just a little concerned that's all. Remember Mr. Murphy's cow was mutilated last night by something. I'm just a little concerned that's all."

"Oh yeah then why did you tell your son to call you if he gets this message, instead of when he gets this message?" Pete asked. I didn't even realize that I had said "if" instead of "when".

"Does anything get past you Pete? Look up ahead there's a car with flashers on. It's Kevin's car."

It had just started getting dark, and I was starting to get real nervous now, Kevin was no where in sight.

As Pete and I stepped out of the sheriff's patrol cruiser, I hollered out for Kevin. Of course there was no answer it wasn't going to be that easy. So I started looking around at the ground.

"Pete grab your flashlight and come over here and take a look at this." I asked Pete as I crouched down beside the car, looking at the shoe prints on the road that I believe was left by Kevin.

As Pete handed me the flashlight, I shined it onto the ground.

"Take a look at this Pete. Don't those look like tennis shoe prints on the road?"

"See Pete, it looks like they take a few steps towards the other side of the road towards the river before they disappear. It looks like there's been several tire tracks go back and forth over them."

"Take it easy Butch. This doesn't mean that your son went down by the river."

"It just means that he walked across the road." Pete was trying to make me feel better. It wasn't working, I was nervous. Big time nervous.

"Butch I'm going to put out an A. P. B. on your son, Kevin. I need to know how old he is, how tall he is, about how much he weighs. You know what I need, a full description of him."

I gave Pete all the information that he needed and while he was issuing an A. P. B., I went to look inside Kevin's car. It was locked but that was ok because I had an extra key. I opened the car door and sat down inside behind the steering wheel.

Everything looked ok so I put my key into the ignition and tried to start the car. It started right up and then died after a few seconds. I looked down at the gauges. Wouldn't you know it? He was out of gas.

"Hey Butch do you want me to call a tow truck for your sons car?"

"No thanks Pete. That brainless kid of mine ran out of gas." I explained to the sheriff. I was more then a little worried about Kevin and irritated that he let his car run out of gas.

"Come on Butch I'll run you back into town to the Short Trip Convenience store and see if your son caught a ride with someone to go get some gas." Pete said as he picked up his radio and told his deputies that he would be heading back into town.

"Butch you better call your wife and tell her what you're doing and see if your son has called in or showed up there."

"Your right Pete, maybe Vickie has heard from Kevin." I said to Pete as I was calling Vickie, hoping that she had some good news.

"Hi Sweet Pea have you heard anything from Kevin?"

"No I was hoping you were calling with the news that you had found him." Vickie responded in a tearful way, she was starting to worry more and more that something had happened to Kevin, and was getting more emotional by the minute.

"Take it easy Sweet Pea we'll find him, it'll be alright. Try not to worry."

"The sheriff and I went to his car and I checked it out. Kevin ran out of gas, so now we're on are way back into town to see if someone had stopped and gave him a ride to the Short Trip Convenience store to get some gas."

"When you find him you call me immediately please. Then you ground him for a year for scaring us like this." Vickie said in a weepy but nervous voice.

"I will and if you here something, call me."

"I need to go now we're here in town now. Love you Sweet Pea, bye." I said to Vickie as we were pulling into the parking lot of the convenience store.

"Butch why don't you go in and check to see if anyone has seen your son? I'll get the gas can out of the trunk and put some gas in it so we can get his car off the side of the road." The sheriff suggested as he popped the truck open from the inside of his car.

Of course no one had seen Kevin since school and by now it was dark and starting to cool down a bit. I told the kids loitering around the convenience store if they happen to see Kevin have him call home immediately. I went ahead and paid for the gas that the sheriff had pumped into the gas can while I was in the store.

"Anybody see your boy Butch?" Pete asked as I walked back out to his patrol cruiser.

"No."

"I don't know what to do next Pete." I was having a hard time concentrating and it was dark now and I knew that the *Prairie Monster* was back.

"I need to go pay for the gas Butch and then we'll go get your sons car."

"Keep in mind Butch that your son disappeared when it was still light out, so the reasonable thing to assume is that someone stopped and picked him up."

"I already paid for the gas Pete, thanks. I know your right but he's a fifteen year old boy who thinks he's a man." I said to Pete as we got back in his patrol cruiser.

As we where driving back to Kevin's car; one of the sheriff's deputies came on the radio and called for the sheriff.

"Calling Sheriff Wells come in please."

"This is Sheriff Wells." Pete answered.

"This is Deputy Barns, Sheriff I think I seen that kid your looking for."

"10-4 Deputy Barns, where?" Pete replied as he looked over at me and smiled.

"While I had someone pulled over writing them a citation along side the highway that red headed Parson's kid drove by with his girlfriend in the front seat and I think he had Butch's boy in the back."

"10-4 Deputy Barns. Thanks I'll check into it." Pete said as he sat the radio back in its holder.

"Well Butch you better call your wife and let her know what Deputy Barns said."

I called Vickie and told her what Deputy Barns saw and reported to Sheriff Wells. She said that she knew the Parson's home telephone number and she would give them a call to see if they have seen Kevin.

As we pulled back up to Kevin's car my cell phone rang. Conway Twitty's Hello Darling. I looked at the sheriff and told him, that would be my wife calling back.

"Hello."

"Ok."

"Ok."

"Ok thanks Sweet Pea." I said to Vickie as I closed my cell phone.

While I was talking to Vickie on my cell phone, Pete had retrieved the gas can from the trunk of his patrol cruiser and had emptied it into the gas tank of Kevin's car for me.

"Good news I hope, you had three oks in your conversation with your wife." Pete said with a wink, telling me that he was paying attention to my phone call and that nothing gets past him.

"Vickie said that she called the Parson's and they said that Ben hadn't been home from school yet."

"She went on to say that Mrs. Parson told her that Ben will drive his girlfriend home after he drive's his cousin home. His cousin lives just a mile down the dirt road from us."

"Vickie said that Mrs. Parson would have Ben call us as soon as he gets home."

"One, two, three, oks, Sherlock." I said to Pete, acknowledging that yes I know how smart you are.

"Alright Butch so I usually observe everything. But that's my job."

"I know Pete I was just having fun with you, but you do have great powers of deduction like the fictitious detective Sherlock Holmes." I said to Pete as I sat down in Kevin's car and started it up.

"I guess calling me Sherlock Holmes is better than you calling me Barney Fife." Pete was telling me that he knew that I had been calling him Barney Fife behind his back.

"Sorry about that Pete."

"Do you want to follow me to my house Pete just in case Kevin's car dies on me again?" I asked Pete as he was walking back to his patrol cruiser.

Pete stuck his hand up and waved for me to go. He would follow behind me down the dirt road to my house. I turned into my driveway and drove up to the house, Pete was right behind me.

As I parked Kevin's car, I could see Vickie looking out the back door. I waited for Pete to park and then I asked him to come in.

"Come on in Pete I'll see if Vickie has heard from the Paterson's."

"Good evening Mrs. Black." Pete said as he walked in the house and took his hat off.

"Oh come on now Pete, I think we know each other enough for you to call me Vickie."

"Please come on into the living room." Vickie asked as she led the way.

"Vickie, have you heard anything at all? I didn't know if the Paterson's had called." I asked as we all stepped into the living room.

"No I haven't heard anything."

"Butch why was his car out of gas? Didn't he have half a tank of gas when he put it in the schools auto shop?"

"Yeah Sweet Pea but you know how kids are; they probably ran the car listening to the radio or something like that."

Just then we heard the back door open and Kevin walked in. We all just stood there for a second.
A second is all it took for Vickie to grab Kevin and hug him.

Then with the wrath of a mother not knowing where her son was, the questioning commenced.

"Where have you been?"

"I've been trying to call you."

"Do you know that you've had your father and I worried half to death?" Vickie was all over the place with her questions.

"I'm sorry my cell phone went dead right after I called when my car died and wouldn't start back up."

"Then Ben came by after dropping off his cousin and offered to give me a lift home if I would ride along with him and Sally to drop her off at her house." Kevin tried to explain what he was doing, and where he had been.

"Why didn't you wait for me?"

"I told you that I was going to load up your brother and sisters and come get you." Vickie asked with her hands on her hips.

"I didn't know. I told you my cell phone went dead. I think I ran out of gas. Dad how did you get my car home?" Kevin asked as he was looking at Pete, probably wondering why the sheriff was here.

"The sheriff put gas in your car and it started right up after that."

"Son you had us worried you need to be a little more considerate of what you are doing. You should have figured that one of us would come looking for you and pick you up." I explained to Kevin in a calm manner.

"Yeah your right dad I didn't think of that."

"Hey thanks Sheriff for helping get my car home I appreciate it."

"You didn't look in the trunk and find my stash of moonshine did you?" Kevin asked the sheriff jokingly.

"Yep that apple doesn't fall far from the tree in this house. Like father like son." The sheriff replied.

"Are you about ready to go Butch?" Pete asked as he started walking towards the back door.

"Sweet Pea the sheriff and I need to go I will call you later." I said to Vickie as I leaned over to kiss her goodbye.

"Sheriff you take care of him. That's the only husband I've got and I would like to keep him." Vickie hollered out to Pete as we walked to his patrol cruiser.

"We'll do Vickie."

"Don't be too hard on the boy." Pete said to Vickie as we sat down into his patrol cruiser.

Pete then picked up his hand held radio and canceled the A. P. B. which he had put out on Kevin.

Pete started up the car and started driving down the driveway when he got to the end of the driveway he asked about my family.

"How many kids do you have Butch?"

"I have nine Pete. Two are already married and have graduated college, three are in college and the other four are at home."

"Two of the three that are in college are twins."

"By the way thanks for being there for me and helping me out tonight."

"You have a real nice family Butch. It was my pleasure helping out tonight. It was real nice to see a family so concerned about their teenage son."

"Now do you think Mr. Murphy would talk to us right now?" Pete asked as we sat there in his patrol cruiser at the end of the driveway.

"I'm sure he would, I'll give him a call and ask him. Go ahead and turn right and start heading that way." I directed the sheriff as I picked up my cell phone and gave Mr. Murphy a call; I hope it wasn't too late to call.

"Mr. Murphy this is Butch, sorry to bother you but I'm with the sheriff right now sir. We were wondering if we could come by and ask you a few questions?"

"You have questions you want to ask me? Questions about what Butch?"

"About trees Mr. Murphy. If you don't mind sir, we have a few questions about trees."

"I don't mind Butch, I'm right in the middle of painting the kitchen right now, but I guess I could use a break." Mr. Murphy said as I could hear him moving something around in the background, it sounded like it might have been a stepladder or chair.

"If this is a bad time Mr. Murphy we could come by later, it sounds like you're busy."

"No, no Butch come on by I told you I could use a break, my back is starting to bother me anyway."

"Butch how far away are you and the sheriff right now?"

"Well I'm glad you asked that Mr. Murphy. We are not far away at all. As a matter of fact we are about to pull into your driveway."

"Butch you're going to have to give me a few minutes so I can do something with my paint brushes and can of paint."

As I said my goodbyes to Mr. Murphy and closed my cell phone the sheriff pulled his patrol cruiser into Mr. Murphy's driveway.

The sheriff and I sat out in his patrol cruiser for about five to seven minutes. Giving Mr. Murphy more time to do whatever he needed to do with his paint and paintbrush before we go talk to him.

As the sheriff and I were walking up to the house, we could see Mr. Murphy walking towards us through the front window of his house. We met on the front porch.

"Good evening Mr. Murphy, again I'm sorry to bother you when your so busy. I don't know if you have ever met the sheriff or not."

"Mr. Murphy this is Sheriff Peter Wells. Pete this is Mr. Murphy."

"Good evening Sheriff it's good to finely be able to meet you."

"Mr. Murphy it's always a pleasure to meet the residents of Rock County." Pete said as he stuck his hand out to shake hands with Mr. Murphy.

"Now Butch, why on Gods green earth do you two want to ask me about trees? I don't know anything about trees." Mr. Murphy explained shaking his head back and forth.

"It all started after I left here this morning Mr. Murphy. When I went in to the office I told the sheriff about your dead cow, and about my suspicions of how it was killed."

"The sheriff agreed to help me in my investigation, and he uncovered some interesting information."

"To make a long story short Mr. Murphy we are looking for a very old tree that we hope is still standing."

"We have no idea what kind of tree it is, all the sheriff and I know is that there was a reporter that was in it the last time anyone ever saw him."

"It's that same reporter I told you about this morning Mr. Murphy, the one that wrote all those stories about the Monster of the Prairie."

"I told Sheriff Wells that it might be worth it to come and speak to you about it."

"I remembered that you told me this morning that your grandfather would tell you stories about the _Prairie Monster_. We think that reporter was trying to kill or capture it when he disappeared."

"I didn't know Mr. Murphy if you had heard any stories about the reporter that had disappeared, and if you had if you would be willing to share them with us. We have no clue where to start at."

Mr. Murphy leaned back against the rail that goes around his porch and then crossed one arm while putting his chin in the hand that was on his other arm. He stood there thinking about what I had just told him.

"Butch I don't know about your reporter, but I do remember that my father told a story about a man that would sit in a tree all night long."

"Do you know that big old Cottonwood tree that's down by the river? The one behind where the old Decker place used to be."

"Butch you know which one I'm talking about. It's that Cottonwood tree that's down there where you and Berry were attacked."

"I think I do Mr. Murphy. Is it the one that everyone calls the big Walnut tree?"

"That would be the one I'm talking about."

"Butch do you know why everyone around here calls it the big Walnut tree?" Mr. Murphy asked me but was looking at both the sheriff and I when he did. Pete hadn't said much the whole time we've been here; he was just standing there listening.

"No I don't know why Mr. Murphy that's just what everyone was calling it when I was growing up so that's what I used to call it too."

"Butch my father told me back when I was a kid that apparently there was some crazy guy that would sit up in that old Cottonwood. Everyone around here thought that he was a nut."

"Now if I remember it right my father told me that the man's name was Wall, and that is why people started calling it the Wall-nut tree."

"Did I help you out any Butch?" Mr. Murphy asked as the sheriff and I stood there and smiled in amazement.

"Yes you did Mr. Murphy, yes you did very much and the sheriff and I appreciate it."

"Thank you Mr. Murphy. Thank you very much." As I thanked Mr. Murphy I then turned to the sheriff and asked if he had any questions that he wanted to ask.

"Pete do you have any questions for Mr. Murphy or are you about ready to go?"

"No I'm good Butch. It was very nice to meet you Mr. Murphy. I hope we can get together under better circumstances sometime." Pete said as he stuck his hand out to shake Mr. Murphy's hand.

"We need to get going Mr. Murphy and you have a kitchen to paint, so thank you again and we'll see you later." I said as the sheriff and I walked down the steps towards the sheriff's car.

"Slow down Butch." Pete said after we sat down in the patrol cruiser.

I knew what Pete was referring to. He was referring to how we needed to take it one step at a time. Don't get ahead of ourselves.

Pete started up his patrol cruiser and he drove down Mr. Murphy's driveway out to the dirt road and then turned towards the river.

"Where are we going Pete?"

"Butch how well do you know Mr. Murphy? Do you think that he would give us a cow to use as bait when we go after this thing?" Pete asked me as he slowly continued driving towards the river.

"Pete I've known him all my life, and I think that he would let us use a cow as long as if it survived we returned it to him."

"Pete you didn't answer my question. Where are we going?"

"Butch I want you to show me where the old Decker house used to stand. If you're up to it I would like you to show me the path that you and Berry took back when you were twelve." Pete was jumping into this with both feet now, and I finally had someone on my side that was willing to help me.

"Alright Pete, but you have to promise me not to get yourself killed. I'm not going to lose another friend to this thing."

"Ok Butch I'll promise you if you'll promise me not to go after this thing alone."

"You got a deal Pete."

The sheriff sat there in his patrol cruiser driving towards the river with a smile on his face. I looked over at him and wondered what in the world could he possibly be smiling at.

"What's so funny Pete you're sitting there with this big cheesy smile on your face, did I miss something?" I asked as I began to smile too, and I don't even know why, or what I'm smiling about.

"Butch I was just thinking that I sure hope I don't ever break that promise I just made to you." Pete said with a chuckle.

As I sat there in the sheriff's patrol cruiser I began to reflect back to when I was a kid. I was teased and picked on by other kids after Berry's death. No one ever believed me before.

Now I'm learning that there were a lot of other people that knew about what was going on and did nothing to stop it.

From either out of fear, which I can understand or they just didn't want to get involved. Which I don't understand. I have to confess that it bothers me that my own people, country folk, stood by and did nothing. I don't understand it.

How can anybody stand by and not say or do anything when two twelve year old boys are attacked and one of them is viciously killed?

All I can go on is what Mr. Murphy said to me earlier. That people were afraid they would be labeled a nut. They were fearful of losing face in the community. Right or wrong sometimes you need to step up to the challenge no matter what.

"You need to slow down Pete."

"Turn into that next driveway. That's the one right there." I said to the sheriff as I pointed to the right.

"Butch that's really not a driveway; it's more of a path." The sheriff said as he pulled his patrol cruiser through the overgrowth of weeds. You could tell that no one has driven on this driveway for years.

It was eerily quiet and there was a sign at the end of the drive on a T-post that read.

No Trespassing by Order of Sheriff. It had several bullet holes in it.

Pete was driving very slowly, not knowing the area and not knowing what to expect it was better to proceed with caution.

The weeds were taller than the sheriff's patrol cruiser. They slowly fell forward as Pete gradually drove up the Decker's old driveway. The sheriff's patrol cruiser pushing down the weeds as Pete ever so cautiously drove into the unknown.

As Pete came to a stop he then turned on his spot light that was mounted on the driver's side door of his patrol cruiser. He began to shine it around the burned out rubble that was still there after all these years.

"Butch is this the old Decker place?" Pete asked as he was stepping out of the car.

"Yeah Pete."

"Yeah this is it."

"This is the old Decker place." I told Pete as I stepped out of the car and stood there.

It had been a long time since I've seen this place. A very long time. It was a little uncomfortable for me standing there.

Pete was strangely quiet; it was as if he was absorbing everything around him.

"Butch you stay here with me by the car. I'm going to call for backup."

"There's something wrong here."

Chapter 7

Returning back to Berry's house.

The sheriff sat back down in the Patrol cruiser and picked up the two radios that he had brought with us. One of them he handed to me and the other one he used to call for backup on.

I believe this is the first time that I have ever seen the sheriff nervous. I wouldn't say that he was scared, like I was earlier but he was definitely nervous.

It feels a bit strange for me, I have an overwhelming urge to go and investigate, continue on and the sheriff wants to call for backup. Thinking back the last time I was here I spent the night here.

Of course those were innocent youthful times, fun times. When Berry and I would play catch right there in the yard. Chase each other playing tag; pick on his little brother Mike. Then let Mike hit balls to us while we would try to field them.

143

I almost feel at ease here now, it's hard to describe. I have this sense that Berry is with me, watching my backside. I hope so because we're going to need all the help we can get, Pete and I. We're about to step into something we know nothing about, and it's going to get dangerous.

"Here Butch, take this radio and clip it on your belt. It's on channel nine. If you need to change channels, switch to five." Pete explained as he handed me the radio.

"This is Sheriff Wells calling for Deputies Barns and Wallace, come in."

"This is Deputy Wallace, sheriff." Frank responded to Pete's call.

"Where are you at right now Deputy Wallace?" The sheriff asked Frank on the radio.

"I'm driving past the Murphy farm right now, checking on old man Murphy's cattle for Butch, heading towards highway 77." Frank told the sheriff, in his usual insensitive manner.

"I need you to turn around and meet me about one mile east of the river on Broken Arrow Road. There's an old burnt out house here where I'm at. This is not an emergency so take it slow and easy Deputy Wallace"

"10-4 Sheriff. That's the old Decker house that you're at. Let me get turned around and I'll be on my way."

"This is Deputy Barns, sheriff."

"I'm about twenty miles north of town on highway 77." Deputy Roy Barns told the sheriff as I listened in on the radio that the sheriff had handed me.

"Ok Deputy Barns I want you to station yourself on Broken Arrow Road where it bends around the river I will give you more instructions later. Call me on the radio when you get there." The sheriff ordered Deputy Barns while he stared off into the night.

"10-4 Sheriff." Roy responded.

"Pete do you see something? You have this distant look about you."

"No I don't see anything Butch."

"I don't see anything at all. Let's just call it a hunch, but there's something wrong here."

"I can feel it. I don't know what it is but it's not good whatever it is." Pete said as he put the night vision binoculars strap around his neck.

As we slowly walked towards the remains of Berry's old house, Pete stopped and looked around. Something was troubling him and he wasn't saying a whole lot right now.

Looking down at the walkway that led up to the burnt out remains of the Decker house, the sheriff knelt down to get a better look. After pushing away some dead grass off of the walkway Pete stared at it for a moment and then proclaimed.

"This was arson."

"Butch you can see here where someone used a liquid accelerant as a fuse to start the fire. Probably kerosene or diesel fuel was used."

"Even after all these years you can still see the burn pattern of an accelerant that someone poured on the sidewalk. See how it travels up the walkway to where the porch once stood."

"Butch this house, for whatever reason, was burned down on purpose. A crime was committed here and someone got away with arson."

"You country folk have some strange customs around here Butch, letting people burn down houses and not doing anything about it." The sheriff said as he stood up and brushed the dead grass from his hands.

"Hey Pete, I don't know about where you come from but here in the country, house fires are a very serious predicament."

"Do you see any fire hydrants sticking up out of the ground around here anywhere Pete?"

"We have to truck water in from everywhere to fight a house fire. Things can get out of hand in a hurry, and you can lose everything you own in just a matter of minutes." I explained to the sheriff.

"I didn't mean anything by it Butch. I was actually referring to the fact that nobody investigated this house fire."

"If they had, they would have found that a crime had been committed." The sheriff told me what the evidence was telling him.

Surveying what was left of the house and looking past the house into the pasture, the sheriff lifted his night vision binoculars to his face and scanned the area.

"Butch go ahead and call Mr. Murphy and see if we can use one of his cows." Pete said as he was looking across the pasture with his night vision binoculars.

"We're going to need it tonight if at all possible." Pete explained as he brought his binoculars down away from his face.

"Are we going to need it delivered, or are we going to pick it up?" I asked Pete while flipping up my cell phone to call Mr. Murphy.

"We can pick it up Butch if Mr. Murphy will loan us his horse trailer and truck to haul it in."

"You should call and talk to Mr. Murphy and let him make that decision. I wouldn't want to impose on Mr. Murphy to much." Pete was right. We were asking for a lot and we should let Mr. Murphy make that decision.

I looked at my cell phone and realized that all I needed to do was hit the call button one time because the last number I called was Mr. Murphy.

"Mr. Murphy this is Butch again. I have a big favor to ask of you. The sheriff and I are going after the *Prairie Monster* and we need some bait."

"We were wondering if you would donate one of your cows? Of course we'll do everything we can to keep it alive, but there's a good chance that it will not survive and would be killed."

"If there's one thing that I've learned over the years Mr. Murphy, it's that things usually don't work out very well for the bait." I said as the sheriff and I stood there looking at each other. It was so quiet out there by the old Decker house; the sheriff could hear Mr. Murphy answer me on my cell phone.

"I don't mind Butch, but I want to be involved in the hunt. As long as I can be a part of being there when you set the bait, you and the sheriff can use anything I've got."

"I'll even bring the cow to you if you need me to. I told you Butch to holler at me if you needed any help, and I meant it."

"It's about time someone went hunting for this thing, and I want to be a part of it." Mr. Murphy said as I looked at the sheriff waiting for an answer. I knew that Pete could hear what Mr. Murphy was saying even though we were about ten feet apart. Mr. Murphy had a voice that carried and it was very quiet out there by the old Decker house.

"You can tell Mr. Murphy we would be glad to have his assistance as long as he doesn't mind sitting stakeout with one of my deputies." The sheriff's thinking was that he didn't want Mr. Murphy too close to the action.

"Mr. Murphy, the sheriff and I would appreciate any help that you are willing to give us. We need someone to work stakeout with one of the sheriff's deputy's."

"You can sit with either Deputy Wallace or Deputy Barns if you don't mind." I tried to be a little more tactful than the sheriff in explaining what Mr. Murphy could do to help.

"I'll do it with Deputy Barns, but I'm not sitting anywhere with that idiot Wallace."

"When do you and the sheriff want to use one of my cows and where would you like for it to be delivered?" Mr. Murphy asked as I began to walk over to where the sheriff was standing.

"We would like it delivered right now if at all possible Mr. Murphy, and we're at the old Decker house." There was a long pause on the phone the sheriff and I just stood there looking at each other.

"Mr. Murphy, are you there? Did you hear me sir?" I asked, puzzled by Mr. Murphy's silence.

"Yeah I'm here."

"Butch are you going to be alright? That's not a good place for you to be at and you shouldn't be tempting fate." Mr. Murphy expressed worry over what had happened to me the last time I was here.

"I'm ok Mr. Murphy. Thanks for your concern."

"Call me if you need help loading up that cow and I'll run right over."

As I said my goodbyes to Mr. Murphy and folded my cell phone down, I noticed that Pete actually smiled for a second and was shaking his head back and forth as he lowered his chin a bit.

"What?"

"What are you shaking your head at and smiling about this time?" I asked Pete.

"I heard your conversation with Mr. Murphy and it seems that he knows Deputy Wallace too." Pete was referring to Mr. Murphy calling Deputy Wallace an idiot. I couldn't hold it in I smiled too.

"Speak of the devil, here comes Deputy Wallace now." The sheriff said as he started walking towards the road. Then Pete abruptly stopped and turned around to ask me to come with him down to the dirt road to speak with Deputy Wallace.

"Butch, would you mind coming along with me please? I'm not going to let you out of my sight as long as we're out here anyway."

"If something happened to you I would never forgive myself. On top of that I wouldn't want to be the one that has to go tell your wife that you've been hurt or something. Especially now that I've seen and heard your wife's verbal wrath." Pete said with a smirk as he put his hand on my shoulder.

The sheriff and I walked down to the road to meet with Frank. Deputy Wallace was just arriving at the end of the driveway in his patrol cruiser.

"Hi Frank." I said to Deputy Wallace as I bent over and put my hands on the side of his patrol cruiser to lean on it a little.

"Deputy Wallace I want you to situate yourself right here where you're at."

"Mr. Murphy will be coming by to drop off a cow."

"I want you to help him unload it and lead it up to Butch and I. We'll be up there by what's left of the old Decker house."

"Are there any questions?" The sheriff was pretty explicate with his orders. I can't imagine Frank having a question, but I would be proven wrong. As I stood there Deputy Wallace asked a question that just proved that he doesn't pay very good attention.

"Do I leave my car here when I lead the cow up to you and Butch or do I bring it with me?" Deputy Wallace asked.

The sheriff looked at me and whispered, don't. But I couldn't help myself.

"No Frank let the cow drive the car." I told Frank with a smile and a chuckle.

"Ok smart guy, I didn't know if I was to tie the cow to the bumper and bring them both up there or just the cow." Frank said as he scrunched his eyebrows down, not appreciating my humor.

"Just bring the cow Deputy, and you can escort Mr. Murphy up to us too if he wishes to come along with you."

"Keep on your toes out here Deputy, there's something wrong here and I don't know what it is yet." The sheriff told Frank, and then we walked back up to the rubble where Berry's family house once stood.

It was a cool evening, not cold just cool. The air was brisk and still. No clouds in the sky and the stars were shining, but not extra bright; tonight the moon was full.

There were no sounds being made. It was quiet, it was very quiet, and then you could hear it in the distance.

The train rumbling down the tracks over five miles away and the sound it made could be heard clearly. It was as if the train was right across the road from us.

Pete began to walk around the rubble with a flashlight and a stick that was about four feet long that he had picked up off the ground.

I stood back and watched the sheriff do his thing. Pete would glance up at me every now and then as if to make sure I was still there. Not saying anything, Pete continued to walk around and jab at the burnt wreckage.

Poking at the burnt debris it looked like the sheriff was looking for something.

"Is there anything in particular you're looking for in all that rubble Pete?"

"Where are the animals at Butch?"

"There should be something, a cat or dog, a skunk or opossum, maybe a rat."

"Why are there no living creatures around?"

"There should be something living in the rubble." Pete was bewildered and for once I think he was confused and unsure of himself.

"I don't know Pete, but it's always like this when I investigate a cattle mutilation."

"The other cows in the pasture would stay clear of the carcass and there would be no birds around either." I answered the sheriff the best I could with what I knew in my investigations.

Just then I heard what sounded like a truck coming down the dirt road.

"It sounds like a truck pulling a trailer coming down the dirt road, that's probably Mr. Murphy. You might want to tell me what the game plan is going to be tonight." I asked Pete, but he just ignored me.

The sheriff and I could hear the truck stop and someone get out of the vehicle, and then we heard voices, it sounded like Mr. Murphy was talking to Deputy Wallace.

Pete and I could hear the back of a trailer door open and the distinct sound of a cow. Just then a call came across on the sheriff's radio.

"Sheriff Wells, come in, this is Deputy Barns."

"Go ahead Deputy Barns." Pete responded.

"Sheriff I'm just now coming up to the bend on Broken Arrow Road."

"10-4 Deputy Barns, I need for you to come on down to where the old Decker house used to stand and pick up Mr. Murphy. He's going to be sitting stakeout with you this evening."

"10-4 Sheriff, I'll be right there."

Just as Pete was finishing up his conversation with Deputy Barns, we could hear Deputy Wallace coming; he and Mr. Murphy were leading a cow with them.

"They're not the quietest pair are they Pete?"

"I'm not going to complain Butch, we are getting a cow to use as bait and we didn't even need to go pick it up."

"Mr. Murphy I want to thank you for helping us out tonight, and providing us with one of your cows to use. Deputy Barns will be here in a couple of minutes to pick you up.   You'll be working with him tonight."

"Mr. Murphy I'm going to need you to stay alert if you're going to help us."

"The last thing I want to see happen is for someone to get hurt."   The sheriff expressed his concerns about having a civilian out here helping us.

"Ok Sheriff, but I'm not an idiot.   I know that you are just putting me with Deputy Barns so I'll be out of the way. I'm ok with that just as long as I'm out here somewhere helping." Mr. Murphy accepted his roll in tonight's endeavor with no misgivings.

"Mr. Murphy, would you happen to know why nobody investigated this house fire?" The sheriff asked. I looked over at Mr. Murphy he just looked back at me; we both knew the answer to that.

"I can clearly see that this was no accidental fire. It was deliberately set and someone got away with arson." The sheriff explained to Mr. Murphy, while pointing towards the burnt out remains of the old Decker house.

All three of us just stood there looking at the sheriff. We all knew the stories about who burned down the Decker house, but that's all they were, stories.

Nobody witnessed anything, and you don't want to go around falsely accusing your neighbors. Besides, there was a lot going on back then and nobody was going to place blame where it needed to go. The Decker's had already been through more then they deserved to go through.

"Ok all three of you are standing there like you know what happened but don't want to tell." Pete was getting increasingly more frustrated with the way nobody seemed to care about the fact that someone committed arson.

It's not that we didn't care. We just understood why it happened. Finally Mr. Murphy begins to tell the story.

"Ok Sheriff I'll tell you what everybody thinks happened to the Decker house. After Butch and his friend Berry where attacked, they ruled Berry's death an accident due to an animal attack. Wild dogs, I think is what they said happened, but we all knew better then that."

"That didn't sit very well with Berry's father, Ray Decker. So literally right after Berry's funeral, and I mean right after the funeral. Ray Decker packed up his family and their belongings and moved away."

"One night I woke up to a red glow in the sky, I looked out a window and knew right away that there was a house on fire somewhere. So I threw on my coveralls and boots and drove over here."

"When I arrived here there were several others already here standing around including the sheriff."

"I asked the sheriff what happened and he pointed at Ray Decker. Mr. Decker was standing right up front watching his house burn."

"I walked up to Ray and asked if he was alright, he told me to leave him be."

"Although no one saw Ray Decker start the fire, everyone assumed he was the one who did it."

"To be honest with you Sheriff we didn't blame him. The man had just lost a son and officials were telling him that a pack of wild dogs had killed his boy."

"Nobody around here believed that then and nobody around here believes it now."

"I'm not saying its right Sheriff; I'm just saying that I understand why Ray Decker did what everyone thinks he did." Mr. Murphy told the sheriff, Deputy Wallace and I just stood there.

"Thank you Mr. Murphy for explaining to me what allegedly happened so long ago. I can understand why everybody is so hesitant in talking about it. After all, a man had just lost a child."

"By the way Butch, I know that you don't want to speak ill of the dead, but you could have explained all of this to me." Pete was basically telling me that I needed to trust him, and he was right. I should have told him about the rumors a long time ago.

"Mr. Murphy, there is something I was wondering if you would give me your opinion on sir?" Pete asked as Mr. Murphy handed me the rope that was tied around his cow's neck.

"My opinion I'm always willing to give Sheriff. Most of the time whether you want to hear it or not."

"When Butch and I got here, I walked around all this debris and I noticed that there wasn't anything living around it or in it. Would you have an idea why that is?"

Mr. Murphy stood there with a stone cold serious look on his face, and then told the sheriff.

"Evil."

Chapter 8

The hunt begins.

Mr. Murphy explains.

"Evil has been here and has let its presence be known."

"Evil doesn't care about any living thing; it just takes what it wants and moves on."

"If you have what it wants it will take it from you. It doesn't matter if you're holding it, or if it's in your body, if it wants it, evil will take it from you."

"The animals around here know this and they stay clear."

"Most of us older residents around here know this too, that's why none of us around here ever tried to buy this piece of land."

"Just stand here and let your senses take in what they see.

"Hear."

"Smell."

"Feel, and can't you taste it in the air."

"Evil, this is a place where it comes."

158

"This isn't the ramblings of an old fool Sheriff. You asked for my opinion and I gave you the reasons why. It's not my opinion Sheriff, it's the facts."

"Evil."

After Mr. Murphy said what he said about evil everyone stood there and looked at him. I've known Mr. Murphy all of my life and I have never heard him talk like that before.

I don't know about everyone else, but I knew what Mr. Murphy was talking about. It wasn't any fairytale he was telling; it was life on the Kansas prairie. I know, I've seen it in person.

Just then the silence was broken by Deputy Barns driving up to Deputy Wallace's patrol cruiser, then you could hear the car door open.

"Mr. Murphy, are you here?" Roy hollered.

"I'm on my way Roy." Mr. Murphy hollered back to Deputy Barns.

"If you have anymore questions Sheriff, you know where I'll be."

"Butch good luck and don't get yourself hurt. This isn't worth it." Mr. Murphy voiced his worries as he and Deputy Wallace walked back towards the road.

I stood there with a very taut rope in my hand that was tied around the neck of Mr. Murphy's cow.

I had to hang on to it with a tight grip, the cow kept trying to pull away. It was like it knew that it didn't want to be there.

I hung my arm over the neck of the cow, to try and calm it down but it wasn't going to stand still, it kept pulling away from me.

The cow seemed to be more nervous than the sheriff and I. It wanted away from there and it wanted away right now!

I can understand why it would be nervous, what I don't understand is how Mr. Murphy's cow knew that it was about to become bait. It couldn't have known.

Or could it have?

It was obvious the cow could sense something was wrong.

Pete and I could hear Deputy Barns and Deputy Wallace discussing the situation and what to do in case of an emergency.

Mr. Murphy was putting in his two cents worth too. Pete and I just kind of smiled at each other.

"Well Pete it sounds like Mr. Murphy is going to tell them what to do." I said to the sheriff as I was trying to calm down Mr. Murphy's cow.

"We better get going Butch, before that cow gets too uncontrollable." Pete was right we needed to get away from the old Decker house. If not for the cow, then at least for me. I was getting nervous again.

"Let me scan the area with these night vision binoculars first. Then I need to make sure my deputies are in position." The sheriff said as he looked across the pasture with his Star Light, Star Bright, night vision binoculars.

"Deputy Barns are you and Mr. Murphy in position yet? You should be out on Broken Arrow Road where it bends at the river." The sheriff called out on his radio.

"10-4, Sheriff." Deputy Barns responded.

"Deputy Wallace, are you ready?"

"I haven't moved Sheriff I'm still at the end of the Decker's driveway." Frank radioed back to Pete.

"Just keep your eyes open and your radio clear Deputy Wallace." The sheriff ordered Frank.

"10-4 Sheriff." Deputy Wallace replied.

#

"Ok Butch, I want you to take the same path that you took the night you were attacked."

"I know it may be difficult to remember, but try to do the best you can."

"One more thing Butch, if you can, I want to know the rock that you and Berry sat down and rested on." Pete said as he stepped to the side of Mr. Murphy's cow and let the two of us pass.

I took a deep breath and closed my eyes. Thinking back I could see in my mind how it looked thirty-five years ago.

I could also see my best friend Berry, right there beside me. I said to myself, I knew you wouldn't let me do this without you my friend.

I was ready now and I knew exactly the way to go. As I started walking Mr. Murphy's cow tugged at the rope that was around its neck, pulling to the far right.

161

Mr. Murphy's cow was giving that burnt out rubble where the old Decker house stood as much space as it could.

When we got past the gate that led to the back pasture, Mr. Murphy's cow relaxed and followed behind me with the rope going limp.

The sheriff was bringing up the rear and he looked somewhat out of place.

"Pete, are you going to be alright?" I asked the sheriff as I looked back at him.

"Yeah I'm alright Butch. Something's not right and it's bothering me."

"I can't put my finger on it, but I can feel it, something's not right." Pete was perplexed, and he wasn't use to this.

"Pete I remember it taking longer to walk this pasture in the past, I must be getting quicker as I get older." I said to Pete as we were getting closer to the rock that Berry and I rested on.

"You were only twelve years old back then Butch. You have a longer stride in your step now and therefore you cover more distance with each step." The sheriff has the need to explain everything.

"This is the rock that Berry and I stopped at and sat down on to rest." I explained to Pete as I stood there and closed my eyes thinking back to when I was here last. Mr. Murphy's cow was standing right beside me, nudging me with its nose.

I could see it in my mind as if it was happening all over again. Berry was sitting there looking up at the stars talking about going into outer space and being an explorer.

Then I grinned inside, Berry stood up and had that beef liver blood all over his leg. I was reliving it in my head. It was funny at the time.

I wish I could tell him to go back home and wash it off. Don't worry Berry I'm going to fix it this time. I said to myself.

"Butch!"

"Butch are you alright?" Pete hollered out.

"I was thinking of old times Pete, just thinking of old times, I'm ok."

"Let's move on. I'm ready to get to the bottom of this." I explained to Pete in a very tranquil way, almost in a laid back fashion. I was much more relaxed now.

"Butch you need to try and stay focused here. I understand that you are reflecting back to when you were twelve and trying not to forget anything but let's try and keep our minds on the task at hand."

"Besides that, the cow is starting to look at you in a funny way now. Even he thinks you're a little strange."

"Pete if you look about fifty yards over there to our left you can see the tree that everybody calls the old Walnut tree."

"That is the only big Cottonwood tree around here. There are some little Cottonwood trees scattered around, but they weren't here thirty-five years ago."

"The river is about a hundred yards in front of us and Broken Arrow Road is on the other side of that row of Hedge Apple trees to our right." It had been thirty-five years since I was last here, but it felt like it was yesterday.

I knew precisely where I was and where we had to go, I explained to the sheriff as we continued on towards the river.

The sheriff and I walked up to the rivers edge and looked around. Pete used his night vision binoculars to scan the area.

I was having difficulties with Mr. Murphy's cow, he was back to tugging at the rope. He did not want to be there. I don't blame it, there was something odd here.

"I don't see anything Butch."

"Do you remember where you were when you first saw the _Prairie Monster_ before he attacked your friend Berry?" Pete asked as he started slowly walking back the way we came.

"Well Pete I guess that I was standing about right here when I first noticed two red glowing eyes off in the distance. I would say it was about twenty yards or so away from where I'm at if I would take two steps backwards into the river."

"Would you say it was about where that rock is sticking up out of the ground?" Pete asked as he pointed over towards a big rock.

"Yeah about there, I'd say."

"Pete that Cottonwood tree that's about twenty feet away wasn't there thirty-five years ago." I told the sheriff as he looked over at the tree.

"Ok Butch, let's tie Mr. Murphy's cow up to that Cottonwood tree and we will position ourselves over by what you call the old Walnut tree."

"If you wouldn't mind Butch, would you go ahead and tie up the cow to the tree please?"

"I will radio my deputies to inform them where we are and that we have set the bait." Pete said as he pulled his radio out of his belt and called in our location to Frank and Roy.

"This is Sheriff Wells calling for Deputy Barns and Wallace, come in please." Pete radioed for Frank and Roy while he walked with me over to the tree that I tied Mr. Murphy's cow to.

I had the feeling that I wasn't going to get very far tonight without Pete right there on my side with me. He was like my shadow wherever I went, Pete went.

"This is Deputy Barns with Mr. Murphy, Sheriff." Roy responded to the sheriff's call first.

"This is Deputy Wallace, Sheriff." Frank called in. I was surprised that Frank was still awake.

"Butch and I have set the bait and are on our way over to what the local folks call the old Walnut tree. Do you copy?" The sheriff explained our location and was asking both deputies if they understood.

"10-4, Sheriff." Frank answered first this time.

"10-4, Sheriff. Mr. Murphy and I understand." Roy answered.

"Let's keep alert out there and I want you to be ready for anything. If anyone sees anything call it in immediately, that's an order."

"From this point on I want radio silence. Do not break it unless you see something strange." Pete told his deputies as we walked up to that old, old Cottonwood tree. The sheriff stuck his hand out and slapped the tree as he looked up into it; it's a huge tree that's been here for a very long time.

The sheriff and I stood up against the tree looking out across the pasture and keeping an eye on Mr. Murphy's cow.

Pete would bring his Star Light Star Bright night vision binoculars up to his face every now and then and scan the area.

Standing out there reminded me of deer hunting. You're usually by yourself and all you have to do is sit and think while you wait for a deer to come by.

It may sound boring but all that quiet time out in the woods gives you time to reflect on everything in your life. You feel at peace. This is my time to talk to and be with God.

I personally feel closer to God when I'm out in the woods deer hunting more so than I do anywhere else. It's almost like taking a spiritual retreat.

The sheriff and I stood there for about a half an hour or so when I whispered to Pete, asking him why he was convinced that tonight was the night we were going to see something.

"Pete why are you so confident that we are going to be able to see something tonight? I've got an idea that you're holding back on me old buddy."

"You know something that you're not saying, don't you Pete?" I asked the sheriff, and he didn't seem too willing to jump right out there and say what he knew.

"I have some hunches Butch. They are nowhere near being facts, there're just hunches." Pete whispered in a very soft voice.

"It's not that I don't appreciate the help Pete, I just don't like being in the dark on this."

"I've spent most of my life seeking out the truth. I don't want to be left out of anything that has to do with getting to the truth."

"Pete I'm glad you're here but don't leave me out of what you might know." I whispered back to the sheriff as we continued standing there by that tree.

"Butch I can honestly tell you that I don't think that we will see the *Prairie Monster* tonight. I'm thinking something else will show up tonight."

"I don't want to discourage you, but I think that there are other forces at hand here." Pete explained to me but left me with more questions than answers.

"Do you mean to tell me that after all that I have told you, and all the evidence that you have uncovered, you still aren't convinced that I'm telling the truth? You don't believe the *Prairie Monster* exists?" I asked Pete, as I was a little surprised to hear him talking that way.

"Don't misunderstand me Butch. I do believe the *Prairie Monster* exists. I also believe that there's more to it than a creature running loose on the Kansas prairie."

"Pete we should really work on our communication skills together, I think I can help you." I told Pete, and I wasn't joking, he needed help.

"Pete I don't know what you're up to, but I have a feeling that I'm going to find out tonight." I said to the sheriff as I walked around the tree we were standing by, to take a look behind us.

"Butch, what's wrong with that cow?" Pete asked as we both looked at Mr. Murphy's cow trying to pull away from the tree it was tied to.

"I don't know Pete other then it may sense that it's in danger and is trying to escape." I said to the sheriff while we watched Mr. Murphy's cow struggling to get loose.

"Butch you keep your eye on Mr. Murphy's cow and I'll watch the surrounding area." Pete said as he started scanning the area with his night vision binoculars.

"I wasn't expecting this Butch."

"Not tonight anyway, I wasn't expecting this at all." The sheriff said in a quiet but nervous voice.

"Pete look over there by the rock that Berry and I rested on. I thought I saw it move out of the corner of my eye." I told the sheriff as I pointed in the direction of what I thought I saw.

"Ok Butch I'll watch over by the rock you keep your eye on Mr. Murphy's cow."

"The cow is the one going to be at risk here, and we need to be ready for anything." Pete was right, the cow was our bait and that's what I needed to keep my mind and my attention focused on.

I began to wonder if this was the safest way to be handling this, but it was too late to worry about it now. Things seemed to be happening rapidly and my heart was pounding faster and faster as I watched poor Mr. Murphy's cow struggling, trying to get loose from being tied to the tree.

"Look Pete!"

"Look just past Mr. Murphy's cow!"

"Do you see it Pete? Two glowing red eye's."

"Do you see it?"

"Oh my God. Where did it come from?" I said to the sheriff as I was pulling my gun out of its holster and aiming it in that direction.

All of the sudden it was gone again. I couldn't see it anywhere. I lowered my gun to my side, but kept it in my hand.

"Pete!" I hollered wondering if the sheriff heard me in all the excitement.

"I saw it for just an instance Butch, but I don't see it now. Mr. Murphy's cow is still tied to the tree and the beast seems to be gone."

"It disappeared as fast as it arrived." Pete said in disbelief as he feverish scanned the area with his night vision binoculars.

"Butch what just happened? What's going on here? Was that what I thought it was?" Pete asked as he continued looking around the pasture.

"Please tell me that you saw it Pete."

"Please tell me that I'm not the only one to witness the _Prairie Monster_." I was pleading and hoping all at the same time, that Pete would confirm the sighting.

"I saw something Butch."

"I don't know what it was, but it was big, and hairy, and fast."

"I didn't hear a thing either, it was very quiet." The sheriff said as he leaned back against the tree having trouble believing his own eyes.

"Calling Sheriff Wells, this is Deputy Wallace, calling Sheriff Wells, come in Sheriff." Frank had broke radio silence, and was radioing the sheriff.

"This better be good Deputy Wallace." Pete responded on the radio.

"I see something strange in the sky Sheriff. Directly north of your location, and its heading your way."

Frank was right; there was something in the sky. It looked almost like a spotlight on a helicopter, way off in the distance.

No it looked like several spotlights on several helicopters. What would helicopters be doing out here, and at night I wondered?

We were hundreds of miles away from the nearest military base and the sheriff's department didn't have anything like that.

As the sheriff and I stood there watching, they begin to get closer and closer.

There were three of them altogether. They were mid-sized helicopters with two rotating spotlights on each one of them.

They almost look like the old military transport helicopters that they used back during the Vietnam War but they were much quieter.

You could start to feel the air flow from their spinning blades as they grew closer. All three of them were painted dark green and were running in silent mode.

They began to circle the area and were sweeping the ground with their spotlights.

"This is Deputy Wallace calling Sheriff Wells, what's going on? Do you need backup?"

"We'll be alright Deputy Wallace. Stay where you're at, and maintain radio silence I will explain things later." The sheriff told Frank as his face had an angry look to it.

"10-4 Sheriff." Deputy Wallace responded.

"What is going on Pete?"

"I don't know just yet, but I have an idea." Pete said as he scrunched his eyebrows down. I felt like Pete was holding out on me, not telling me everything he knew.

One of the helicopters hovered above us for a moment and then drifted off to the east and landed in the pasture. The other two continued to circle and hover above us.

A couple of men dressed in black suits stepped off the helicopter. Right behind them a couple of men dressed in camouflage carrying automatic weapons stepped off and flanked the men in the black suits.

All four of them started walking towards the sheriff and I.

I looked around the area and made sure nobody was coming up from behind us. Mr. Murphy's cow looked as confused as I did, but at least he was a lot calmer then he was earlier.

I don't know what Pete and I could have done at this point to protect ourselves. All we had were hand guns and they were no match for automatic weapons.

"I knew it Butch!"

"I knew it, deep down from the get go, I knew it!" Pete said as the men from the helicopter walked closer to us.

"Pete what did you know? I don't understand."

"Would you please holster your weapon Butch?" One of the men dressed in a suit asked.

"I don't know you, how do you know me?" I asked as I put my gun back in its holster.

"What is going on here?"

"Pete you seem to know something. Who are these people?" I wasn't just asking at this point, I was demanding to know from the sheriff.

"Butch these two gentlemen in suits work for the United States government." Pete explained as he hung his night vision binoculars on a tree branch.

Chapter 9

G-Men.

I didn't want to believe it, but it was starting to look like the United States government was behind this and Pete knew something about it.

Could this have been a government experiment gone wrong? Maybe it was an accident that the United States is trying to cover up?

That can't be it. The *Prairie Monster* has been around longer then Kansas has been a state.

The more people that get involved in this the more confusing it all gets.

It's a good thing that these two guys dressed in suits have a couple of armed escorts with them. I'm not a violent person but somebody is going to give me some answers.

The other two helicopters continue to circle around us but they did climb higher up which made it a little easier for us to talk.

"Sheriff Peter Wells, and Fish & Game Officer Butch Black, what are you two doing out here in the middle of this pasture at night?" The older of the two men dressed in suits asked.

"Butch let me introduce to you Special Agent Brian Cook." The sheriff wasn't really introducing me to the government agents; I would say that he was just telling me who they were.

"Of course I can't tell you which arm of the government he works for. I was never privy to that information; it was considered Top Secret and was classified." Pete said as he glared at the men dressed in suits. I could tell that the sheriff didn't care for Special Agent Brian Cook.

"Pete what makes an agent for the United States government special anyway?"

"I'm not for sure Butch, but my guess is that they need to have a lower then average IQ."

The four men just stood there motionless, and stone faced as they stared at the sheriff and me.

"Enough with the pleasantries, Cook what brings you and your entourage out here in the middle of the night disturbing Butch and I star gazing?" Pete asked after insulting the two gentlemen.

"You're a little out of place here in the middle of nowhere aren't you Peter? The plains of Kansas are a long way from the streets of Chicago." The older man said as he stood there in front of us.

"Butch we have never been introduced, my name is Brian Cook and this is Robert Hudson. You can call me Brian." The older gentleman said as he stuck his hand out for a handshake.

"Mr. Cook I don't know you and like the sheriff said, you are disturbing our night out star gazing. Besides that your helicopters are scaring my cow."

"Ok let's just cut the act here gentlemen. I know what you two are doing out here. You're out here with Shawn Murphy's cow, using it as bait."

"You have a Deputy Wallace standing by in a patrol cruiser at the front of this property."

"You have a Deputy Barns with the civilian Shawn Murphy, in his patrol cruiser on the other side of those trees." Special Agent Cook said as he pointed at the row of Hedge Apple trees.

"You two are out here trying to capture a mythical creature you call the *Prairie Monster*."

"My orders are to take you two in for debriefing." Special Agent Cook said to the sheriff and I. But I wasn't going to stand by and let this happen willingly.

"You can't just take us in!"

"Who do you think you are?"

"I know my rights."

"Say something Pete; you're the sheriff around here." I said as I looked over to Pete expecting him to say or do something.

"Butch they are going to take us with them one way or another, and they're going to tell us that it has to do with national security." Pete explained as he never took his eyes off of Special Agent Cook.

"What about Mr. Murphy's cow?" I asked the sheriff.

"You may call your deputies following our lift off and have them pick up the cow after we have cleared the area Peter."

"Cook how did you know that Butch and I were out here? You didn't just happen to be out flying and spot us down here. Somebody informed you and I want to know who." The sheriff demanded to know who was informing the government from Mr. Cook.

"Come on Peter you taught me how to be a good investigator. All I had to do was keep my eyes open."

"Now can we please get going?" Mr. Cook motioned with his hand for us to walk to the helicopter.

"Come on Butch lets go before there's an accidental shooting while someone's out hunting and we end up dead." Pete said as he started walking towards the helicopter.

The other two helicopters that where circling above us lowered down closer to us as we boarded the helicopter. It was as if they where providing cover in case of attack.

After all of us boarded the helicopter and we lifted off Mr. Cook told the sheriff that he could radio his deputies now.

"This is Sheriff Wells calling Deputy Wallace and Deputy Barns, come in." Pete called on a headset radio that Mr. Cook had handed him.

"This is Deputy Wallace, Sheriff." Frank responded.

"Deputy Wallace I want you to help Mr. Murphy retrieve his cow from the old Decker pasture. I will have Deputy Barns bring Mr. Murphy to you. You will find the cow tied to a tree down by the river."

"I also want you to help Mr. Murphy take his cow back to his place and help him unload it." The sheriff explained to Frank.

"This is Deputy Barns Sheriff, I heard and I'm on my way." Roy told Pete.

"10-4. Call me on my cell phone after you drop off Mr. Murphy." The sheriff told Deputy Barns.

"Do you mind telling us where we are going Cook?" The sheriff asked as he handed back the headset.

"It's not far."

"It's someplace we can talk without being disturbed." Mr. Cook explained.

"By the way Peter you're not going to hide anything from the United States government by using a cell phone." Mr. Cook told the sheriff with a smirk on his face.

"You'd be surprised what you can do on a cell phone Cook. Try to keep in mind who the teacher is here."

As we flew across the countryside, not following any roads or highways we were the lead helicopter and we were flanked by the other two helicopters. It was amazing to me how quiet these helicopters were.

"We're going to be landing very soon, so please prepare yourself." The pilot turned around and informed us.

Mr. Cook was right it wasn't very far. We landed in the middle of a pasture that was fenced off. It was about five acres squared with a ten foot chain link fence and razor wire that ran across the top of the fence.

There was what looked like a small house made out of concrete blocks sitting in the center of this fenced off pasture.

Mr. Cook stepped out of the helicopter and motioned for Pete and I to follow him. After we did, the helicopter lifted off and all three of them flew away, heading east along the tree tops.

"Ok Cook where are we?" Pete asked.

"I know where we are Pete. We're at an abandoned missile silo. My guess is that it's not really abandoned though." I said to Pete as his cell phone began to ring.

"This is Sheriff Wells." Pete put his cell phone on speaker phone and answered it so we could all hear his conversation with Roy.

"This is Deputy Barns, Sheriff you wanted me to call you after I dropped Mr. Murphy off?" Roy said as we could hear him on Pete's speaker.

"I was talking to a friend of yours and he told me to tell you hi." The sheriff told Deputy Barns.

"Oh yeah who would that be Sheriff?" Roy asked.

"Special Agent Brian Cook."

"Special Agent Brian Cook?" Roy repeated what Pete had said. You could tell that he was not sure that he should say anything.

"Yeah he told me that you two used to work with each other." The sheriff was fishing to see if Deputy Barns knew Special Agent Brian Cook.

"Oh yeah, I didn't realize that he had told you about us." Roy fell for it, hook, line, and sinker.

"He told me that you were his eyes and ears down here in Kansas." The sheriff told Deputy Barns.

"Next time you talk to Brian tell him I said hi, would you please?" Deputy Barns asked the sheriff.

"I'll do you one better than that Deputy Barns."

"You get to work with him again, because you're fired!"

"You take that patrol cruiser back to the office and turn in your badge immediately!" The sheriff told Deputy Barns.

Special Agent Brian Cook stood there slowly shaking his head back and forth; he couldn't believe that one of his agents fell for one of the oldest tricks in the book.

"Wait a minute Sheriff, you can't fire me I did nothing wrong, besides that my salary is supplemented from the government." Roy tried to explain.

"You have one hour to turn in your equipment, or I will have Deputy Wallace arrest you for obstructing justice, interfering with a police investigation, and impersonating an officer."

"Do I make myself clear?" Pete said as he handed his cell phone to Special Agent Cook.

"Do what he says Barns."

"The next time you address me you better address me as Special Agent Cook, or as Mr. Cook, or your next assignment will be in Alaska."

"Yes sir Mr. Cook." Deputy Barns knew he was in trouble. Special Agent Cook was very upset with him, and Deputy Barns would be explaining his actions first thing Monday morning in Special Agent Cooks office in Washington D.C.

"I will see you in Washington on Monday at 9:00am in my office, don't be late."

"I want you to know that Sheriff Peter Wells didn't know anything. He was guessing and you fell for it."

"I will be dropping you a grade in rank and pay. So think about that between now and Monday." Mr. Cook said to Roy as he folded down the sheriff's cell phone.

"Very good Peter. You out-smarted an idiot." Special Agent Cook said to the sheriff as he was handing him back his cell phone.

"Now let's step inside please." Mr. Cook said as he led the way over to what looked like a door to a storm cellar.

Special Agent Cook placed the palm of his right hand on some sort of sensor and then a light came on in the doorway, and the door opened.

All three of us stepped through the doorway with Mr. Cook leading the way. The door automatically shut behind us. The hallway was poorly lit, and it had a steep angle heading downwards.

The only light visible was coming from a room that was at the end of the hallway.

As we approached the room, I could see that it had a table with twelve chairs around it. Special Agent Cook asked us to please be seated.

"Ok this is how it's going to work tonight gentlemen. First I'll ask the questions and if you two give me honest answers, I will answer your questions, and give you honest answers." Mr. Cook explained to Pete and I.

"I have a couple of questions before we get started." I said to Special Agent Cook.

"Are we in any danger, and why should we answer any of your questions?"

"No you're not in any danger."

"At least from the United States government you're not in danger." Mr. Cook explained.

"If you answer my questions, I'll tell you what you want to know about the *Prairie Monster*. That's what you want isn't it Butch? To find out the truth about what or who killed your friend."

"That's what you have been searching the last thirty-five years for isn't." Special Agent Cook said. Well I can't speak for the sheriff, but he just grabbed my full attention.

"Cook you can take your questions and stick them where the sun doesn't shine. We're not interested in what you have to say." The sheriff told Special Agent Cook while pointing at him with his finger.

"Now wait a minute Pete." I said as we sat there at the table together.

"Maybe Butch, you and Peter should talk between yourselves for a moment. I'll go and get us something to drink." Special Agent Cook said as he stood up and walked to a door that slid to one side and then slid back after he walked through it.

"We don't need him Butch."

"Pete, I appreciate all your help, and I value your advice and friendship, but I want you to hear me out on this."

"I have been living with this for thirty-five years and this is as close as I've been since I was attacked back when I was twelve years old."

"I made a promise to my best friend Berry to find his killer and I will do anything that I need to do, to keep that promise."

"If Special Agent Cook can help me achieve my goals then so be it. I'm willing to help him if he is willing to help me."

"Butch, be careful what you say. The walls in here have eyes and ears. I know what is going on and I know what to do."

"I need for you to trust me on this Butch. I'm telling you we don't need his help." Pete had leaned over and whispered to me.

"Pete you better be right, this is too important for me to treat like it was nothing."

"I'll keep my mouth shut Pete and we'll go ahead and do it your way." I told the sheriff, although I disagreed with him. I trusted him, I had to. He had taken me further then I was able to do on my own.

"You won't be disappointed Butch." The sheriff said to me as he patted me on the back.

"How do you know so much Pete? Where are you getting your information?" I whispered.

"I will tell you later Butch; remember the walls have eyes and ears." Pete leaned over and whispered back to me.

Special Agent Cook came walking back into the room with three bottles of water. He placed all three on the table and told us to pick one.

"I realize that Peter doesn't trust me so I will let you two select a bottle of water first and I'll take whatever is left over." Mr. Cook said to Pete and I as we sat there looking at him.

"It's not that I don't trust you Cook, I don't trust the way you do things." Pete said as he reached for a bottle of water and opened it.

The sheriff then sniffed the bottle of water as if it was a bottle of fine wine, took a sip and turned to me and nodded, signaling to me that it was ok.

I picked up a bottle and noticed right away that it was ice cold.

"Wow Mr. Cook your refrigerator must be turned up very high to keep your drinks this cold." I said to Special Agent Cook as he took the remaining bottle of water, opened it and started drinking it.

"We have a soda machine back in another room that we keep turned up high. It can get very hot here in Kansas in the summertime."

"I'm here tonight to find out everything that you two know, and how you found out what you know."

"After I find out all that I need to know from the two of you. I have been authorized to tell you the truth about what the United States government knows, and how involved we are with this situation."

"Cook are we being recorded right now?" Pete asked as he leaned back in his chair.

"Yes you are Peter. Audio and video."

"I can assure you that this is kept top secret and in our business we take keeping things secret very serious, and we keep it secret."

"We know Peter that everybody around here knows about the _Prairie Monster_. They're afraid to talk about it for fear of being labeled a nut."

"We know about those individuals who do talk about it, like Butch for instance. Our job is to keep it covered up."

"Mr. Cook if the United States government knows more then the sheriff and I, why do they need to know what we know?"

"I can answer that Butch." Pete said as he leaned forward in his chair and interlocked his fingers while resting his hands on the table.

"The government wants to plug the leaks. They want to get rid of all the evidence that is out there available to anybody willing to spend the time looking for it." The sheriff told me as he was looking right at Mr. Cook.

"Peter is right Butch. We need to plug the holes in the system."

"The information that you two provide us will mysteriously disappear from wherever you obtained it." Special Agent Cook continued to explain.

"Butch you and Peter need to understand that the public can not be allowed to see this information."

"There would be mass hysteria and the call for retribution against…. Well I've said way too much already. Are you and Peter going to help us or not?"

"How do we know that we can trust you Mr. Cook? How do we know that we can trust the United States government?"

"I'm not at liberty to discuss all the details of our offer until we get all the information we can from you and Peter."

"I will tell you that we were caught off guard tonight by you and Peter."

"We would have been in touch with you two earlier if we would have known that you were moving this fast in your investigation. Butch, we have been monitoring what you have been doing for years now."

"You're the reason that we had to assign an agent to the sheriff's department."

"The United States government has had a copy of your *Prairie Monster* file for years. We were content with letting you be until now."

"I am willing to tell you everything Butch, but you're going to need to trust me first." Special Agent Cook explained.

"You do realize that a murder was committed thirty-five years ago, don't you Cook?"

"Yes Peter and that has been taken care of a long time ago. The United States government is not in the habit of letting any of its citizens get murdered and not do something about it. We just don't make it public knowledge."

"I can understand why you want to speak to Butch but how do I figure into all of this?"

"You Peter are too smart for your own good. You are a very good investigator and we know that it is your fault that we had to scramble tonight."

"I had plans to meet and talk with the both of you tomorrow at the county courthouse, but the two of you moved faster then I had anticipated."

Pete smiled after he heard that, he seemed to get some comfort in knowing that he caused problems for Mr. Cook, and the government.

I stood up and started walking around this big table that we were sitting at, trying to think things out. A lot was happening and I needed to consider everything that was laid out in front of me.

Mr. Cook and Pete sat there staring at each other, not wanting to trust one another. It was like watching two heads of state from opposing countries; it's hard to believe that they both work for the same government, one federal, and one state.

I needed to call Vickie and let her know that everything was going good, and I was ok.

"Mr. Cook I need to call my wife and let her know that I'm alright. Is there going to be a problem with that?" I asked Special Agent Cook, as I flipped open my cell phone.

"I'm afraid that isn't possible in here Butch. All electronic devises are jammed while you're in this complex."

"As a sign of good faith Butch you can step outside and call your wife Vickie to let her know you're alright if that will help things along."

"How did you know my wife's name was Vickie? I never mentioned her name to you." I asked Special Agent Cook while I looked down at my cell phone and noticed that I had no signal strength.

"Come on Butch, he works for the United States government. He knows everything about you. He probably even has copies of your tax returns." Pete said as he stood up to stretch.

"What's the catch for me being able to go outside?" I asked Mr. Cook expecting him to restrict me in some way or another.

"No catch."

"Why don't you step out with Butch, Peter and discuses whether or not to trust me? If you choose not to I will call for you a ride and we can go our separate ways."

"Are we going to be spied on out there?" Pete asked as he walked up to me and looked at my cell phone.

"There are cameras that will most certainly keep an eye on you. You can talk to each other freely; there is no audio equipment outside the building. Don't be talking to each other while you are on your cell phone though."

"We do monitor all your cell phone calls around here Butch." Mr. Cook told Pete and I as we walked back up the hallway.

Once we arrived at the door and stepped out my cell phone lit up with eight missed calls. They all came from Vickie, she was probably worried sick.

She wasn't going to be very happy about me being out of touch and I really didn't have the time to explain everything to her right now.

"Pete I need to call Vickie first if you don't mind."

"You go ahead Butch." Pete said with a nod of his head as he took a couple of steps away and turned his back to me.

I called Vickie. The phone rang one time then she picked it up and instead of saying hello, Vickie answered with are you alright.

"Hey Sweet Pea I can't explain things right now but I wanted to let you know that I'm ok and that I love you."

"I understand Butch, please be careful out there I love you too, and call me when you can."

"I will, I need to go now. Goodbye." I said to Vickie as I turned to Pete to ask him what we should do next.

"Ok Pete what are we going to do?"

"Butch do you still want to tell them how we found our information?" Pete whispered to me.

"I will go with whatever you recommend Pete. You took me this far we'll do what you want to do."

"I don't trust Special Agent Brian Cook, Butch. I just don't trust him."

"Somebody is going to need to start so it might as well be us." The sheriff was giving in.

"If he can help us solve your friend's murder then maybe we should give him a chance. I just don't like dancing with the devil, that's all." Pete said as he was not making this decision very lightly.

"How do we get back in Pete?"

"That's easy Butch all you need to do is wave. Somebody is watching us on a camera somewhere." Pete said as he raised his right hand and waved it back and forth.

After about a minute and a half the door opened and there stood Special Agent Cook.

"Alright Cook you win. We'll talk first." The sheriff told Mr. Cook.

Chapter 10

Face to face with the Government.

Pete and I followed Special Agent Cook back down that dark hallway to the room that had that big table with the twelve chairs around it.

Whenever I had to arrest someone for poaching I would always video tape their statement. It was no big surprise that Mr. Cook didn't have a tape recorder or video camera with him to take our statements.

There were probably several of them hidden all around us in that room. I wondered how many people are watching us right now.

"Who would like to start?" Mr. Cook asked as we all sat down at the table. The sheriff and I on one side with Mr. Cook in his black suit on the other side.

"Why don't you start by asking Butch and me your questions you wanted to ask?"

"Ok I will. Peter why didn't you draw your weapon like Butch did when the cow you were using as bait was in trouble?"

"I didn't need to."

"I knew the government was somehow involved and would be showing up."

"Matter of fact, I didn't plan on seeing the _Prairie Monster_. It was as much of a surprise to me as it was to Mr. Murphy's cow."

"You, on the other hand, I knew would show up. Well maybe not you personally but somebody from the government was going to show up." The sheriff proudly told Mr. Cook with a smile.

"What about you Butch?"

"Did you know somebody from the United States government was going to be showing up?" Special Agent Cook inquired as he was clearly getting irritated.

"No Mr. Cook. I didn't know the sheriff's entire plan. I thought we where going hunting for the _Prairie Monster_. I didn't realize that we were flushing out weasels." I explained to Mr. Cook, this time it was my turn to ridicule the government.

"Butch I know that country folk are raised to respect people, and to address them as Mr. and Mrs. and I do indeed appreciate you calling me Mr. Cook."

"At least while we're sitting around here would you please start calling me Brian?" Special Agent Cook said to me as he sat there and folded his arms.

"If it will hurry things along I'll call you whatever you want me to call you." I replied to Special Agent Brian Cook as Pete was still sitting there with a big smile on his face.

"How did you figure out which tree to stand by and where to set up your bait?"

"Sheriff Wells figured that one out."

"Ok Peter you seem to be the one that holds all the cards. Would you like to tell me how you figured that one out?"

"No I wouldn't, but I will."

"It's all right there in Butch's *Prairie Monster* file in his pictures and in his notes. All you need to do is be smart enough to look past the obvious."

"In the pictures that Butch took of cattle mutilation's in the far background there is always a huge rock sticking up out of the ground. Big heavy boulders that look like they've been there forever."

"Besides the cow being mutilated that's the only other common factor in those photos that Butch took. My guess is that they move the rock to one side or the other, and that's how they are able to come and go without being seen."

"They live under the ground don't they? Of course you already knew that though didn't you."

"They use the big rocks as some sort of a door into our world." The sheriff was very impressive as he spoke of his deductions of my photographs.

"That was the easy part to figure out. I started to concentrate next on the reporter that disappeared, John Wall."

"John Wall was just a pen name that he was using to write his articles under. His real name was Jonathan Wallace."

"Jonathan Wallace was born right here in Rock county, the oldest child of Mary and William Wallace.

"He is the great, great uncle of one of my deputies. Deputy Frank Wallace, and like most families he had some childhood stories about his great, great uncle."

"His grandfather would tell him stories about how the _Prairie Monster_ killed his uncle, and that they never found the body of his uncle."

"Deputy Wallace never believed the stories that his grandfather told, but they did provide us with more clues."

"Deputy Wallace told us that his great, great uncle had warned his grandfather to stay away from the large stones. That right there told me that I was on the right path."

"Deputy Wallace told Butch and me that his grandfather had told him about the time that he had ridden a horse out to see his uncle the night his uncle disappeared."

"This is where Deputy Wallace's story gets interesting; his grandfather told him that his uncle was hidden in a tree."

"That was the last time that anyone ever saw his uncle Jonathan Wallace, a.k.a. John Wall."

"After talking to Deputy Wallace, Butch and I began to look for trees that were old enough to have been around back then."

"We enlisted the help of Mr. Shawn Murphy. He was able to tell us about the story behind the Cottonwood tree that is referred to around here as the Wall-nut tree. It was Mr. Murphy that directed us to that old Cottonwood tree."

"He explained to us that his father had told him that a nut or crazy person would sit up in that old Cottonwood tree."

"The nuts name was Wall. So people started calling it the Wall-nut tree. And that's how we happen to be out there tonight." The sheriff had explained the whole story to Special Agent Cook on how we ended up out there tonight.

"How did you find out that John Wall was actually Jonathan Wallace and that he grew up around here?"

"Oh come on Cook. Are you going to sit there and try to tell us that you don't have access to that information? I have a feeling that you had that information faster than I did." Pete said to Special Agent Cook.

"Peter we are well aware that you retrieved information from the Philadelphia Star."

"It was the same information that was in Butch's file. There was no mention about Wallace changing his name to Wall." Brian was trying to explain to the sheriff that he didn't have a clue about the name change, which came as a surprise to him.

"Cook if you would have taken the time to look in the employment records of the Philadelphia Star, you would have known all of this."

"That's not my department Peter but I would say that we didn't go that far. I will be discussing this with my superiors."

"I have a question Brian. How does the United States government know that Pete was retrieving information from the Philadelphia Star?"

"If Special Agent Cook doesn't mind I can answer that Butch."

"The United States government tracks everything that you do on a computer if you key in the right word. They have certain words that are red flagged, and if you type in that word then you're going to be monitored from that point on."

"It's like when you go to the Library if you check out certain books that are red flagged you will fall under there, we need to watch this guy file."

"Is that about it Cook?"

"Something like that Peter."

"Excuse me gentlemen I need to step out for a moment." Special Agent Cook said right after a little light came on in the corner of the room.

"They must need to change batteries in the camera so they want Cook to stall for time." Pete said with a snicker as Mr. Cook left the room.

"Pete is Special Agent Cook going to tell us anything useful or is this going to be just a big waste of time?"

"I don't know Butch. He might but I don't know if it will be intentional or not. You need to realize that Special Agent Cook is going to follow orders."

"He will only do what he is told to do and nothing more." Pete said as he stretched his arms up and outward, twisting his back at the same time.

Special Agent Cook came back into the room and proclaimed that he was ready to tell us what the government knew. He was going to share their information with the sheriff and I.

Whenever the government is involved and they tell you that they are going to let you in on something you better be prepared to take it for what it's worth.

"Ok gentlemen I need you two to take an oath." Special Agent Cook said as the sheriff and I looked at each other. Why should we take an oath?

"Don't worry it's not a blood oath or anything like that. We need to swear you to secrecy due to national security."

"I want you gentlemen to understand that if you talk to others or try to publish what I'm about to say, you will be prosecuted and sent to a federal prison."

"Look it is very important that this doesn't get out to the public. If that is going to be a problem then I need to know right now?" Mr. Cook asked the sheriff and I.

"Butch and I don't need to swear an oath of secrecy; we already know what the government knows. We know that there is a whole culture of creature's living under the ground."

"We also know that the United States government has known about them and has kept the public from finding out the truth!" Pete told Special Agent Cook in a loud and angered voice.

"How did you know all of this Peter? Who gave you this information?" Mr. Cook asked as he was starting to get angry himself, he thought that there was a leak somewhere.

"You did." The sheriff explained. Special Agent Cook wasn't expecting that.

"We didn't know positively until right now. You confirmed it for us. I want to thank you for that. Cook you could use some work on your interviewing skills."

"Butch and I had a theory that something was living under the ground. That's why they never come out during the day; their eyes can't handle the sunlight."

"Our intentions are to capture the one that attacked Butch and murdered his friend Berry Decker."

"Justice!"

"That's all we're after Cook." The sheriff was showing why he is what he is. The best investigator in the country. Now the government knows he's the best there is too.

That light in the corner of the room came on again; Special Agent Cook excused himself and left the room. I flipped open my cell phone to check for service. No service, they have something blocking the signal in here.

"Pete I have a couple of questions."

198

"Shhhhh. Butch the walls have eyes and ears remember."

"You told Mr. Cook that you and I had a theory." I whispered to the sheriff as I cupped my hand around my mouth and leaned in towards his ear.

"Yeah I told him that."

"Knowing that other people are listening, I didn't want them to think that you were only a opossum hunter." Pete whispered with a smile.

"Thanks." I whispered back sarcastically.

Special Agent Cook came walking back into the room. He had a brown folder with string around it under his arm.

Mr. Cook laid the folder on the table and opened it up. He pulled out two documents that had government seals on them and closed the folder back up, and wrapped the string back around it.

"I have been authorized to offer you two gentlemen jobs with the United States government."

"You may continue your regular jobs, and continue performing your regular job duties while you're doing specialized work for the government, and no one needs to know that you're working for us too."

"Except you Peter they want you to come to Washington with me. They want to not only offer you a job; they want to offer you a position in the agency." Mr. Cook explained the governments offer. I don't blame the government for offering Pete a job; I'd want him on my side too.

"I don't know about Pete but my goal right now is to find my friend, Berry Decker's murderer, so I'm not interested right now."

"I like it here Cook, and besides that I can't ever see myself taking orders from you."

"I told them that neither one of you would be interested but they wanted me to make the offer anyway. I was also told to tell you to take a couple of weeks to think it over." Special Agent Cook relayed to Pete and I.

"Cook if you don't mind Butch and I have some work to do. We're ready to go now."

"Ok I'll arrange transportation for you and Butch. If the both of you don't mind, it will be ground transportation?"

"That's alright with us, but the sheriff and I want to wait outside for our ride." I told Mr. Cook answering for the both of us.

The sheriff and I walked up the hallway and out the door.

We stood outside waiting on our ride surveying our surroundings and not talking to each other.

After about fifteen minutes or so a black S.U.V. pulled up to the outside of the fence, the gate then automatically opened.

The sheriff and I looked at each other. I motioned with my head to walk over, Pete grinned and we both walked over to the vehicle.

I walked around the back side as Pete climbed into the back seat of the black S.U.V. on the passenger side.

I noticed a government license plate on the bumper as I circled the rear of the vehicle.

I climbed in the back seat on the driver's side. The driver said that he was instructed to drive us back to our vehicle on Broken Arrow Road.

Nothing was said on the drive back by either our driver or one of us, it was an uneventful trip back to the old Decker house.

When we arrived back to the sheriff's patrol cruiser, Pete and I thanked our driver and walked over to the sheriff's car. It was still sitting in the driveway where the Decker's use to live.

After sitting down in the vehicle and closing the car door I looked over at the sheriff and smiled at him while I commented on his life.

"Well Pete, you certainly live an interesting life. I'm going to start hanging out with you more often. You're like a James Bond and Indiana Jones all rolled up together aren't you?"

"What are you talking about Butch?"

"We don't have the windy city monster, up in Chicago that lives beneath the streets and comes out at night to attack the public." Pete said to me as he picked up his radio and called for Deputy Wallace.

"Deputy Wallace this is Sheriff Wells come in."

"Deputy Wallace are you there? Come in please."

"I'm here Sheriff, at Mr. Murphy's house."

"I didn't know what you wanted me to do after I helped Mr. Murphy put his cow back in the pasture. I thought it best if I hang out here for awhile to make sure nothing happened to the old man."

"Good job Deputy. Good job indeed."

"I want you to go to the station and see if Deputy Barns has returned his patrol cruiser."

"If Deputy Barns is still there I want you to arrest him immediately. Do you copy Deputy Wallace?"

"10-4 Sheriff. I'm on my way."

"What shall I say to Deputy Barns is the charge he's being arrested for?"

"Tell him he's being arrested for being an idiot and that I will formally file charges on him tomorrow."

"Butch your friend Deputy Wallace surprises me every now and then and does the right thing without being told."

"Although he's still a little rough around the edges, he means well." The sheriff said to me as I sat there and flipped open my cell phone to call Vickie, I needed to let her know that I was ok.

"Before I call Vickie and let her know how things are going, Pete."

"How are things going?"

"Things are going well, very well indeed."

"You can tell her not to worry, we have a plan, and everything is going as scheduled." Pete said with a big smile on his face.

"We do? They are?" I was puzzled.

"We most certainly do Butch. We most certainly do, and it's a good one."

"And believe it or not the United States government is going to help us." The sheriff was on a roll; his mind was working in overdrive. It was obvious that he had things worked out in his mind and was confident with his plan.

"Butch when you call your wife I want you to tell her a few things that aren't going to be completely truthful."

"Is that going to be a problem with you?" Pete was asking me to lie to my wife.

"I guess that really depends on the circumstances Pete, and what all it involves."

"Butch I want you to be brief, tell her that everything is going as planed and that you're ok."

"Tell her that we should have Berry's murderer in custody soon. Then tell her that you will explain everything later." The sheriff explained to me exactly what to say to Vickie.

"Are we Pete, are we going to have Berry's murderer in custody soon?"

"I honestly don't know Butch. It wouldn't surprise me if we did, and it wouldn't surprise me if we didn't."

"I think that we are going to know what happened that night you and Berry Decker were attacked, and why you were attacked."

203

"Butch I want you to know that I don't think the United States government is going to let us capture it and go public with it. So don't get your hopes up to high."

I called Vickie to inform her how things were going. This time the phone actually rang more than a couple of times.

"Hi Sweet Pea it's me, how you doing?" I asked Vickie when she answered the phone.

"I'm worried sick, what do you think?"

"Can you please tell me what's going on?"

"Everything is going fine. Pete and I are right on track with our plans."

"Sweet Pea, we should have Berry's murderer in custody by morning."

"I can't go into details right now but I'll explain everything to you when were finished." I tried to put everything into plain words without being too informational. I didn't want Vickie to ask a lot of questions that I wasn't prepared to answer at this time.

"I swear Butch not knowing what's going on, is the worst. Not knowing if you're alive or dead. Not knowing if you're laying out there hurt somewhere and not knowing were to look if you are."

"I'm worried Butch, very worried." Vickie said as she fought back tears.

"It's ok to worry Sweet Pea, just don't let it consume you." I tried to calm Vickie's nerves.

"You need to stay strong for the kids, don't let them know that you're worried. I promise that I'll be alright, and you know that I don't break my promises."

"Ok, I'll find something to occupy my mind with and try not to dwell on it. Please be careful and call me when it's over. I love you very much Butch."

"I will Sweet Pea; I love you very much too." I said to Vickie as I closed my cell phone.

I looked over at Pete sitting next to me smiling from ear to ear.

"What?" I asked Pete as I stared at him.

"Aren't we sweet?"

"Yeah, yeah, you wish you had someone like I have."

"Now would you like to tell me what's going on, and how we're going to get the United States government to help us?"

Chapter 11

A plan to trick the government.

Pete started up his patrol cruiser and backed out of the Decker's old driveway. We headed down Broken Arrow Road towards town. It was like Pete was in a race. Not the kind of race that you run, but the kind of race you're in when you're on a scavenger hunt. Pete seemed to be driven.

It was starting to get late, as I looked down at my watch I noted the time, it was 11:15pm. This has been a long day and it doesn't have an end to it in sight.

I wasn't feeling tired, just the opposite I seemed to be energized. I was ready to do what needed to be done to bring this thirty-five year mystery to an end. It wasn't quite thirty-five years yet but it would be this coming August.

I hadn't noticed that I was calling it thirty-five years until just now. It's been a long, long time, and I'm now ready to do battle.

I would like to say that Pete and I had this great plan and we were going to do battle with my monsters from the past.

I would like to say that, but the truth is that I didn't have a clue what the plan was. Pete was the one that came up with all the information that led us to where we are right now.

"Pete, I'm going to guess that we are heading back to town for a reason."

"We need a few things from my supply room." Pete explained.

"Ok Pete this is going to be like pulling teeth."

"Are you going to tell me what's going on willingly? Or are you going to make me ask you everything?"

"I'm sorry Butch, I've got different ideas running through my mind and I just haven't been very considerate of your involvement."

"I need to start bouncing my ideas off of you, that way you'll know what I'm thinking and where we're going." Pete apologized and began to explain what he had in mind.

"I have a couple of Taser guns in the supply room at the courthouse."

"Butch I was thinking that when we return to the old Decker place, we should be better prepared for anything."

"Do you know anything about Taser guns Butch? How to use one? How they work? What they do?"

"I'm happy to say that I don't know a thing about Taser guns Pete. I've never caught someone out in the woods poaching an animal with one."

"Come to think of it Pete, it wouldn't surprise me if that was the next big thing poachers tried using to poach deer." I said to the sheriff thinking to myself that I need to watch what I say. I don't want to give poachers any ideas.

"Ok Butch let me give you a quick lesson on Taser guns and what they can do, while we ride into town together. If that's alright with you?"

"I tell you what Pete; I'm always willing to learn something new anytime I can." I told Pete as he began to explain what Taser guns did.

"Butch the Taser weapons I have deliver about 50,000 volts of electricity. You need to treat these guns like you would treat any other gun."

"The big drawback to these guns is that you need to be within fifteen to twenty feet of your target." Pete explained.

"Pete I've seen these guns used on television, and I've always wondered what discharge's the projectile?" I asked Pete, thinking that a blank cartridge must fire the projectile out.

"Butch air cartridges will launch two probes up to twenty feet using compressed nitrogen."

"I can't express enough how these Taser guns need to be treated with the same care that you would treat a regular gun."

As we were pulling into the parking garage of the courthouse Pete looked over at me and with one eyebrow raised he suggested that I wait for him out in the car.

"If you would wait here Butch I will be back in about ten minutes?"

As I sat there in the sheriff's patrol cruiser I watched Pete walk towards the employee's entrance of the courthouse.

Deputy Wallace came walking out the door as the sheriff approached the entrance. The two of them stopped and talked for a moment.

Deputy Wallace continued walking towards me after the sheriff was finished talking to him.

I opened the door of the patrol cruiser and stepped out to speak to Frank.

"Hi Frank."

"Hey thanks for your help tonight."

"I appreciate you helping Mr. Murphy with his cow and then sticking around to make sure that nothing happened to him. That was very professional of you. I owe you one Frank." I said to Deputy Wallace as I raised my right hand to shake hands with him.

"Butch can you tell me what's going on with Roy?" Frank asked about Deputy Roy Barns. I don't blame him for being curious about someone he worked with.

"I'm sorry Frank, I don't know exactly what's going on, but what I do know I can't discuss with anyone."

"That's ok Butch I understand. Roy had already been here and gone by the time I arrived at the courthouse so it wasn't even an issue for me."

"Butch it looks like we'll be working together tonight, the sheriff told me to not go anywhere and to wait for him out here in the parking garage."

"Frank I know I don't have to tell you this but I'm going to say it anyway. Be careful tonight don't take any unnecessary chances." I told Deputy Wallace as we both turned our heads and looked at the employee's door open.

"Butch here comes the sheriff, are you going to tell me what we are about to do tonight, or is the sheriff going to fill me in on what to do?"

"Frank I'd be more than happy to let you know, only if I knew what we are going to be doing later tonight." I said to Frank in a loud voice so Pete could hear me. I was hoping the sheriff would inform Frank and me both on what the plan was for tonight. I don't like being kept in the dark on what's going on, but I trust the sheriff with my life.

The sheriff walked up to Frank and me. Pulled his car keys out of his pocket and opened the trunk of his patrol cruiser.

Pete tossed four Taser guns and a couple of pairs of handcuffs in the trunk. After closing the trunk Pete turned to Frank and told him to meet us at the old Decker house.

"Deputy Wallace I want you to follow Butch and I in your patrol cruiser to the burnt out old Decker house. Stay close to us when we get to our turn off at Broken Arrow Road I will give more details to you at that time. Do not use your radio to call me unless it's an emergency." The sheriff explained to Frank as he motioned with a nod of his head for me to get into the patrol cruiser.

"Ok Pete lets have it, what's the game plan tonight? I've waited long enough and I want to know what you suspect is going to happen." I asked the sheriff as I put my seatbelt on; I was starting to get a little frustrated.

"Butch we're not getting the whole story from the United States government, and I'm getting tired of being jerked around. I think that its time we were told everything about Berry Decker's death. We're going to get the truth one way or another tonight."

"Special Agent Brian Cook is still holding out on us, and he's going to tell us what happened or I'm going to shoot him with one of those Taser guns in the trunk." Pete said with a grin, and at this point I don't think he's kidding. As a Matter of fact I know he's not kidding, Pete don't like Special Agent Cook.

"If my hunch is right Butch, there will be a couple of black S.U.V.'s with government license plates on them when we get back to the old Decker place."

"I would imagine that Special Agent Cook will be in one of them. He's going to think that he's there to stop us." The sheriff explained as he began to drive out of the courthouse parking garage and towards the old Decker house.

"I'm catching on Pete, that's why you had me tell Vickie that we were going to have Berry's murderer in custody soon. Knowing that the United States government couldn't allow this to happen you used my conversation with Vickie as bait to draw them out again."

"You knew that the government would be listening in on my cell phone calls, and would probably try and stop us. Am I right Pete?"

"You're doing pretty good for an old opossum hunter, Butch."

"We need to get Special Agent Brian Cook to give us more details about these creatures that live underground. He knows more than he lets on and its time that he shared it with us." Pete explained to me as we drove towards the old Decker place with Frank right behind us.

"Pete you saw how fast the _Prairie Monster_ can move, how in the world are we going to get close enough to do anything to it?"

"We're not."

"There's something you haven't mentioned yet Butch, which is how intelligent these creatures can be. It's no mistake that they have been hidden all these years."

"No one has any real evidence of their existence. They're not stupid so we have to be very cautious in what we do. We have to be smarter than they are."

"Butch I don't know if the plan I have will work but I'm willing to give it a try and who knows with some luck it might just work, we'll see what happens." Pete said as he hesitated a moment before he began to tell me about his plan.

"I don't want you to laugh at my plan Butch, so just hear me out. This is what I had in mind. We're going to set up four Taser guns around that big rock that you and your friend rested on back when you were twelve. These creatures are using large stones as doorways into our world."

"We're going to aim the Taser guns upwards and towards the big rock. I have some twine in the trunk that we'll use to wrap around the big rock and through the trigger guards of the Taser guns. By wedging the Taser guns in between smaller rocks we should be able to aim them just about anywhere we need to."

"When the big rock is raised it will pull on the twine and if everything goes well it will activate the triggers on the Taser guns."

"I'm hoping it will stun the creature enough for us to put handcuffs on it." The sheriff explained his plan to me as we turned onto Broken Arrow Road.

Pete came to a stop and waved for Deputy Wallace to pull up beside us.

"Deputy Wallace I want you to go to Mr. Murphy's place and see if we could use his cow again, and ask him to come along if he wants to."

"If he agrees, help him load up the cow and bring it back to where you picked it up at earlier tonight."

"Under no circumstances do you use your radio or your cell phone. Do you have any questions Deputy Wallace?"

"No I got it Sheriff. I'll be back in less than an hour."

As Deputy Wallace drove off towards Mr. Murphy's farm Pete slowly drove towards the old Decker place.

"I take it we're not in any hurry to get there Pete?"

"We want to give the government time to respond to our trap." The sheriff explained as he continued ever so slowly down the dirt road. Pete turned into the driveway of the old Decker place and slowly drove forwards.

As we pulled up and parked where we had parked earlier I started getting that overwhelming urge to go and confront my past again.

As the sheriff and I stepped out of his patrol cruiser we both stood there and listened.

We could hear vehicle's coming down Broken Arrow Road from both directions.

"Do you think that's the government boy's coming our way Pete?" I asked as we walked to the front of the sheriff's patrol cruiser and sat on the hood.

"I think were about to find out Butch."
Pete said to me as he folded his arms.

Right about then two black S.U.V.'s
pulled into the driveway. The passenger
side door of one of the vehicle's opened and
Special Agent Brian Cook stepped out and
walked up to Pete and I.

"What took you so long Cook?" The
sheriff asked sarcastically.

"You two think your funny don't you?
You're walking a fine line with national
security right now."

"Don't you two understand that you need
to drop this before someone gets hurt? Will
you please let it go?" Special Agent Cook
said, not really asking Pete and I but
telling us to back off.

"Cook I want to know why the United
States government didn't bring a twelve year
old boy's murderer to justice!!!!!" The
sheriff asked Mr. Cook in a very loud and
angry voice.

"The United States government didn't
just stand by and do nothing!!!" Mr. Cook
hollered back.

"First of all we didn't prosecute Mr.
Raymond Decker for arson. We had him for
burning down his old house. The United
States government offered a deal to Mr.
Decker and he accepted it."

"Just what kind of a deal did the
United States government make with Mr.
Decker?" I asked Special Agent Cook.

"Butch the government and Mr. Decker
signed a confidentiality agreement, so what
I'm about to tell you will be breaking that
agreement."

"Because of Mr. Decker's untimely death I can explain to you some of the details of the agreement between the United States government and Mr. Decker, and not get in any legal problems."

"The United States government agreed to not prosecute Mr. Decker for arson; we agreed to pay off the loan on the house that Mr. Raymond Decker allegedly burned down, and the government agreed to pay for his new house that he had moved his family into."

"We also agreed to pay the college tuition for his kids so all of them could attend the university of their choice. All we asked of Mr. Decker was for him to not bring attention to himself and what had happened to his son."

"Mr. Decker was to never talk about what happened to his son Berry to anybody, anywhere at anytime."

"Butch there was nothing that was going to bring Berry back, so Mr. Decker decided to concentrate on providing the best life for the rest of his kids and making them safe. He really had no choice, his back was against the wall, and he did what he had to do for the rest of his family." Special Agent Cook described what had happened thirty-five years ago between the United States government and Mr. Decker.

"Let me get this straight Cook, you're telling Butch and I that if Mr. Decker didn't agree to the government's deal that they were going to throw him in federal prison. Is that about it?"

"Hey I don't make the deals!! Let's keep in mind that Mr. Decker is an arsonist. We could have just arrested him and thrown him in jail." Special Agent Cook replied trying to defend the government's decision to keep this under wraps.

"Well Butch lets see what you would do if you were Mr. Decker. You get a free house and all your kids can go to college free, or you get to go to prison. Which one would you elect to choose Butch?" Pete was pointing out the obvious that the government didn't give Mr. Decker much of a choice at all.

"Look Peter, Mr. Decker's children are a lot better off now then they would have been if he hadn't made the deal that he did with the government's attorneys."

"What about Mr. Decker, is he better off now?" I asked Special Agent Cook knowing that Mr. Decker died of liver disease a long time ago.

"Listen to me Butch, the United States government didn't tell Mr. Decker to drink himself to death; he did that on his own." Replied Special Agent Cook as he put his hands on his hips as if he was as pure as the driven snow.

"No they didn't, did they Mr. Cook!"

"The United States government just made it so that Mr. Decker had to sell the memory of his son, my best friend Berry."

"The government gave Mr. Decker no choice, and you know that. That's the same as putting a bottle in his hand and forcing him to drink, as far as I'm concerned." I told Mr. Cook as I looked over at the sheriff, he was nodding his head up and down in agreement with me.

"Ok Butch I understand that you're a little upset right now, and I know how Peter is, he wants to arrest everybody."

"The bottom line is that we have a treaty with these creatures and I can't let you break the government's agreement." Special Agent Cook explained in a softer more somber tone of voice.

This was something new, a treaty. That would mean that the United States government has found a way to communicate with these creatures.

All of the sudden there was an uneasy silence with Pete and I staring at each other. Special Agent Cook had finally given us something tangible. Neither one of us was willing to believe that our government was hiding this information from the public.

Not knowing what Mr. Cook had in mind when he told Pete and I that he couldn't let us break the government's treaty, the sheriff told Special Agent Cook what the government wanted to hear. Pete is good at that. Getting information from people by telling them what they want to hear.

"Brian I understand now what you have been trying to tell Butch and I. To be honest with you it never crossed my mind that the United States government was in direct communications with these creatures." Pete began to try and fish more information out of Special Agent Cook. I don't think it's going to be very easy; Special Agent Cook is starting to catch on.

Still it didn't stop the sheriff from trying, even though Special Agent Cook knew the way the sheriff operates.

"Tell me Cook, the government's treaty probably has a clause in it that states that the creatures have to stay out of sight and keep to themselves under the ground. Am I right?"

"Peter there are other factor's that I just can't discuses with the two of you."

"Butch I am truly sorry about what happened to you and your friend Berry Decker it was a very unfortunate incident and it caused a diplomatic nightmare."

"If it will put your mind at ease Butch, I can tell you that it was taken care of in a very aggressive and military way many years ago."

"Peter this is one case that you need to let go there's nothing there to investigate, it's over. It has been closed and forgotten for years, and needs to stay that way." Special Agent Cook told the sheriff as if he was trying to convince us it was for the better to let it go.

"You know Brian you could have explained all of this to Butch and I a long time ago and saved everybody a lot of time and heartache."

"Butch and I will put it to rest and I think we'll be getting back to you in a week or two about the government's offer to help keep their secret." Pete told Special Agent Cook as he stuck out his right hand to shake hands with him.

"Thanks Peter, I hope I can count on your help in the future." Special Agent Cook said as he shook hands with the sheriff and me. I don't know about Pete but for me it felt like I was shaking hands with the devil. Something just didn't feel right with this whole thing. I was a little surprised that Pete was willing to back off so easy.

Pete and I stood there and watched Special Agent Cook return to his vehicle, get in, and back out of the driveway. The other government S.U.V. followed right behind him.

"Tell me Pete, we're not going to just drop this are we?"

"Not on Special Agent Brian Cook's life Butch, not on his life!"

Chapter 12

The capture.

As the sheriff and I stood there, I realized that it didn't matter what the government tried to do, Pete was going to help me get to the truth.

At this point I didn't know if the sheriff was doing this because we had become good friends or because of his overwhelming desire to see that justice is done. After all he was still Sheriff Peter Wells and he did have a bit of a problem with a "the law is the law and if you break the law then you need to be punished" attitude.

It could be that Pete just didn't like to be pushed around by the government especially when the United States government is wrong. I also think that Pete doesn't like Special Agent Cook at all, personally or professionally.

The both of us were just standing out there not saying anything to each other just waiting; waiting on Deputy Wallace and Mr. Murphy to show up.

This gave me time to reflect on what had happened so long ago. I thought to myself how would I have handled it if I was Mr. Decker?

The United States government really didn't give Mr. Decker much of a choice. I may not agree with his decision but I'm not sure that I would have done it any differently under the circumstances.

And what about Mrs. Decker? How come nobody has taken into account her feelings?

Pete and I both raised our head up as we could hear a vehicle coming down the dirt road.

"Sounds like there's a truck coming and it sounds like its hauling a trailer." I said to the sheriff in a soft, almost whispered voice.

"Come on Butch let's walk down to the road and make sure it's Mr. Murphy and Deputy Wallace that's coming." Pete said to me as he started walking down the driveway.

Mr. Murphy was driving his old truck and pulling a trailer. Deputy Wallace was right behind him in his patrol cruiser. Mr. Murphy rolled down his window as he pulled up to the sheriff and I.

"Where do you want the cow dropped off this time?"

"Go ahead and pull your truck and trailer into the driveway as far up in there as you can if you don't mind Mr. Murphy, we'll unload your cow up there off the road." The sheriff asked as he was pointing up towards the old burnt Decker house.

"Deputy Wallace wait here for a moment please, I want to talk to you after I talk to Butch." Pete told Frank as he walked up to me.

"Butch would you go and help Mr. Murphy unload his cow please?"

"Sure Pete but what about the government boys? I don't want the government to stop us again."

"Don't worry Butch I'm going to take care of that right now with the help of Deputy Wallace." Pete said with a smile as he turned and walked back to Frank.

"Deputy Wallace I'm going to call you on the radio. After you answer my call all I want you to say is 10-4 Sheriff. You got that?" The sheriff explained as Frank shook his head up and down and gave the sheriff a thumbs up.

Pete walked back up to his patrol cruiser and sat down inside with the door shut. I'm sure he did that to block out any noise that Mr. Murphy and I were making while we were unloading Mr. Murphy's cow from the back of Mr. Murphy's trailer.

The sheriff picked up his radio and called for Frank.

"Deputy Wallace, come in please."

"This is Deputy Wallace." Frank answered on his radio after pausing for a few seconds. He didn't want it to look like he was expecting the sheriff to call.

"I'm going to call it a night Deputy Wallace; I'll see you in the morning." Pete told Frank so that if the government was listening they would think that everybody was giving up for the night.

"10-4 Sheriff."

Pete stepped out of his patrol cruiser and motioned for Deputy Wallace to walk up the driveway where Mr. Murphy and I had just unloaded the cow that we planned to use as bait.

"That's pretty slick Pete. Do you think the government boys fell for it?" I asked the sheriff as Mr. Murphy shook his head back and forth, he couldn't believe the sheriff could be so deceitful.

"I don't know Butch, I hope so. We shouldn't underestimate the government though."

The sheriff opened the trunk on his patrol cruiser and pulled out four Taser guns, some twine and the extra handcuffs he had put in earlier. He handed me the Taser guns to carry and then shut the trunk.

"Ok now that everybody's here I can tell you we plan to use Mr. Murphy's cow as bait to lure the *Prairie Monster* out of its hiding place and stun it with these Taser guns. After stunning it, we hope to put handcuffs on it. I carry two pair's with me and I have a couple of extra pair's for its feet." The sheriff finally explained his plan.

"What about Frank and Mr. Murphy? What do you want them to do?" I asked Pete as Frank stood there with his hands on his hips and Mr. Murphy stood there holding the rope that's tied around the cow's neck.

"While Butch and I are setting up our trap I want Mr. Murphy to tie the cow up to the same tree that they untied it from earlier. Deputy Wallace will act as a lookout for all of us." The sheriff laid out the assignments for tonight.

"I won't let you down Sheriff, I'm ready and I'll do whatever needs to be done." Deputy Wallace said to all of us.

"Good. Is there anything that anybody wants to say before we get started?" Pete asked while he looked back at all of us. We all looked at each other. Then Mr. Murphy stepped up to speak.

"Yeah I would like to say something to the two of you right now before we take another step."

"When are you two going to start calling me Shawn?"

"Why thank you Shawn." Deputy Wallace responded.

"Not you Wallace. You can still address me as Mr. Murphy." Mr. Murphy said as he winked at Pete and I with a smile on his face.

"Alright now if no one has anything else to say lets get started?" The sheriff suggested.

All four of us walked past the old burnt out Decker house with Mr. Murphy's cow in tow.

We walked through the pasture and right up to where we were earlier this evening.

Mr. Murphy tied his cow up to the same Cottonwood tree that we had it tied to earlier while Pete and I set up the Taser guns around the big rock we think is the doorway to the *Prairie Monster* world.

Mr. Murphy and Deputy Wallace walked over to Pete and I as we finished setting up.

The last thing that Pete did was pull the twine tight that was wrapped around the big rock, and through the trigger guards of the Taser guns. Pete was being careful not to pull too tight on the string that went through the trigger guards of the Taser guns; he didn't want to set them off prematurely.

Pete stepped away from the target area and stood there looking over our job.

"Well men I think this is going to work. All we need is a little luck." The sheriff explained as we all started walking towards that big old Cottonwood tree that everybody calls the Walnut tree.

As we walked up to the tree Pete reached up and grabbed his night vision binoculars off of a limb that he had hung up there when the government helicopter's showed up.

"You knew didn't you Pete?"

"You knew that we were going to be back here tonight. That's why you left your night vision binoculars hanging up there on that branch." I said to the sheriff as he just stood there and grinned.

"Deputy Wallace I want you to stand behind Butch and I. Do not draw your weapon unless somebody's life is in jeopardy."

"When this all starts it will happen fast, and we will be running full throttle I want everybody to be ready." Pete was understating the obvious in my mind.

"Pete you need to tell Mr. Murphy and Frank about how fast the *Prairie Monster* is." I told the sheriff as I leaned back against the tree we were standing by.

"Butch is right, this thing is fast, very fast, and strong. When Butch and I saw this thing earlier it pushed up that huge rock came out from under it looked around and went back down."

"It did all of that in less then three seconds." Pete explained how dangerous the *Prairie Monster* could be, and then looked at me and asked me why I was smiling.

"Ok Butch what's so funny? I'm not exaggerating, you were there, and you saw it too." The sheriff was puzzled over me smiling.

"I'm sorry Pete. It just came to me why Special Agent Brian Cook was so protective of these creatures earlier." I couldn't help myself from smiling over what I was thinking.

"Well are you going to tell us?" Mr. Murphy wanted to know what I was smiling at now.

"I was just thinking that the *Prairie Monster* crawled out from under a rock just like those government agents did." Everybody smiled.

After about ten or fifteen minutes everybody squatted down against the tree. We all sat there looking around in different directions but focused mostly towards Mr. Murphy's cow and the big rock where we had set up our trap.

"Wallace you do know that your family was one of the first group of settlers that came to Rock County don't you?" Mr. Murphy whispered to Frank.

"I really didn't start paying much attention to that kind of stuff until earlier today when the sheriff and Butch talked to me about my great, great uncle Jonathan Wallace the newspaper reporter." Frank whispered back.

"Well Frank I don't know about Mr. Murphy but my family doesn't have a tree named after any of its past members." I said to Frank in a soft voice as I winked at the sheriff.

"Yeah I guess that is something after all." Frank replied.

Mr. Murphy asked Pete about his heritage and the fact that he grew up in Chicago. I don't know if the sheriff wanted people to know that he was an orphan.

I wonder if that's a sore spot for Pete or something that he's proud of. Coming out of an orphanage and making something of himself. I'm not in Pete's shoes, but I'd be proud if I was him.

"What about you Sheriff?"

"We all know that you came from the big city, but what about your family?" Mr. Murphy asked in a deep but whispered voice.

"Mr. Murphy I would love to tell you about my ancestry but I don't know anything about my family. I'm an orphan sir."

"I grew up in an orphanage in Chicago." The sheriff began to explain to Mr. Murphy.

"I'm so sorry Sheriff I didn't mean to be so nosy." Mr. Murphy apologized as we all sat there feeling a little uncomfortable that he had asked about the sheriff's past.

"That's ok Mr. Murphy. As a citizen of Rock County you should know about your sheriff."

"I don't know much about my parents other than what the orphanage had told me when I left there after graduating high school."

"I was told that at the time when I was left there at the orphanage, there were a lot of unwed teenage mother's that didn't know what to do."

"So out of desperation they would leave their newborn babies at the orphanage."

"They told me that my father probably never knew I existed. I still hold on to that idea hoping that some day I'll find him through DNA."

"The staff at the orphanage told me that when I was abandoned there I was severely underweight and I had been born premature."

"So growing up I had a lot of medical problems, and no one back then wanted to adopt a child with medical problems."

"That's how I ended up staying at the orphanage until I graduated from high school. I didn't mind though, they treated me real good. After graduation they gave me a thousand dollars, rented me an apartment for three months and helped me get into community college."

"I donate ten percent of my salary to the orphanage every month. It's just my way of thanking them for being there when I needed them, and it helps me feel good inside about myself. I was raised in a good environment and taught good values." The sheriff explained a lot more to Mr. Murphy than he ever did with me when I had asked him.

"How did you end up with your name being Peter Wells, if they didn't know your parents?" Deputy Wallace asked the sheriff. That's a pretty good question coming from Frank, I was surprised, maybe the sheriff was rubbing off on his deputies.

"The women at the orphanage would pick first names out of the Bible for the kids that didn't have a name. The last names they went in alphabetic order. When I was abandoned they just happened to be on W's."

"That's an amazing life you've lived there Sheriff. I can't speak for Wallace but I know that Butch and I are glad you're a part of our community now." Mr. Murphy expressed his gratitude to Pete.

"Now wait a minute, as a Deputy I've learned a lot from the sheriff since he took over the Sheriff's department. He has taught me more since he's been here then I ever learned at the academy"

"I'm glad he's here too, I'm a much better law enforcement officer because of him." Frank said as he stood up. We then all stood up; our knees were getting tired of squatting against the tree.

"Thank you gentlemen for making me feel wanted and appreciated. That's why I took this job to begin with here in Rock County, Kansas. Everybody around here makes you feel right at home."

"I would treat you the same way I treat everybody else even if you weren't my superior. We just don't know any better Sheriff. That's the way we were raised around here."

"I think what Frank is trying to say Pete, is that we like to live a slow and easy life around here and it's just easier if everybody treats one another with respect, that's the way we all were raised when we were kids."

"Even though Mr. Murphy has told me on several occasions to call him Shawn, I still address him as Mr. Murphy. It's done out of respect." I tried to explain to Pete about the values taught to us from people like Mr. Murphy and our parents. That's just the way it was growing up in the country.

"I'm very proud to be Sheriff of Rock County, Kansas, and I hope to someday get married and settle down here." The sheriff told us as he raised his night vision binoculars to his eyes and began to scan the area again.

So there we all were, four grown men standing out in the woods in the middle of the night next to a tree named after a reporter that everybody thought was crazy. It makes you think, I wonder who the crazy ones are now. Is it me or is it the ones that follow me? It's good to have friends.

Standing out there waiting on a creature that most people think only exists in fairytales I'm feeling a bit foolish but yet this is as real as it gets, and it's dangerous.

I'm beginning to think that this has gotten out of hand. This was my fight and now I have put three other people in danger.

Maybe I should call this off and come back another day by myself, that way I know no one else will get hurt.

"Hey guys I was just thinking maybe we should call it a night and rethink all of this." I said to Pete, Frank and Mr. Murphy. I could never forgive myself if one of them got hurt because of me.

"It's to late Butch; look at Mr. Murphy's cow trying to pull away from the tree that it's tied up to." The sheriff whispered.

All four of us stared at the rock that Pete and I had set our trap up around. The sheriff was looking through his night vision binoculars.

And then it happened.

In an instant the big rock came up and all four of the Taser guns shot all eight of their probes.

With a heavy thud the *Prairie Monster* fell next to the big rock. We all just stood there looking at it for a second or two, then Pete took off running towards the creature, I ran behind him and Frank and Mr. Murphy were coming behind me.

"Here Butch put these handcuffs on its feet, I'll take care of its hands." The sheriff said as he handed me a couple of pairs of handcuffs.

"I got you!!!"

"Do you hear me I got you!!!?" I hollered out to the *Prairie Monster*.

"Butch!"

"Butch are you alright?" Pete hollered out.

"Yeah I'm alright Pete." I said to the sheriff as I locked up the handcuffs around the feet of the *Prairie Monster*.

I can't believe it. We did it and now the world was going to know what I have known for almost all of my life.

Some fairytales are true.

I was angry, very angry. Everything that had happened in the past came rushing back.

"Berry Decker!!! I want you to remember that name, Berry Decker. Do you hear me?" I hollered again at the creature.

"Ok Butch just what are you trying to accomplish by hollering at this thing?" The sheriff asked me as he stood up and stepped back away from the beast that I call the *Prairie Monster*.

"I want some answers!!!"

"I've lived most of my life with people telling me that this thing didn't exist!!! Now that I have proof that it does I want some answers Pete!" I found myself hollering at the sheriff now.

"Do you want to put it in a chair under a hot light and interrogate it? Maybe beat it with a rubber hose." Pete was being sarcastic now, but I've waited too long for this and I plan to get some answers someway, somehow. Somebody is going to pay for what happened to Berry.

I had just confronted my demons from the past and I wasn't even breathing hard. I stood at its feet and looked into its glowing red eyes.

It just laid there staring at me. Every now and then its eyes would look right and then left without turning its head. Just then I noticed something around its neck, something tied with what looked like a piece of old leather.

"Hey Pete what is that tied around its neck there?" My eyes were fixed on the object that hung around the creature's neck. I couldn't quite make out what it was.

"Can you see it? What is that?" I asked the sheriff as I strained to see what it was. There was a full moon out tonight, and for being night time it was pretty bright out. But it still wasn't quite enough light to see what was around the creature's neck.

"There's something tied around its neck Pete. What is it; can you see what it is?"

"I don't know what it is, but there's something there Butch." Pete replied as he leaned forward a little to get a closer look, but not too close the sheriff was still a little unsure about what we had here.

"Frank can you shine your flashlight over there to give us some light on it?" I asked Deputy Wallace as I pointed towards the *Prairie Monster*.

"I don't think that's going to be a good idea Butch. Remember the creature is sensitive to light and we don't want to agitate it right now." Pete reminded me as all four of us stood around staring at what we had just captured.

Nobody really wanted to get too close to the creature. Keeping in mind that it had killed once before and probably would kill again to escape if it had the chance. We were all being cautious not to get within striking distance of the *Prairie Monster*.

Somebody needed to get in a little closer to the beast to see what was around its neck. Since it was my promise to Berry that brought us out here, I guess it should be me that steps up.

"I'll take a closer look." I said as I very carefully moved closer to the creature.

"No!"

"No it can't be!" I said as I started backing up away from the creature.

"What is it Butch?" Mr. Murphy asked.

I stepped back and told everybody what I had seen, even though I had I hard time believing it myself.

"It's."

"It's a crucifix."

Chapter 13

Catch and release.

A crucifix. What would a wild animal be doing with a crucifix around its neck? How did he get it? Where did he get it? Is religion a part of their customs?

This I wasn't expecting, could it be that this thing worships the same God I worship?

What's going on here? I have more questions now than I ever had before. We finally captured the *Prairie Monster*, and this just keeps getting more and more confusing each step of the way.

Mr. Murphy and Frank had kept back about ten or twelve feet from the sheriff and I. They still looked a little uncomfortable and nervous standing that close to the *Prairie Monster*.

We would soon find out that they should have been. Things were about to get dangerous, very dangerous and we were about to be out-numbered five to one.

All of the sudden the big rock came up and about twenty of these things came running out of the ground and surrounded us. It happened so fast they looked like a stream coming out of the ground.

This was bad, real bad and it didn't look like it was going to have a good ending to it.

Deputy Wallace immediately pulled his gun from his holster; I put my hand on my gun ready to pull it, but I didn't.

I don't know why I didn't other then it would be like pulling a peashooter out to defend yourself against a tank. Pete was the calm one instead of pulling his gun he used his head.

"Deputy Wallace, holster that weapon immediately!" The sheriff ordered Frank with a loud and commanding tone in his voice. I'm sure that Pete hollered at Deputy Wallace in a loud voice so the creatures that surrounded us could hear him too. He didn't want to be the first to show any signs of aggression.

As Deputy Wallace put his weapon back into his holster Mr. Murphy slowly began to lift his hands, as a sign of surrender.

I thought I better say something and start trying to discuss a way out of this before someone gets hurt.

"Mr. Murphy, lower your hands we're not going to surrender to these things. We'll fight if we have to but we'll try to negotiate with them first." I said to Mr. Murphy as I motioned with my hands for him to lower his.

"Ok Butch I want to see this. How are you going to try and communicate with these creatures?" Deputy Wallace asked in a calm, soft almost whispered voice.

"Is there anyone among you that can speak English?" I begin to try and communicate with them.

"Can you understand what I'm saying?" I looked around at all these creatures looking at me. They all just stood there in the night, each one of them staring back at me.

"Well this isn't getting us anywhere." I tried the nice approach I guess I'll have to try the tough guy approach now.

"I don't know what you call yourself but we have placed this creature under arrest!!!"

"Do you understand!!!?" I hollered at them in an angry voice. Again they all just stood there staring at us with their glowing red eyes.

"Aaaa Butch do you think yelling at them is the wisest thing to do?" Frank asked while he cocked his head to one side.

"For once I have to agree with Deputy Wallace on this one Butch." Sheriff Wells said but didn't offer any ideas of his own this time.

And then it happened.
A voice came up from the ground where the big rock had been pushed up and now there was an opening there. It was a male's voice and it was speaking in English.

"Did I hear someone being addressed as Wallace?" A well dressed man came walking up what appeared to be steps leading up and out of the ground where the big rock once laid.

As he stepped up and out of the ground we could see that he looked to be in his early sixties, and he looked like he was some kind of a business man, maybe a CEO of a large corporation.

"Good evening gentlemen. My name is Webster, Henry Owen Webster." The old man said as he stepped forward.

"How." Pete said.

"How what?" I asked the sheriff. I didn't understand what he was referring to.

"That's pretty good Sheriff Peter Wells, you picked up on that right away." Mr. Webster said to Pete while he stood there with his hands crossed in front of him.

"Picked up on what, I don't understand?" I inquired, I was confused, and I wasn't picking up on what they were talking about.

"My initials, they spell out the word how, and Mr. Wells, I'm sorry, Sheriff Wells, caught that right away." Mr. Webster congratulated the sheriff for being so observant.

"Yeah I know he does that all the time. Nothing gets past Pete." I said bragging on the sheriff's observation skills.

"So this must be Deputy Wallace." Mr. Webster asked as he walked over to where Frank was standing and looked at him.

"Yes sir, my name is Deputy Frank Wallace. Does that mean something to you? Have we met somewhere before?" Frank asked Mr. Webster trying to be more personally involved in the situation at hand. Frank usually doesn't get much of a chance to be involved, so he's trying to show the sheriff that he knows what he's doing.

"Are you related to a Jonathan Wallace from long ago?" Mr. Webster asked Frank as he moved his head up and down looking at deputy Wallace, sizing Frank up.

"I have a great, great uncle named Jonathan that disappeared right over there a long, long time ago." Frank said as he pointed at the old Cottonwood tree that everybody calls a Walnut tree.

"May I shake you hand sir?" Mr. Webster asked as he put his hand out.

Frank leaned over to his right so he could see around Mr. Webster, and looked at Pete. Looking for authorization to shake hands with Mr. Webster I would suspect. The sheriff nodded his head up and down as if he was giving Frank his approval. Frank extended his right hand and Mr. Webster shook hands with Deputy Wallace. It seems to mean something to Mr. Webster, shaking hands with Frank.

"It is a pleasure to meet you and to shake your hand. Your great, great uncle Jonathan Wallace was our first ambassador to the Sandstone people many, many years ago."

"Can you imagine how brave your uncle had to have been to step into their world not knowing what to expect." Mr. Webster told Frank about his uncle, solving the mystery of his uncle's disappearance.

"Sandstone people, that's a rather odd name for a culture of creatures. Why are they called Sandstone people Mr. Webster?" Deputy Wallace asked as he adjusted his hat. Everybody seemed to be a little more relaxed now than they were a couple of minutes ago.

I don't feel as threatened now as I did earlier, but I know things could change in a hurry.

"Deputy Wallace, your great, great uncle Jonathan Wallace gave them that name after he was welcomed into their world."

"If you don't mind Mr. Webster I have a question. How did Deputy Wallace's great, great uncle Jonathan come up with the name Sandstone people?" Mr. Murphy asked as he looked around at the creatures that had us surrounded and out-numbered.

"You must be Mr. Shawn Murphy." Mr. Webster said as he turned his attention towards Mr. Murphy.

"If you could see their world you would understand why. Most of their furnishings in their world are made out of Sandstone rocks, everything from their buildings to their furniture. They have some really beautiful furnishings made out of sandstone."

242

"Sheriff Wells, would you be so kind as to remove those handcuffs from Mr. Rockford please?" Mr. Wallace asked Pete as he was pointing towards the creature we had handcuffed on the ground.

"Now just wait a minute here!!! Pete don't you do anything yet! I don't think you understand. I have put this creature under arrest for murder Mr. Webster!"

"He is in my custody!" I told Mr. Webster in a loud and angry voice so that he would know that I wasn't going to let him go without a fight.

"That's where you're wrong Mr. Black. You have the wrong Sandstone creature."

"You may go Mr. Murphy and you too Deputy Wallace. Sheriff Wells you may leave after you remove those handcuffs off of Mr. Rockford." Mr. Webster said as if he was giving us permission.

After I was attacked over thirty years ago as a twelve year old boy, and Mr. Murphy not doing anything back then, he wasn't about to walk away and leave me there alone.

Needless to say what Mr. Webster said did not sit very well with Mr. Murphy. As a matter of fact, it down right made him mad.

"I don't know who you think you are, but I'm not about to walk away and leave Butch here alone with you and these creatures!!!" Mr. Murphy hollered out in an argumentative way.

Pete looked over at Deputy Wallace and gave him a short and quick nod with his head.

I didn't know what was going on or what was about to happen but apparently Deputy Wallace knew what to do. All of the sudden the sheriff drew his gun and pointed it at the head of the *Prairie Monster* that we had handcuffed on the ground.

Deputy Wallace drew his gun at the same time and pointed it at Mr. Webster. This was starting to get bad, very bad for all of us.

I was the only one that didn't pull my gun. I felt like I was out of the loop on something. The Sandstone people that had us surrounded moved in a little closer to us.

"That's close enough!!!" Pete hollered.

"I don't want to shoot this thing, but I will if I have to." The sheriff was making what I hoped was an idle threat.

"Mr. Black will you talk to your friends please, before someone gets hurt? This could get out of hand in a hurry and then there will be no going back."

"I am willing to take you into their world for a brief tour and bring you back here, but first you must let Mr. Rockford go." Mr. Webster had proposed a solution to our problem at hand, and a chance for me to go into their world.

Pete started shaking his head back and forth, he did not agree with the solution, and he didn't want me to go, this was not an option in his mind.

"How about I take you into my world for a tour Mr. Webster? I can show you what the inside of a jail cell looks like." The sheriff was telling Mr. Webster he would arrest him if he had to.

"This is what you wanted isn't it Mr. Black? To know what happened."

"This is your chance to find out what happened to your friend Berry Decker's killer, and to fulfill a promise you made to him and to yourself."

"I can show you what happened to Berry Decker's killer right now, and give you closure on what happened to you and him over thirty years ago. You need to stop this right now Mr. Black before something happens that can't be undone."

He was right, and I had come too far tonight to give up now. Not only did I want to know, I needed to know. I paused for a moment and thought about it.

It was time to put my fears aside and keep moving forward. It was time for me to make good on a promise I had made a long time ago.

"Pete, would you go ahead and take the handcuffs off please?" I asked the sheriff, but I was clearly uncertain of what I was about to do, and you could tell it in my voice.

"I don't think that's a good idea Butch." Pete expressed his displeasure on the whole situation, and he wasn't going to agree with Mr. Webster's solution.

The sheriff was probably right, but I sure was hoping he was wrong. I had made up my mind about this, I was going in.

"Go ahead put your gun away and take the handcuffs off of please. It's my decision, it'll be my responsibility."

"You can go ahead and put your gun away too Frank." I told Pete and Frank while looking over to Mr. Murphy, and assuring him everything was going to be alright with a grin and a little nod of my head.

"It's going to be ok Mr. Murphy. I'll be alright." I reassured Mr. Murphy while trying to reassure myself.

After holstering his gun the sheriff leaned down with his handcuff key and slowly removed the handcuffs from Mr. Rockford's feet and then from his hands.

Not knowing what was going to happen next Pete backed away from the creature, keeping his eye on him, and his hand on his gun.

The creature slowly rose to his feet and stared at the sheriff. Not knowing what was going to happen next the sheriff and I were a bit uneasy.

Then the unexpected happened.

It spoke, and it spoke in a deep voice.

"Thank you." The creature said to the sheriff.

Then in a flash he was gone down the hole, where the big rock was covering what looked like a staircase earlier.

"They can speak?" I asked Mr. Webster.

"Thanks to the work that Deputy Wallace's great, great uncle Jonathan Wallace did."

"It was he who taught the Sandstone people how to communicate with the world above, and to be more respectful and understanding of other cultures in and around the world."

"So why don't the others that are surrounding us say anything?" I asked as I pointed to the ring of Sandstone creatures that was around us.

"They understand you Mr. Black, and will talk if they see the need to."

"Butch they're shy creatures and they sometimes have a small amount of difficulties speaking in English."

"They have names like everybody else, they live their lives in a very social setting, and they don't like being referred to as monsters."

"There's one more thing Butch, you are not going to be allowed to bring a weapon with you into the Sandstone people's world." Mr. Webster informed me, as he explained the conditions of entering their world.

"I understand how that might present a problem for these creatures. They don't seem to possess any weapons other then the ones that they were born with." I explained referring to their strength and speed.

"We are visitors to their world and we have to abide by their laws and customs while we are down there." Mr. Webster was basically laying down the ground rules for me to be able to enter their world.

"As Sheriff of Rock County I cannot allow Butch to go alone with you! These monsters tried to kill him once before. I must insist on being allowed to go with him."

"The Sandstone people will not allow you into their underground world Sheriff Wells."

"If Mr. Shawn Murphy would care to attend the tour with Butch and I he may if he so wishes too." Mr. Webster extended an offer for Mr. Murphy and I to go with him into the Sandstone people's world. At this point I honestly thought that this was going to be their best offer.

"My Deputy and I will not stand by and allow this to happen." The sheriff said as he motioned for me to back up.

"It's ok Pete I'm willing to go with Mr. Webster and take the chance. What about you Mr. Murphy. What are you going to do?"

"Let's do this together Butch." A very proud and defiant Mr. Murphy replied as he stepped forward and put his hand on my shoulder.

"Just wait a minute! Nobody is going anywhere yet."

"I want some reassurances first before Butch and Mr. Murphy go anywhere." The sheriff said to a very calm and confident Mr. Webster.

"I'm sorry Sheriff Wells but you are just going to need to trust me on this one." Mr. Webster explained to Pete not really caring if the sheriff trusted him or not.

"Pete this is something I have to do, so please understand." I tried to make it clear to the sheriff that I was going with Mr. Webster. I had hoped that it didn't upset Pete too much. I tried to be respectful to my friend.

"It is my responsibility to make it safe in this county for all its residents Butch, which includes you, and Mr. Murphy."

"If you are absolutely positive that you want to do this I will not try to stop you."

"I want to go on record saying that I am against this and I think this is a very bad idea." Pete told me with real concern in his tone of voice.

"Would you do me a favor and please hold my gun for me my friend?" I asked Pete as I handed over my sidearm.

"Sure Butch. Just so you know though I think your making a mistake." Pete said as he took my gun. He was right it probably is a bad idea, but it had to be done. Time had come for me to put my fears aside.

All of the sudden the Sandstone creatures went back down under the ground, they are amazingly quick and agile as they disappeared from sight.

All of them but two, they hung back and stood over by Mr. Webster one on each side of him as if they were his bodyguards.

It was apparent that they recognize English because they understood what the sheriff and I had said to each other.

They understood that Mr. Murphy and I were going with them and I was going unarmed. They seem to be more intelligent than I had ever anticipated, and they were well organized too.

As Mr. Murphy and I walked over to the entrance of the Sandstone people's underground world we were joined by Mr. Webster and the two creatures that stayed behind.

At this point I thought I better try to be a little friendly with our new acquaintances.

"Mr. Webster do your two friends have names that they would prefer to be called by?"

"You did say that they didn't like being called _Prairie Monster_." I had inquired about names before we stepped into their world.

"The taller one with the light brown hair and with the more muscular arms is called Mr. Magma. The shorter one with dark brown hair is called Mr. Granite." Mr. Webster introduced our two escorts to Mr. Murphy and I as we all gathered there at the entrance to their world.

"Butch, ask that Webster guy why he calls these things Mr." Mr. Murphy whispered in my ear as he leaned over towards me.

"Mr. Webster I noticed that you are real formal with these creatures. Addressing them as Mr. Magma, and Mr. Granite, why so ceremonial with them?"

"Respect Mr. Black."

"They have always treated me with respect and kindness so it's just a matter of returning the gesture." Mr. Webster explained as he reached over and patted Mr. Granite on the shoulder.

"Sheriff Wells, we will be back here to this same spot in about two hours."

"If you would care to wait on us I will assure you your safety will be guaranteed by the Sandstone people."

"Oh you bet I'll wait, and nothing better happen to Mr. Murphy or to Mr. Black. Or trust me there won't be any place on earth or below it for you to hide. Do you understand me Mr. Webster?" Mr. Webster smiled at the sheriff.

"That's not a threat sir, I don't make threats. That's a guaranteed promise to seek justice." The sheriff told Mr. Webster as he was staring down the two creatures.

"If you gentlemen will follow me we will enter the world of the Sandstone people." Mr. Webster said as he started down the staircase.

Chapter 14

Stepping into their world.

Mr. Murphy and I walked down the long poorly lit staircase made of rock, following behind our guide, Mr. Webster, and being followed by what we refer to as _Prairie Monsters_ whose names appear to be Mr. Granite and Mr. Magma. I reached out for a handrail and all I could feel was solid rock walls on both sides of us.

The only light that seems to be here was at our feet on the stairs, it was a dim light that lit up each step. I'm guessing about a seven watt light, not much but enough to see each step, and there were a lot of steps. Many, many steps chiseled out of solid rock each one of them perfectly shaped in size and in height.

I could see a light in the distance at what looked like the end of the stairs. As we walked down the stairs and I stepped off the last step I could see that it was a staging area that was lit up with little more light than the stairs had on them.

There were three hallways leading away from the staging area that we just stepped into, and there were four more creatures guarding another staircase that led deeper into the ground.

Mr. Webster started walking down the long hallway to the right of us. Mr. Murphy and I followed behind Mr. Webster with Mr. Granite and Mr. Magma right on our heals. I don't know where we are going, but it keeps getting deeper and deeper underground.

After walking about two hundred yards or so we came to a room that reminded me of the room that the sheriff and I were in earlier tonight with Special Agent Brian Cook.

It had a big table with twelve chairs around it, the only thing different was that the table was made of sandstone and the chairs looked to be made out of some kind of tree root. I did take note that the table and the chairs were very well crafted.

"If you and Mr. Murphy would care to have a seat here I will go and get someone that wants to see you before we get started." Mr. Webster said as he turned and went through a door that slid to one side and then slid back. I walked around the table looking at it and the chairs. Whoever made them did a good job.

It was just like the room that the government had at the old abandoned missile silo.

"Deja vu." I whispered out load.

"You've been here before Butch?" Mr. Murphy asked as we both sat down in these chairs made of tree root.

"No not here, but a room just like this that the United States government has hidden away in an old missile silo." I explained to Mr. Murphy as our two guards stood watch over us.

"Are you two allowed to speak?"

"Or do you just stand there like a couple of idiots, because you are forbidden or too afraid to talk to us no good humans?" Mr. Murphy asked Mr. Granite and Mr. Magma.

"We can talk if we see a need to." Mr. Magma told Mr. Murphy as we sat there and looked at each other. It was eerie hearing these creatures talk and show signs of intelligence.

"Do you and Mr. Granite have mates that you share your lives with?" Mr. Murphy inquired of our two guards.

"I am married with two offspring; a young male and a female, my wife's name is Shale and we are very happy together." Mr. Magma told Mr. Murphy and I.

"What about you Mr. Granite, are you married too?" Mr. Murphy asked as he looked over at me and winked.

"I am, and my wife and I have two male offspring I am very proud of. My wife's name is Limestone and I too am very happy to be sharing my life with my wife and offspring." Mr. Granite very proudly explained his marital status to Mr. Murphy. I just sat there and listened to them talk between themselves.

"I was once married to a very special woman myself that I considered my soul mate. She meant the world to me. I too was very happy." Mr. Murphy told our two new acquaintances.

"Your mate has gone to be with the holy one?" Mr. Magma asked Mr. Murphy about the passing of his wife. Gone to be with the holy one, that's the first time I've ever heard it put that way.

"Yes about twenty years ago and I haven't quite been the same ever since."

"I miss my mate very, very much and I think about her everyday." Mr. Murphy seemed to be opening up to these creatures. I don't know who was being more cordial, Mr. Murphy or our two guards.

"We are very sorry to hear of your wife's passing." Mr. Magma said to Mr. Murphy as he bowed his head slightly.

"Thank you for your compassion and kind words you seem to be very understanding." Mr. Murphy said as he stood up and stuck his right hand out to shake hands with Mr. Magma.

This was an awkward moment; and more than a little different. There stood Mr. Murphy with his hand out and the two sandstone creatures didn't know if they could trust him or not.

Mr. Magma and Mr. Granite looked at each other; they were unsure and cautious on whether to shake hands with Mr. Murphy.

Then with a little hesitation, very, very slowly Mr. Magma put his hand out and actually shook hands with Mr. Murphy. Not wanting to be left out of the moment Mr. Granite put his hand out to shake hands with Mr. Murphy too.

"You are the first topside creature I have ever shook hands with." Mr. Granite said as he was shaking hands with Mr. Murphy, and then they both smiled at each other. Mr. Murphy rarely smiles at someone he doesn't know.

Just then the sliding door opened, Mr. Webster and another Sandstone creature walked into the room. It felt like tension just walked into the room and everybody was on pins and needles again.

"Did I miss something here?"

"What's going on?" Mr. Webster asked as the door behind them slid shut.

Mr. Granite and Mr. Magma stepped back and bowed there heads slightly keeping their eyes looking forward and trained on the Sandstone creature that came in with Mr. Webster. It was obvious that this was someone of high importance and stature in their community.

There was an uneasy silence in the room now; it was as if Mr. Magma and Mr. Granite had done something wrong. I stood up and told Mr. Webster that we were just trying to get to know each other.

"There's nothing going on here. We're just sitting around shooting the breeze with Mr. Magma and Mr. Granite. That's what us humans raised in the country will do when we're left alone."

"Besides that, you're the one that left us here with nothing to do. Mr. Murphy was just asking about the marital status of Mr. Granite and Mr. Magma and about their families." I explained to Mr. Webster and his friend that had come into the room with him.

"Mr. Black, Mr. Murphy I would like to introduce you to the Sandstone people's leader, this is the honorable King Lava."

"We don't much cotton to monarchies in these parts." Mr. Murphy told Mr. Webster and King Lava as he looked over at me with a small grin on his face.

"I think what Mr. Murphy is trying to say is that we believe in electing our leaders. We don't think it's fair that you become a leader just because you were born into the right family." I tried to be a little more diplomatic then Mr. Murphy was.

"The Sandstone people take great pride in electing their leaders too." Mr. Webster began to explain their electoral process.

"They may call their leader king, but he is elected just like we elect our president."

"There are a couple of differences, their king is elected for a ten year term and after he is finished with his term the Sandstone people vote on how well he did in office."

"This will determine what kind of retirement he receives after he leaves office, and where he lives in their social structure."

"So you see their system of government is not too much different than ours. Some people think that it's better than ours." Mr. Webster enlightened Mr. Murphy and me on the Sandstone people's way of electing their governing council.

"So is the king allowed to marry and have a wife by his side?" Mr. Murphy asked Mr. Webster as he was staring at King Lava.

"I have a mate and her name is Queen Gypsum, we are blessed with one offspring male child that we received permission to name Berry." King Lava said to Mr. Murphy as he stared back at him, neither one of them wanting to show any weakness.

"Berry!"

"You named your son Berry?"

"Why would you name your son Berry?" I asked King Lava wondering what was going on.

"If I may Mr. Black, I don't mean to interrupt you and King Lava but you will get the answers to your questions as we tour the Sandstone people's world." Mr. Webster explained as he tried to intervene between King Lava and myself.

"Why would you need to get permission to name your son Berry?" I asked again, I wanted to know what was going on and I wanted to know right now.

"Mr. Webster will be happy to explain to you about our laws as you tour our world and see how we live and work down here. I will meet back up with you and Mr. Murphy at the end of your tour in a couple hours. So watch your step and enjoy yourself."

"I'm going to send Mr. Granite and Mr. Magma with you as escorts on your tour. They will be there for your safety and the safety of our citizens"

"They will try to answer any questions that you may have along with Mr. Webster and they will keep curiosity seekers away from you and Mr. Murphy while you are walking around down here." King Lava said just before he stepped back through the sliding door and out of sight.

"I don't think we will have a problem with curiosity seekers at this time of night. All of the businesses are closed up tight and most of the Sandstone people are at home in there living accommodations right now." Mr. Webster explained to Mr. Murphy and I standing in front of the sliding door as if he was giving King Lava time to get where he needed to be.

"Before we get started I would like to know why Sheriff Wells was not allowed to take the tour with us, and why was I invited to come along on this little adventure?" Mr. Murphy asked Mr. Webster.

"Sheriff Wells refused to follow orders from the United States government. He could have caused problems down here, and we don't need anymore problems down here."

"When we get towards the end of the tour the Sandstone people would like to apologize for their actions to you Mr. Murphy and ask you a very important question that would help them out tremendously in their culture." Mr. Webster told Mr. Murphy and I which again just caused more questions about our tour that we were about to take.

"Ok that's fair enough as long as Mr. Granite and Mr. Magma are there with me." Mr. Murphy was almost making demands to Mr. Webster. You know they say that you can tell a lot about a man just by shaking hands with him. I would say that Mr. Murphy felt something when he shook hands with our two escorts.

"Mr. Black do you have any questions about the tour that we are about to take? Or would you prefer to ask them as we walk?" Mr. Webster asked me as he slid the door open that led deeper into the world of the Sandstone people.

"I'll ask my questions as we walk if you don't mind Mr. Webster." I said as I stepped through the sliding door.

Mr. Murphy walked through the door right behind me, and then Mr. Webster behind him. Our two escorts Mr. Granite and Mr. Magma were bringing up the rear.

"Are we going to have any kind of light to take with us on this tour?" I asked Mr. Webster as we stepped onto what looked like an old cobblestone street from centuries ago.

"Flashlights are forbidden down here. They are considered weapons since they can temporarily blind the Sandstone people." Mr. Webster started explaining why they have so little light down here in their world.

"The more time you spend down here the more your eyes will adjust to the darkness and the less light you will need to see."

"Just imagine if you were born down here and spent all of your life underground what it would be like if all of the sudden there was a bright light shined in your face." Mr. Webster was starting to make sense now.

"What about you Mr. Webster? How do you get around down here?" I asked as we all stood there at the end of this street.

"I have my problems from time to time but just like your eyes will my eyes adjusted to the darkness and they make due with what little light there is down here. It's really not that bad down here if you would just give it a chance"

"If you will notice that all of the street lights shine upwards and reflect their light off of the rock ceiling and back down towards the street. That is so none of the Sandstone people have light shining directly on them." Mr. Webster was being very informative letting us know what the Sandstone people's biggest weakness is. I was a little surprised that he gave us this information.

"How long have you been the ambassador to the Sandstone people Mr. Webster?" Mr. Murphy asked.

"It's been about thirty-four years now. About one year after Berry Decker and Mr. Black here were attacked."

"The ambassador before me was pulled out after young Berry Decker was killed as a protest to the Sandstone people."

"So you see Mr. Black the United States government didn't abandon you or your friend Berry. Things got really tense at that time and it was the Sandstone people's king that defused the situation." Mr. Webster was finally giving me some answers that I should have received a long time ago.

"Ok Mr. Webster I would like to know how the king back then resolved the situation. After all I was the one that was there when my friend Berry was killed."

"As we get towards the end of our tour you will get to witness the great sacrifice that the king made over thirty years ago." Mr. Webster said to me without revealing everything about what happened.

"Is the Sandstone people's king from back then still alive?" I asked Mr. Webster as I was noticing that my eyes were starting to adjust to the darkness.

"Sadly no. He passed away some time ago a very lonely soul. My guess is that he never forgave himself for what he had to do." Mr. Webster said as he bowed his head slightly.

"If you don't mind me asking Mr. Webster how old are you?" Mr. Murphy asked Mr. Webster a rather personal question, but that was Mr. Murphy's way.

"No I don't mind at all. I'm ninety-nine years old now; I was sixty-five years old when I undertook this job." Mr. Webster told us with some pride in the tone of voice with his chest stuck out.

"You look pretty good for being ninety-nine years old. I would have guessed that you were in your sixties." I said as I looked over at Mr. Murphy.

"This is what happens when you live underground and you're not subjected to the harmful rays of the sun. The aging process slows tremendously down here underground, and I live a lot healthier down here."

"I think we'll give our eyes a couple more minutes to adjust to the darkness and then we'll get started." Mr. Webster said as we all stood there at the end of this street.

We were far underground and I wondered what the sheriff was doing up there on the surface waiting on Mr. Murphy and I, not knowing if we were ok.

If I know Pete his mind is probably working in overdrive trying to figure out how he could reach us if he had to.

The sheriff had his own ideas. Right after we left with Mr. Webster Pete ordered Deputy Wallace to find Berry's mother.

"Deputy Wallace do you know Berry Decker's mother? Ray Decker's wife." The sheriff asked an eager to please Frank.

"Yeah I know her. She and Mr. Decker used to own all of this land." Deputy Wallace told the sheriff as he pointed around where they were standing.

"Deputy do you think you can find her and bring her here? That's if she is willing to come along with you."

"Yes sir I think I can find her, and if she wants to come along with me I can bring her here."

"Do your best deputy; I think she's going to want to be here. And remember I want radio silence." The sheriff told Deputy Wallace as Frank turned and started walking back to his patrol cruiser.

After Deputy Wallace left, Pete flipped open his cell phone and called Vickie, knowing that the government was probably listening in but at this point the sheriff didn't care.

"Mrs. Black this is Sheriff Wells I'm sorry to bother you but I need to talk to you."

"Is Butch alright Pete? Has something happened to him?" Vickie asked, but was fearful of the answer.

"He is ok for now but I would like to show some force around here, I know that Butch has a couple of brothers. Do you think that they would be willing to help us out this late at night?"

"They're family Pete of course they'd be willing to help out. That's what family does around here in these parts, that's how everybody is raised."

I think Pete knew it wouldn't be a problem but just didn't want to presume anything. After all he was the outsider in all of this.

"Do you think that they could get some friends to help us?" The sheriff asked Vickie, not really knowing what he just asked for.

"Of course they can Pete. You're going to have so much help you won't know what to do. I'll give Butch's brothers a call and let them know what's going on and their brother needs them."

"Where do you want them to meet up with you at Pete?" Vickie asked the sheriff. She was feeling a little better about things knowing that the sheriff was going to have some local help.

"Tell them to meet me at the spot where Butch was attacked when he was a boy almost thirty-five years ago."

"Ok Pete you better be prepared for these people because they will do what's right, not necessarily what the law is."

"I understand and I think that's what we are going to need." The sheriff told Vickie as he closed his cell phone and sat down to wait on my brother's.

Chapter 15

The tour.

My eyes had finally adjusted to the low light that was being reflected down from the street lights off of the rock ceiling above us.

I could see that there were several little shops that lined both sides of the narrow cobblestone street. It was very clean and well maintained; these creatures seem to take great pride in their community.

It was a street that was for pedestrian travel only. As a matter of fact it was more like an extra wide sidewalk then a street. It reminded me of a turn of the century cobblestone street. I felt like I had just stepped backwards in time.

There were benches to sit on carved out of sandstone about every thirty feet on both sides of the street, and there was a small trash receptacle next to each bench. It could have been a Norman Rockwell painting. It was really quite beautiful; it seemed very inviting and peaceful.

I didn't see anyone or anything around and all of the shops were closed up tight. I guess our night time is their night time too.

There was one thing that I thought strange though, there were no birds, or cats, or dogs around.

Don't they have pets I wondered? It's just another question to be asked in a long line of questions about how the *Prairie Monster* lives.

I guess if I had seen an animal running around I would have thought it odd. I don't know why, I just would have.

I can hear water running, it's like a small trickle, not a lot but it is definitely the sound of water running. I don't see any water anywhere but I hear the faint sound of it trickling through and over rocks like there was a creek nearby.

"Mr. Webster I can hear water trickling through what sounds like a small creek." I let our tour guide know what I was hearing, hoping that he would give me an explanation.

"Please keep in mind that you're standing underground Mr. Black. You're surrounded by water down here running through the ground from above, its mother nature's way of filtering water for us to drink."

"The Sandstone people have worked very hard and gone through great pains to divert all ground water around their living area. There are small channels and canals built throughout the rock walls that surround us." Mr. Webster explained to Mr. Murphy and I a very elaborate water displacement system that they had perfected over the years.

"Mr. Webster, my family and I get our drinking water out of a well deep in the ground. What about the Sandstone people's drinking water, where do they get theirs from?"

"If you will follow me I'll be happy to show you." Mr. Webster said as he walked up to what looked like an office cooler water spigot sticking out of the rock wall beside one of the benches.

"All you need is to walk up to one of these water dispensers and fill your water bottle with ice cold clean filtered water; you will find them just about everywhere." Mr. Webster said as he pointed out several more spigots scattered around in the rock walls along the cobblestone street.

We started to slowly walk down the street; I stopped and looked into the window of a shop that had a sign on it that read, The Grinding Wheel Bakery.

It had what appeared to be some kind of pita bread behind the glass cased counter. There were several small pastries on top of the counter.

I didn't ask any questions about the bakery and Mr. Webster didn't offer any words of wisdom about what I was looking at.

We continued our journey and the next shop looked like an old fashion hardware store. The next little shop after that was a bit surprising, it was a music store. It had violins hanging in the window.

"The Sandstone people appreciate music I see." I said to Mr. Webster as I gazed into the little music shop.

268

"Classical music Mr. Black, they enjoy the classics. Boris Tchaikovsky, Ludwig van Beethoven, Johann Sebastian Bach." Mr. Webster replied referring to the great composers of classical music.

"What about their schools, hospitals, and sleeping accommodations?" Mr. Murphy asked as he and Mr. Granite and Mr. Magma walked a couple steps behind me and Mr. Webster.

"The hospital and school and the Sandstone peoples residences are deeper into the ground. You will not be permitted to tour that part of their world due to security reasons. I hope you will understand that they are not trying to hide anything. They just want to protect their families."

"That's highly understandable Mr. Webster, I don't blame these creatures at all for securing their living quarters and looking out for their young. That's just basic survival skills that they need to do to insure their continued existence." Mr. Murphy said to Mr. Webster as he stopped and sat down on one of the benches.

"Mr. Murphy are you alright? Do you need to rest for a little bit?" I was a little concerned for the health of Mr. Murphy.

"I'm ok I had a pebble in my boot that's all. See." Mr. Murphy said as he took his boot off and turned it upside down, and a small rock fell out.

Mr. Webster continued to tell us about the Sandstone people's living quarters.

"Do you remember the four guards that were guarding that other staircase when we first came down into there world?"

"I remember." Mr. Murphy said to Mr. Webster as he stood up after putting his boot back on.

"That is one of many entrances into their protected living accommodations."

We continued slowly walking down this beautiful cobblestone street. It felt like we were out for an evening stroll.

"What is this place Mr. Webster?" I asked as we all had stopped in front of an arched hallway, and I peered down it trying to see what was down there.

"If you don't mind Mr. Black we can come back to this later, there's something I think you should see that's in the park." Mr. Webster said, peaking my curiosity about the park, and diverting my attention away from the arched hallway for now.

"A park, they have a park down here?" I asked wondering just what kind of park would you have underground?

"Yes they do and it gets relatively busy at lunchtime. The Sandstone people are very sociable."

"A park usually has trees in it and grass under your feet, dogs running around chasing things and each other." Mr. Murphy asked.

"Their park is more like a social meeting place for couples. It's impossible to grow trees and grass without sunlight so there are a lot of benches and tables, and a fountain in the middle. The Sandstone people don't believe in having pets so you will not see any down here." Mr. Webster explained.

As we walked up to the entrance to the park and I looked at it I thought the park looked more like a big warehouse with tables and benches in it.

The ceiling was up higher and there seemed to be more light in the park than there was on the street.

There was water circulating in the fountain and there was a stone statue in the middle of the fountain spraying water out of the base of the statue.

As we walked closer to the fountain I could see that it was a statue of a human, it appeared to be a statue of a young boy.

It was a statue of Berry carved out of solid rock and there was writing carved into the outer base of the fountain that read, "Let all that rest here know of Berry."

"Why would they kill Berry and then honor him like this?" I asked Mr. Webster. At this point I didn't know if I should be angry or impressed that they seem to be trying to atone for their sins.

"There's a lot that you don't know Mr. Black. The Sandstone People are friendly creatures if you will just give them a chance." Mr. Webster tried to sway me into believing that the _Prairie Monsters_ are misunderstood, I'm not buying it though.

"I was there Mr. Webster. I know how they are so don't try to tell me that they are friendly!!! No offense to Mr. Magma and Mr. Granite here but I still think that they are monsters!!!" I said with an angry and very loud voice.

"Why don't you give us a chance Mr. Black? All we're asking for is that you to keep an open mind about us until you have seen everything." Mr. Magma asked as he gestured with his hands, holding his palms up and out away from his body.

"It might not have been you Mr. Magma but one of your kind viciously attacked and killed my best friend Berry Decker!!!" I wasn't going to let anyone change my mind at this point.

"You rush to judgment Mr. Black. You don't know everything there is to know."

"Maybe so Mr. Granite but I feel I have a right too." I replied back to Mr. Granite very quickly and sternly. I'm not about to be pushed around.

"You haven't seen everything that was done so something like that doesn't happen again to someone else!" Mr. Webster was irritated as he explained that there was more for me to see.

"Shall we continue the tour?" Mr. Murphy suggested, trying to defuse the situation at hand.

"Yes I agree with Mr. Murphy I think we need to continue the tour!" Mr. Webster said as I had clearly angered him with my comments and attitude.

As they all started walking away I stood there and looked at the statue of my friend. They really did do a good job on it. I wonder what Berry would have thought about a statue of him in the middle of a park.

"Goodbye my friend." I said in a whispered voice as I lowered my head and walked away.

"Are you ok Butch?" Mr. Murphy asked as he turned back and looked at me.

"Yeah I'm ok." I replied to Mr. Murphy as I caught up with them just getting to the entrance to the park.

"I want to apologize for getting angry back there Mr. Black, that wasn't very professional of me, and that's not like me at all." Mr. Webster explained, sounding just like a bureaucrat.

"We all have our own opinions about what happened Mr. Webster. I have mine and you have yours." I said as I walked past them all and continued along the cobblestone street. I could feel them staring at me as I continued walking in front of them.

Mr. Granite broke the silence when he commented about his father as I walked up to what looked like an old book store.

"This is where my father works."

"What is this place?" I asked Mr. Granite as I climbed up about six rather large steps.

"It is our Museum of History."

"Is it ok if I look in?" I asked as I was leaning forward to get a better look.

"Of course you can Mr. Black, matter of fact you might see some of the same things that we have in our own museums." Mr. Webster told me when I peered into the Museum. It was dark in there and hard to see, of course down here its dark everywhere.

"I see a lot of Indian artifacts in there. What does your father do for the Museum Mr. Granite?" I asked while still trying to see things inside the Museum.

"He teaches history to our young and to anyone who is willing to listen."

"My father lives by the old saying that if you don't remember your history you are doomed to repeat it." Mr. Granite sounded like he was very proud of what his father does, and he enjoys telling people about it.

"He sounds like he's a very smart man." I said to Mr. Granite, still standing at the top of the stairs looking around the inside of their Museum.

"We are not men Mr. Black don't you remember we're _Prairie Monsters_." Mr. Granite said as he stared at me. I probably deserved that but I didn't respond to Mr. Granite's little dig.

"I think that we all are starting to learn more and more about each other." Mr. Murphy was trying to break the tension that had come up between our hosts and me. I didn't care what they thought or how they felt towards me. They weren't going to convince me that they were misunderstood creatures.

"I'm glad you said that Mr. Murphy because the next stop on our tour involves you." Mr. Webster told a surprised Mr. Murphy.

"Why don't you go ahead and start calling me Shawn Mr. Webster and I'll start calling you Henry if that's ok with you."

"I think that would be fine sir, just a fine idea." Mr. Henry Webster said as he stuck his hand out to shake hands with Mr. Shawn Murphy.

"Mr. Webster I don't understand why anything down here would involve Mr. Murphy, but I going to assume that we're about to find out."

"We need to keep moving it's starting to get late, and we still have a lot to see and discuss. If we don't get going your Sheriff Wells is going to get worried." Mr. Webster recommended.

As we continued our walk I could see a shop that had furniture carved out of rock.

There was a shop that had clocks in it called the Time Bandit. They had a grandfather clock that was made out of rock and a beautiful pendulum that swung back and fourth. It looked quite unique, I wished I had the time to stick around and hear it chime.

There was a shop that had mushrooms in it several different kinds and sizes. The shop itself was shaped like a mushroom.

And then I could hear it. The sound of cattle in the distance.

"Do I hear cattle down here Mr. Webster?" I asked as I came to a stop.

"Yes you do Mr. Black, straight ahead of you if you will continue walking."

Mr. Murphy had taken the lead in our little tour. As we walked around a corner there it was, a cattle feedlot with about twenty head of cattle in it that looked like they were underfed.

"What are you doing to these cows down here?" Mr. Murphy asked in amazement.

"The Sandstone people are trying to raise their own cattle and are having difficulties in their attempts." Mr. Webster stated the obvious. Even he looked embarrassed over the whole thing.

"What are you feeding them?" Mr. Murphy asked in disbelief that they were attempting to raise cattle underground.

"Mushrooms." Mr. Webster explained.

Mr. Murphy couldn't believe it.

"Mushrooms!"

"You're feeding them mushrooms!"

"I'm surprised there all not dead."

"Where's their water trough?" Mr. Murphy asked. He was starting to get angry.

"They get watered four times a day everyday Shawn. The Sandstone people are trying to do the right thing." Mr. Webster proclaimed.

"Four times a day you say."

"Everyday, four times a day."

"Wow that much you say." Mr. Murphy said sarcastically.

"Butch would you look at this?"

"Can you believe this?"

"I have never seen anything like this in all of my years of ranching." Mr. Murphy said as he shook his head back and fourth in disgust.

"Why have you brought Mr. Murphy and I here to see this?" I asked as I looked around at this pathetic attempt at a feedlot.

"The Sandstone people have been trying to raise their own cattle for years now and they haven't been very successful at it." Mr. Webster said as he turned to another entrance to the feedlot. There in the shadows stood another Sandstone creature.

"I would like for you to meet Mr. Boulder. He is the manager of the feedlot down here."

As Mr. Boulder came walking out of the shadows he was hanging his head down like he was ashamed or embarrassed about something. He came walking up to Mr. Granite and Mr. Magma and stood beside them. It was obvious that something was bothering Mr. Boulder and everyone new what it was but me and Mr. Murphy. I looked at Mr. Murphy and wondered what was next.

"The Sandstone people would like to make a formal invitation to Mr. Shawn Murphy to take over as manager of their cattle feedlot." Mr. Webster said just as Mr. Murphy folded his arms and began shaking his head back and fourth.

"I can't do that Henry. I'm not going to put someone else out of a job."

"You're not going to be putting anybody out of a job Shawn. Mr. Boulder will become your assistant for now and he is willing to learn all there is to learn about running a feedlot."

"Where would I be teaching Mr. Boulder how to take care of cattle?" Mr. Murphy asked as he turned and looked back at the cows in the pen.

"They would like for you to live with them down here underground in their world while you are teaching them how to run a feedlot and take care of their cattle." Mr. Webster explained to Mr. Murphy.

"How is Mr. Boulder going to feel about this?" Mr. Murphy asked as he hung his arms over the fence.

"Well Shawn I think it would be best if I just let Mr. Boulder explain to you how he feels about the whole thing." Mr. Webster said as Mr. Murphy turned and faced the manager of this feedlot, Mr. Boulder, standing over by Mr. Magma and Mr. Granite.

"I was the one that went to King Lava and asked for your help Mr. Murphy. I'm losing cattle and I don't know why. I can't fix it and I need help. I don't want to lose any more cattle needlessly." Mr. Boulder seemed sincere and concerned about his cattle.

"Lift your head up son there's nothing to be ashamed of. Theirs a lot of ranchers above the ground that can't raise cattle either, but they keep trying. So don't give up now." Mr. Murphy said to Mr. Boulder feeling a little sorry for him.

"My shame is because of Mr. Black."

"You see it was my brother that attacked him and killed his friend so long ago." Mr. Boulder said as I began walking up to him. I could feel the blood rushing to my head.

"I am part of a security force responsible for my people's safety down here Mr. Black and I cannot allow you to touch Mr. Boulder." Mr. Magma said as he stuck his hand out to stop me from getting too close to Mr. Boulder.

"I'm not going to touch Mr. Boulder but I want to know why. Why did your brother kill my best friend?" I asked in a rather loud and angry voice.

"I'm sorry Mr. Black but I'm not allowed to speak of what happened." Mr. Boulder said as he hung his head even lower.

"Well someone is going to tell me what's going on!!!" I said as I was in no mood for double talk from anybody, and right now I was willing to fight anybody or anything to get to the truth.

Mr. Webster wisely intervened.

"Berry's name is sacred down here Butch, and what happened to him is not allowed to be spoken about."

"You have to understand the worst thing to happen to the Sandstone people was the accident that killed your friend Berry Decker."

"Why would they kill him then?"

"If that's the worst thing to happen to them why would they allow it to take place? You're not going to expect me to believe that, are you?"

"I think that it will all be clear when we get to the end of our tour Mr. Black. You've came this far, give it a little more time." Mr. Webster suggested.

"What's next then?" I asked wanting to continue the tour so I could get to the bottom of this, and get the answers to my questions before I explode in anger.

"We need to head back to the arch that you asked about earlier, and go down its hallway. I think that you will find your answers there." Mr. Webster said as I stood there staring at Mr. Boulder with hatred running through my veins, wondering what was going through his mind.

"I have a couple of questions I would like to ask the brother of Berry's killer, your Mr. Boulder here if you don't mind."

"If the killer of my friend is your brother then you must know if he is still alive or is he dead."

Mr. Boulder closed his eyes and answered.

"Yes I know."

"My brother still lives."

Chapter 16

Brothers.

The sheriff was starting to worry about what Special Agent Brian Cook might try and do to stop this after he found out what we had done.

There's no doubt that the government knew by now what we had done, and that Mr. Murphy and I had gone down into the Sandstone people's world with Ambassador Webster.

I'm certain that Special Agent Cook had a boss somewhere that was pretty upset with him right now. Everybody has superiors that they have to answer to and the government is no different.

I'm sure that Special Agent Cook had told his superior that this had been taken care of. That they weren't going to have anymore trouble out of the Pete and I for a while.

Special Agent Cook was wrong.

Sheriff Wells was just about to realize what he had unleashed, asking for help from country folk, when Deputy Wallace came walking back across the pasture towards the sheriff where he had left him a couple hours earlier.

"Is that you Deputy?" The sheriff asked in a soft voice.

"10-4 Sheriff."

"Were you able to find Mrs. Decker?" Pete asked Deputy Wallace as Frank stumbled and almost fell in the dark.

"Yes Sheriff I drove over to her house and talked to her personally." Deputy Wallace said with pride as he was able to locate Mrs. Decker on such a short notice.

Frank had a good idea where Mrs. Decker lived. He had pulled over one of Mr. Decker's cousin's about a year ago for speeding. When Frank noticed the last name Decker he asked how the Decker's were doing.

Mr. Decker's cousin had told Frank that they were living in a nice house a couple of towns over.

"What did Mrs. Decker have to say when you spoke with her?" The sheriff asked as he stood up and strained to listen to some noise that he could hear in the distance.

"Mrs. Decker was quite enthused about the whole thing Sheriff, and was more than happy to come with me but said that she would rather wait in my patrol cruiser until you need her. She's old and the night air bother's her."

"Deputy Wallace do you hear something? I think I can hear voices in the distance like a group of people walking through the pasture heading this way." The sheriff asked Frank as they both strained to listen.

"No I don't hear anything."

"Wait I do hear something." Deputy Wallace told the sheriff as he turned and squinted trying to see in the darkness.

All of the sudden, without warning Sheriff Wells and Deputy Wallace were surrounded by about twenty-five or so gun toting rednecks in cowboy hats.

"Deputy please tell me that these fellows are friends of yours." The sheriff leaned his head over and whispered to Deputy Wallace.

"I wouldn't say that they were friends but I do recognize some of their faces. I can tell you that I know some of them, and they're not very friendly when it comes to the law." Frank whispered back to the sheriff a little nervous himself.

"I'm not sure who makes me more nervous out here, the _Prairie Monster_, or these guys." The sheriff said to Frank in a low soft tone of voice so the men approaching couldn't hear him.

"Can I help you gentlemen with something?" The sheriff asked as he looked around at all the men that had surrounded him and Deputy Wallace.

"Which one of you two is Sheriff Wells?"

"Wallace is that you?" My brother Roger asked Frank as he stepped closer to the two of them and recognized Deputy Wallace.

"Yeah it's me." Deputy Wallace answered back to Roger rather reluctantly.

Deputy Wallace and my brother Roger had run into each other in the past and Roger had always picked on Frank. So Frank didn't like Roger at all. He always considered Roger as a bit of a bully.

My brother Roger stands about 6'2" and weighs about 300 pounds. He has long hair and a big bushy beard. He actually looks more like your basic motorcycle gang member. Although Roger does ride a motorcycle from time to time, my brother has never belonged to anything in his life. Except maybe the Big Red One when he was drafted into the army, but that was many years ago.

My brother Roger can be rough around the edges, but once you get to know him and he gets to know you it doesn't take you long to figure out that if you needed the shirt from off his back he would gladly give it to you.

"You must be the sheriff then."

"Hi I'm Leon and this is my brother Roger."

"You called Vickie and told her that our brother Butch was in trouble and needed some help." My brother Leon said to the sheriff as he came walking up closer to shake hands with Pete.

My brother Leon is the oldest one of all of us brothers and sisters. Leon is short, only standing about 5'8" tall, and weighing about 190 pounds. Leon is clean shaven with short hair. He is short and stocky. When he was a younger man he would get into a lot of fights. Brother Leon is older and wiser now, and he uses his wits instead of his fists to settle problems.

Leon usually does all of the talking in a situation like this. That's if he can keep Roger from running his mouth.

"Hello sir. My name is Sheriff Peter Wells. You will have to excuse me I wasn't expecting this many men to show up." The sheriff said as he shook hands with my brother Leon, surveying all the other men that had come along with my brothers.

"Hi, I'm Sheriff Peter Wells." Pete said as he stuck his hand out to shake hands with my brother Roger and introduce himself.

"I don't know you and I'm not near as friendly as my older brother Leon is, so take your hand back and stick it in your pocket." Roger said with an icy stare as he stood there and didn't shake hands with the sheriff.

"You'll have to excuse my brother Sheriff, he doesn't trust strangers and he takes a little getting used to anyway."

"You don't need to make excuses for me big brother; I can handle myself. Besides that, there's no one here I need to impress anyhow."

"Now where's my brother Butch at." Roger asked as he stood there with his cold stare aimed towards Pete. Roger never did like the law around here.

"Do you see that hole in the ground over there?" Pete asked as my two brothers looked over at where the big rock once was.

"Butch went down that hole with some government bureaucrat after what he calls the _Prairie Monster_." The sheriff was trying to explain as he looked over towards Deputy Wallace wondering and hoping that Frank had something to add to this conversation.

"You let him go by himself!!!?" Roger hollered at Pete in a loud and angry deep voice, loud enough that I'm sure that even Mrs. Decker heard him sitting in Deputy Wallace's patrol cruiser.

"Wait a minute. The sheriff didn't just let Butch go off by himself." Deputy Wallace tried to help but my brothers knew Frank back when he was a kid and they still thought of him that way.

"Shut up Wallace, when I want you to speak I'll let you know, and I'll tell you what to say." Roger told Frank as he was still staring at Pete but speaking to Deputy Wallace.

"Ok that's enough; I don't care if your Butch's brother or not I will not have you treat my Deputy that way." Pete was trying to take control of the situation. He had been warned about asking for help from my brothers. They do things their way.

"You need to listen to me and you need to listen to me good Sheriff. You better hope nothing happens to my brother. I'm holding you personally responsible for his safety." Roger threatened the sheriff. The only thing Roger was seeing was that there was a family member in trouble and the sheriff had a chance to stop it and he didn't.

"Roger, will you back off for just a minute so I can talk to the sheriff." Leon said as he stepped over to the staircase that led down the hole in the ground and tried to look down it.

"You called for help Sheriff, just exactly what do you need us to do?" Leon asked Pete while he was still trying to look down that deep dark hole. The lights had been turned off of the steps so he could only see a few feet into the hole.

The sheriff didn't know what to think about Roger, but respected Leon's help with him.

"Thank you sir, I appreciate the help."

"I need some backup just in case the United States government sends someone to try and stop us. I want to be here when Butch returns to make sure he's alright, and I don't want the government stepping in and trying to run me and my Deputy off. We've already had a couple of run-ins with them tonight."

"That government bureaucrat that went with Butch down in that hole, told me that they would be returning here at about sunrise, and I want to be here when Butch returns."

"Leon, I want you to know that I tried to stop Butch but he said that he had a promise to keep and that he was going to take care of it tonight." The sheriff was trying to explain to my brother Leon my reasons for going down into the Sandstone people's world without any backup.

"Ok Sheriff we'll just hang back and see what happens for now. I'll go and talk to the guys and explain the situation." Leon told Pete as he walked away and motioned for everybody to come towards him so he could speak to them.

"I'm still keeping my eye on you Sheriff!" Roger told Pete as he tilted his head just a bit and smirked at him.

"Roger get your butt over here." Leon hollered out trying to stop Roger from causing anymore trouble. Sometimes it's an overwhelming task.

"I'm glad those guys are on our side Deputy Wallace. Or I think they're on are side." Pete whispered to Frank.

Deputy Wallace and the sheriff stood there and watched my brothers talk to everybody that came out to help. After a few minutes everybody fanned out and took up positions surrounding the entrance to the Sandstone people's world. Pete was amazed how well everyone blended into the background; it was if they were part of the pasture.

Leon came walking back over to the sheriff and Deputy Wallace with a sack in his hand.

"Here you go Sheriff; here are a couple bottles of water and a couple of roast beef sandwiches for you and Wallace. The women made them up for us before we came out here." Leon said to Pete as he handed him the sack that contained the sandwiches and a couple of quart Mason jars with water in them.

That would be considered bottle water in Kansas. Our natural spring water in Kansas is every bit as good as what you can buy in Chicago or New York City.

"Thanks." Pete said as he reached out and took the sack from Leon, thinking that he was actually going to get a couple bottles of water.

Pete handed Frank a sandwich and a Mason jar of water, smiling over the fact that Leon called it bottled water. The sheriff was still getting use to country folk in Kansas.

After Leon walked back over to Roger they sat down behind a couple of rocks about twenty yards away from the sheriff and Deputy Wallace.

"I wouldn't swear to it in court Sheriff but I think that Butch's brother Roger doesn't like you." Deputy Wallace said with a smile.

"You think!"

"I should have made you a detective." The sheriff said sarcastically.

So there they all sat out there in a pasture in the dark waiting on me to come walking back up out of the ground. All of them but Mrs. Decker she was still in Deputy Wallace's patrol cruiser.

They were going to have to wait a little while longer. I was about to confront my past and take care of a promise that I made to a friend a long time ago.

After Mr. Boulder told me that his brother was the one that killed Berry and that his brother is still alive I was speechless. I had anger and hatred in my heart.

I know that wrath is one of those seven deadly sins, but right now I was having a hard time remembering that there are seven virtues to go along with those deadly ones, and patience just wasn't in my heart right now.

I thought to myself that I wished that I had brought my gun with me although it was probably best that I didn't. It was quite possible that I could have started a war between the Sandstone people and the United States.

"Let's go!!!" I demanded as if I was in charge and running this tour.

"You going to be alright Butch?" Mr. Murphy asked as he put his hand on my shoulder.

"Yeah I'm alright."

"I'm going to be just fine, just fine indeed. Let's get going!" I said to Mr. Murphy but my eyes were clearly filled with rage.

As we all left the cattle feedlot Mr. Webster was leading the way and he let me know that we had to make one more quick stop along the way.

We slowly walked several hundred feet before we came to a stone doorway carved out of solid rock in the shape of a cross.

"What is this place?" I asked with a softer tone in my voice. The slow walk had actually done me good. I had started to calm down a bit.

"This is the place where we come to worship our creator." Mr. Boulder explained.

Mr. Boulder, Mr. Magma, Mr. Granite, and then after a few seconds Mr. Webster all stepped through the doorway leaving Mr. Murphy and I standing by ourselves just outside the entrance to their church.

"Mr. Murphy would you like to come in and join us as we pray for Mr. Black, to find forgiveness and compassion in his heart." Mr. Granite asked as he walked out of sight inside, not waiting for an answer from Mr. Murphy.

"Come on Butch lets go in; it can't hurt to ask the almighty for guidance." Mr. Murphy suggested as he walked through the doorway and into their church, their sanctuary, their house of worship. It just seemed strange.

I stood outside the doorway by myself for a couple of minutes thinking about what I should do. I guess it wouldn't hurt to go inside and take a look around and see for myself what their church looked like.

I walked down a short corridor and into the most beautiful church I have ever seen in my life. It was amazing; I stood there in awe. It had polished stone pews with a polished stone pulpit that looked like it was carved out of one piece of solid rock.

There were carvings everywhere and there was a huge polished stone cross above the pulpit with carved Bible verses on it.

I sat down in a back pew that had velvet cushions on it and bowed my head. Instead of praying to God, I thought about my friend Berry and about the promise I had made to him at his grave so many years ago.

I thought to myself what am I going to do? This was weighing heavy on my mind. I guess you'd say that I was in the right place at the right time with the mental anguish I was having. It didn't look like I was getting any help from the big guy upstairs.

What's going on here Berry? I said to myself as I lifted my head. I sure could use some help old buddy I know you're with me.

Maybe Pete was right. Maybe he needs to put me in a cell, after all asking for help from dead people I don't think is quite normal. Then all of the sudden I felt a chill, like a cool breeze.

I looked around and saw that everybody still had there heads bowed. I looked at all of the candles burning and noticed that the flames on them were not flickering; they were burning with a still flame, as if there were no breeze blowing, no air flowing in or out of the church.

If that was the case then why did I feel a cold chill? I got up and walked back outside and waited on the others. This whole thing just didn't feel right.

One by one they all came out walking out of the church. Mr. Webster was the last one to exit their house of God.

I had thought it best that I did not speak of the chill I felt. My credibility with these creatures at this point in time was next to none.

"We are going to wait here for King Lava to show up. At this time he would like to speak to you Butch before our next stop." Mr. Webster explained.

"How long is that going to take?" I asked in a low key and more considerate way, trying to present myself as a calmer and more understanding person.

"Not long. King Lava is on his way even as we speak." Mr. Granite told us as we all just stood there waiting, not talking between ourselves. The only sounds I heard were water running through the rock around us.

As King Lava approached the three Sandstone people stepped back and bowed there heads slightly while keeping there eyes trained on the king, just as Mr. Granite, and Mr. Magma did before.

I felt like I was doing something wrong not bowing, but that's just not our way of greeting people. By all means I wasn't trying to offend anyone it's just not the way we do things.

"Hello gentlemen, I hope that the tour went well for you and Mr. Murphy and that you learned a little something about us along the way." King Lava was dispensing pleasantries like a politician.

"The tour was just fine sir, it was very educational." I don't mind pleasantries but there's a time and a place for everything and right then all I wanted was answers to some questions that I've already asked and just gotten the runaround on.

"You have spent more time touring down here than I had anticipated gentlemen." King Lava expressed some concerns about how much time we had spent in his world touring the way they live.

"I didn't realize that there was a time limit on how long we could spend down here looking around." I was starting to get frustrated over the lack of information I was receiving, and what I felt like is their king's stalling techniques.

"I'm afraid you've misunderstood me. There's no time limit Mr. Black."

"It would just be easier if you and Mr. Murphy weren't down here when all the shops opened and our people started their daily routines."

"It's a security issue that's all, we don't get very many topside people down here and there's bound to be curiosity seekers that just want to see you and Mr. Murphy."

King Lava was right, I could just imagine what it would be like if I were to take a couple of Sandstone people on a tour of our town. I'd want to do it at night too so there wouldn't be a problem with crowds.

"King Lava, why did you need to get permission to name your male offspring Berry?" I asked the king the same question I had asked him earlier, wondering if I was going to get an answer this time.

"Your friend Berry is considered a hero down here and it is written in our law that no newborn shall carry the name of Berry unless their parents first get permission from our governing counsel."

"We had to make it law because of all of the requests from new parents to name there male offspring Berry. We couldn't have everybody calling there offspring Berry." King Lava gave a very good and informational explanation this time, and it made sense to pass a law like that if that was the case.

"Why is it that you consider Berry a hero down here?" I asked King Lava; it seemed that I was finally going to start getting some answers.

"Life is sacred to us, and Berry Decker paid the ultimate price in a terrible mistake." King Lava replied, this time with a short answer and he wasn't being very informative. King Lava then turned towards Mr. Webster to thank him for his help.

"Thank you Mr. Webster for your assistance in giving Mr. Black and Mr. Murphy a tour of our world. I will have Mr. Black, and Mr. Murphy brought to you at the staging area after they are through."

"I will wait for you and Mr. Murphy at the staging area Mr. Black." Mr. Webster said to me as he walked away leaving Mr. Murphy and I standing there with three Sandstone creatures and their king.

Meanwhile Sheriff Wells had his own troubles on the surface. Special Agent Brian Cook and his partner Special Agent Robert Hudson had just showed up with ex-Deputy Roy Barns and a couple of other agents.

"Sheriff Wells I'd like to talk to you!"

"I thought we had an understanding!" Special Agent Barns said as he and the other agents approached Pete and Frank.

"Hold it right there!!!" Roger hollered out at the agents as he and Leon stood up.

"You are interfering with a federal investigation. Who do you think you're messing with?" Special Agent Barns replied.

"Oh yeah I want to see your federal warrant, because if you don't have one you're trespassing, and we tend to shoot trespasser's in this part of the country." Roger was being a little dramatic, but that was Roger.

"Listen here." Was all that Special Agent Barns said to Roger and Leon when he realized that he and the other agents were surrounded and out-numbered by about six to one.

"Like my brother said if you don't have a warrant then you need to go before someone in a suit gets hurt." Leon said referring to the government agents; they were the only ones wearing suits and ties.

"Do you know that I can have all of you arrested for interfering with a federal agent?" Agent Barns tried threatening everybody.

"Do you know that I can strip you naked and paint your butt green?" Roger threatened back and was probably more serious with his threat then agent Barns was with his.

"Ok Sheriff Wells you win this time, but the next time we meet you're going to need more than a bunch of hillbillies to save you." Agent Barns told Pete as he and the other agents backed out of the pasture. Leon and Roger sat back down into their positions.

That was quick Pete thought as he walked over to Roger and Leon to thank them for there help.

"I want to thank you gentlemen for your support and for your help." Sheriff Wells said as he crouched down by Leon and Roger sitting on the ground.

"I'm still going to keep my eye on you." Roger said to Pete as Leon shook his head back and forth.

"I wouldn't have it any other way." Pete replied back with a smile.

Chapter 17

We meet again.

With Mr. Webster gone and Mr. Murphy and I standing outside their church with King Lava and our escorts, Mr. Granite and Mr. Magma, it was still hard to not feel hatred towards Mr. Boulder standing just ten feet away from me. After all it had been his brother that had killed Berry and attacked me. It was his brother that had put this scar on my back.

Mr. Murphy walked over to Mr. Boulder and started talking to him. I think that they were talking about cattle but I'm not sure I had a lot on my mind and I really wasn't paying that much attention to what they were saying.

This morning started out with a telephone call from Mr. Murphy wanting me to come over to his farm and take a look at a dead cow. I couldn't have dreamed all of this was going to happen in one day, but it did, and it wasn't over yet. There was still more to come before this day would be over.

This morning Mr. Murphy wanted to shoot whoever or whatever was killing his cows. Now he's standing next to and talking to the same creatures that have been killing his cattle for years.

This morning I was pretty much the only one that believed in the *Prairie Monster* and now there are several people that not only believe, but have seen it for themselves.

I've got a funny feeling that there's something not being told to me. I'm not getting the whole story and I get the feeling that they think that I'm stupid.

"King Lava, are you willing to take me to visit with Mr. Boulder's brother?" I asked as Mr. Murphy stopped talking and started walking my way.

"Of course I am."

"Let us begin to walk in that direction while I tell you about our laws." King Lava said as we all started walking back the same way we came.

"Butch are you sure that you want to do this?"

"After all he is responsible for young Berry's death and for that scar you carry around that's on your back, and the one in your heart." Mr. Murphy was somewhat worried about how I was going to react when I came face to face with Berry's killer.

"I'm sure Mr. Murphy."

"I'm more than sure. I've waited a long time for this and now it's time to bring this nightmare to an end. I've been preparing for this moment for almost thirty-five years now."

"Am I sure that I want to do this? Yeah I'm sure Mr. Murphy." I then turned to talk to King Lava.

"Your laws, King Lava, you were about to tell me about your laws down here." I asked as we were slowly walking back the same way we had came earlier.

"We have laws down here just like you have laws above the ground. Just like your world above us we have some citizens who break our laws." King Lava was explaining as we continued walking.

"I am glad to say that we don't have near the problem down here with our citizens breaking our laws that you have up there with your citizens breaking your laws."

"With that said I will tell you that we do have a few citizens that break our laws every now and then. It doesn't happen very often but it does happen, and when it does we deal with it immediately."

"When someone breaks our laws and they are caught they are usually punished by being sentenced to perform community service work."

"The work they must perform is done in and around the park where other citizens can see them." King Lava continued to educate me and Mr. Murphy as we came closer to that arched hallway I had asked about when we walked past the music store earlier on our tour.

"King Lava every culture needs to have laws to survive, and every culture has some of its citizens break those laws. There is no such thing as a perfect world, everybody wishes there was but there isn't."

"The real sign of a great culture is does its form of punishment fit the crime that was committed? That is where several cultures differ, and disagree on." I was just about to ask about how they punish killers when the King stopped walking right in front of the arched hallway.

King Lava sat down on a bench just outside the arched hallway and motioned for Mr. Murphy and me to sit on the bench across from him. He had something to tell us and he wanted us to be seated while he explained it to us.

"I need to tell you about a tradition that is against the law down here but is considered a right of passage for young males into adulthood. It was something that was started by our ancestors."

"I myself did this many years ago as a young male. Of course I don't agree with it now. It was something that our ancestors did and a lot of the older ones down here wish to hang onto tradition." What King Lava was telling us was making him and the other three Sandstone people with us nervous. You could see it in their eyes and how they bowed their heads slightly when the King continued his speech.

"Many, many years before my fathers, father was born it was thought that young males couldn't crossover into adulthood unless they first went above the ground and retrieved some fresh organs from a living animal."

"Back then it was generally a deer that lost its life and became the vessel that was used to cross over into adulthood."

"When many of our males reach twenty years of age they would sneak to the topside and kill a cow then retrieve some of its organs to bring back down here to prove that he had indeed crossed over into adulthood."

"Most of our older males down here have been through this ritual. Before a young male goes topside he will sharpen his claws on a grinding stone for hours. They will work at this until their claws are as sharp as a scalpel."

"When a young male attacks an animal he will use his speed to run up on it. Grab it, and in one fluid motion puncture a main artery while lifting it above their head. While holding the animal above his head he will suck all the blood out as the animal's heart pumps it out at the same time."

"We don't normally drink blood, but as part of the ritual it is considered disrespectful not to accept the blood of your kill. It lets the spirit of the animal you have chosen to live on inside of you."

"After all of the blood is taken, the young male will use its sharpened claws to remove an organ or two so when he returns back down here he has proof that he has crossed over into adulthood." King Lava was starting to show signs of embarrassment at this point, not making eye contact with Mr. Murphy or me.

"Excuse me King, but do you realize how many cattle I have lost to your little tradition over the years." This ritual into adulthood wasn't sitting very well with Mr. Murphy.

"Are you saying that this is against the law down here but is still practiced by your young males? Including yourself when you were a young male? All this was done at my expense." Mr. Murphy asked in a manner of disbelief, and shock.

"Yes we are very much aware of the cost that we have put upon you, and as we get older and wiser we realize that it was done for no reason other than old-fashion tradition."

"On behalf of all of my people I would like to take this time and opportunity to offer an apology to you for all the trouble and expense we have caused you in the past." King Lava said to Mr. Murphy as he bowed his head towards Mr. Murphy and I.

Mr. Murphy looked at me sitting next to him and with a slight grin on his face he shook his head back and forth.

I couldn't believe Mr. Murphy wasn't steaming mad. This isn't the Mr. Murphy I know, he's usually more spirited then this. Spirited, yeah that's a good word to use to describe Mr. Murphy.

"What do you say to somebody Butch, when they apologize for something that they have done and you understand why they did it, but don't necessarily agree with it?" Mr. Murphy whispered to me just before he accepted King Lava's apology.

"I will accept your apology only if you can assure me that you are trying to stop this from happening in the future. I want it stopped not only against me but against other ranchers too."

Mr. Murphy expressed his concerns to King Lava in a sincere jester to make things right between the Sandstone people and himself, and others.

"I will pledge to do everything within my power to see that we put an end to this tradition of our young males going above ground and retrieving fresh organs from a living animal." King Lava was at least honest with Mr. Murphy. It was obvious that they no longer approved of this practice.

"That would explain why Mr. Murphy has lost so many cattle over the years King Lava, but why would your people attack Berry?"

"Berry Decker was not an animal and he did not deserve to die." I was more than willing to listen to any explanation that the king could offer as long as someone was paying for Berry's death.

"Mr. Black I'm sorry to say that accidents happen every now and then, and when your friend Berry was accidentally killed some thirty-five years ago the citizen responsible for his death was put in jail for his crimes immediately."

"At the end of this arched hallway we have two jail cells. One of them holds no one and has been that way for decades. The other one holds the brother of Mr. Boulder."

King Lava was right to hold this for last. I would say that I was just about as nervous as I could get right now, but I also know that I need to go and confront Mr. Boulder's brother.

"What is Mr. Boulder's brother's name, and how long has he been in jail." I asked not really caring what they call him but I was curious about how long he has spent in jail.

"Mr. Gemstone is his name and he was put in that jail cell about four hours after your friend's death almost thirty-five years ago."

"He has been there ever since then, and not once has he ever been let out. Not even to attend his father's funeral." King Lava went on to explain about Mr. Gemstone's life behind bars, and some of their rules for being locked up.

"He is allowed visitors twice a week and they can spend up to six hours with him each time."

"His family can bring him food, books, and music to listen to, but that's all." King Lava pretty much laid out the prisoner whole daily and yearly routine of life behind bars.

"So when do I get to go down that arched hallway and see him for myself?" I asked King Lava while I sat there across from him on a bench with Mr. Murphy.

Just then Mr. Murphy put his arm around me and gave me a hug, knowing that I was close to confronting my monster from my past, he was giving me some emotional support.

"You may go anytime you want to Mr. Black."

"Mr. Gemstone knows that you're here and he is looking forward to getting the chance to talk with you." King Lava said as he stood up and motioned with his right hand for me to go ahead and go down the arched hallway.

"Is there anything else I should know before I go visit the prisoner?" I asked as I stood up and looked down the arched hallway that led to the Sandstone people's jail. I still had that feeling that I wasn't being told everything.

"Yes there is but I think that Mr. Gemstone should be the one to tell you for himself. I think that you'll find it somewhat revealing." King Lava told me as I turned towards Mr. Boulder and looked intently into his eyes.

"What about you Mr. Boulder do you have anything to say before I go visit your brother?" I asked a rather humbled Sandstone creature that was just standing there. He hung his head down as if he was ashamed of something or someone.

"No sir." Was all Mr. Boulder said in a quiet unassuming way.

I walked over and stood at the entrance for a moment gathering my thoughts. This is where I've wanted to be for many, many years. I'm on the threshold of finally confronting the _Prairie Monster_ that killed Berry.

With my back to everyone, as I looked down the long hallway that led to the jail cell that contained my best friend's killer, I asked the king something that even he wasn't expecting.

"King Lava is it alright if Mr. Boulder accompanies Mr. Murphy and myself to visit with his brother?" I thought if I'm going to get to the bottom of this I might need a family members influence.

"Of course. If that is what you so desire, I'm sure that Mr. Boulder would be more than happy to accompany Mr. Murphy and yourself to visit with his brother Mr. Gemstone." King Lava said as he motioned with a nod of his head for Mr. Boulder to go along with Mr. Murphy and myself.

All three of us began to walk down a rather long hallway, with myself in the lead and Mr. Murphy right behind me with Mr. Boulder walking quietly behind him.

As we walked I could hear Mr. Murphy's footsteps along with my own, but I couldn't hear the footsteps of Mr. Boulder. I had forgotten how quiet the Sandstone people are when they move.

I stepped slowly and cautiously down the arched hallway, my breathing was a bit on the heavy side but under the circumstances I think that it's to be expected.

To my surprise as we walked closer to where the two cells are, in what seemed to be a big cavern. It was a little brighter in there than it was outside on the benches; there were more lights around the jail cell area making it a bit easier to see. They still shined upwards and reflected off of the ceiling, but there where more of them.

Finally there we were in front of the jail cell that held Mr. Gemstone, and there he was sitting on the edge of his bed. The cell itself was a lot bigger than I had anticipated. It was nothing like the jail cells that we have in our world.

It was still a jail cell with solid rock walls and a rock ceiling with thick bars across the front and two sets of thick bars that separated the two cells. It was no place that I would care to be or spend the rest of my life in.

It appeared that they were using the other cell that was in there as an area for visitors to sit while they visited with Mr. Gemstone.

"Hello my brother." The creature behind the bars in the cell said, while he continued sitting there on his bed not moving, just sitting there.

"Hi brother. I brought Mr. Black and his friend Mr. Murphy with me today to visit with you."

"I know that you've been waiting a long time for the chance to talk with Mr. Black, but I think you should let him speak first."

Mr. Boulder said to his brother Mr. Gemstone as we walked into the other jail cell and sat down on some chairs that were in there.

Mr. Boulder greeted his brother just like I talk to my brother's; I found that a little uneasy to think that we were that much alike.

I always thought it was a sign of respect and of acknowledgment that we were brothers. It also told others that we were brothers.

I tried very hard to find the hatred that I had felt for most of my life but for some reason it wasn't there anymore. Don't get me wrong I was still very upset but the deep down anger I had felt for years seemed to have vanished for now.

All I could do at the time was sit there and stare at this creature that I've hated for years sitting on the edge of his bed. Sitting there like he didn't have a care in the world.

I wondered why he did what he did, and why he didn't have the courage to look at me. I wanted to holler at him to look at me.

I didn't know where to begin. What to say first, or which questions to start asking first. Of course the biggest question would be why. Even though I wanted to start out with why, I figured I better start out slowly.

"Do you believe in God Mr. Gemstone?" Was the first thing that came to mind to ask.

"Yes sir, I pray to him everyday." Mr. Gemstone said as he stood up and walked over to a chair that was facing us on his side of the bars.

"What do you pray for?" I asked, wondering what the beast that had killed my friend, and ruined so many lives would ask of God.

"Forgiveness."

"I pray for forgiveness everyday Mr. Black."

"I also pray for my mother and my father, God rest their souls in heaven."

"I pray for my brother and I pray for the soul of Berry Decker and for his family."

"I also pray for you Mr. Black. I pray that you find peace within yourself and that you and your family are healthy." Mr. Gemstone explained to us about all the praying that he did. Of course if I were in jail with nothing to do I imagine that I would be doing a lot of praying too.

"Do you remember the last time you saw me?" I asked as I started remembering back to that night that Berry and I were attacked.

"Yes I do, I remember it well."

"That was the worst night of my life, and I'll never forget it." Mr. Gemstone said as Mr. Boulder reached over and put his hand on my shoulder as if he wanted to say something.

"So who's decision was it to attack Berry and me!?" I wanted to know if there were others involved that night, I was starting to get angrier just thinking about what happened to Berry.

"It was totally my fault and my responsibility, I made a terrible mistake and your friend was killed because of my actions."

"It was me Mr. Black and only me."

"I was the one that killed your friend."

"I know that what I did can't be undone, but I hope and pray that this never happens again between our people Mr. Black." Mr. Gemstone seems to be sincere but I was already starting to get angrier after thinking about what he had done in the past and what he said just made me more furious.

"Why did you kill my friend Berry!!!?"

"Why!!!?"

"Why did you do it!!!?" I hollered at this creature as I lunged forward grabbing the bars.

"Don't you hear me I want to know why!?" I asked again as the *Prairie Monster* that I've been chasing for years just sat there staring at me.

"I'm sorry Mr. Black I thought your friend Berry was a cow. I made a mistake, a horrible mistake, and if I could trade places with your friend Berry I would." Mr. Gemstone apologized but I wasn't about to believe it.

"I don't believe you!!!"

"There's no way you could have mistook Berry for a cow!!!"

"Why do you just sit there staring at me like you don't have a care in the world!!!?"

"You deserve to have the same thing happen to you that you did to Berry."

"You monster!!!"

I was vary frustrated and angry at Mr. Gemstone as I stepped back and stared into those glowing red eyes, he didn't scare me anymore.

"Just wait a minute Mr. Black." Mr. Boulder said as he stood up and walked up to me ready to defend his brother.

"It's alright my brother let him be, Mr. Black is right." Mr. Gemstone said trying to smooth things out as he takes responsibility for what he did.

"No he's not right. He doesn't know everything, nobody has told him yet." It seems that Mr. Boulder was starting to get upset with the way I was verbally attacking his brother. So Mr. Boulder told us why.

"My brother went above the ground to try and be normal, and partake in a tradition that would have allowed him the respect he deserves."

"He could smell the fresh liver that your friend had in his pocket and thought that he was a cow."

"You see Mr. Black… my brother is blind!"

Chapter 18

Justice prevails.

With the sheriff, my brothers and friends waiting on me above the ground and with sunrise right around the corner, Mr. Murphy and I down here were finally getting to the truth.

I didn't know whether or not to believe it at first, but I was bound to get the whole story one way or another. This was my chance, and I might not get another one so I wasn't going to leave until I felt I knew everything, and I believed it.

"He has been blind ever since birth."

"He was just trying to be normal." Mr. Boulder explained about his brother as I sat back down.

"If he's blind then how did he know that you were with us when we came down here?" I asked, remembering that Mr. Gemstone was the first one to say anything when we arrived. Then in a polite and calm manner with no apprehension Mr. Gemstone said.

"I can explain that to you Mr. Black if I may."

"I know my brothers smell, he could walk in down here with a group, and I would be able to pick him out. Being blind since birth has enhanced my other senses." Mr. Gemstone appeared to be telling us the truth about his blindness.

I thought to myself as I put my face down and into my cupped hands, with my elbows on my knees while sitting on a bench next to Mr. Murphy.

Oh my God.

All these years, all that anger, and this was truly just a big accident.

Mr. Murphy put his arm around me and asked if I was going to be ok.

"Butch this isn't what I thought it was going to be down here. Are you going to be alright with what you found out about the night that you and Berry were attacked?" Mr. Murphy whispered to me knowing that we had made a huge mistake thinking that these creatures were monsters.

"Mr. Boulder would you go and get King Lava for me please?" I asked Mr. Boulder as he looked over at his brother, not wanting to leave him alone down here with me.

Mr. Boulder was wondering if his brother was going to be ok while he went to get the king. Of course I can't blame him because of the way I treated him and his kind.

"I will go and get King Lava if you will assure me that no harm will come to my brother?" Mr. Boulder wanted to be helpful but didn't want anything to happen to his brother. I can respect the love that they share between each other.

"I give you my word Mr. Boulder." I said as he nodded and then turned and starting walking back down the hallway towards the entrance where we had left King Lava and our two escorts.

"I owe you an apology Mr. Gemstone."

"I was wrong and I was wondering if you would accept my apology and find it in your heart to forgive me?" I said as I walked up to the bars and grabbed one bar with each hand.

"There is no need for an apology Mr. Black, I was wrong thirty-five years ago myself and someone lost their life because of it. I understand and feel your anger." Mr. Gemstone tried to make me feel better about myself.

"Butch what are you going to do now? You know that you need to do the right thing here."

Mr. Murphy was right, I needed to do something, and I just didn't know what I could do. I heard some noises Mr. Murphy and I both looked towards the arched hallway, we could hear talking; it was King Lava and Mr. Boulder coming towards us as they talked between themselves.

"King Lava what can we do to get Mr. Gemstone released? He has already spent too much time in jail and I intend to see him released." I asked a surprise and stunned King Lava. Mr. Boulder began to shed tears of joy. I looked over at Mr. Murphy he had a big smile on his face.

"Butch, I'm so happy for you, you've found forgiveness in your heart and hatred doesn't consume you anymore." Mr. Murphy said to me as he seemed to be happier himself.

"Well King Lava can we get these bars opened and Mr. Gemstone out of there?" I asked again this time I could see King Lava tearing up himself.

"Are you sure Mr. Black? You want him released?"

"I do have the power to pardon the prisoner, but even his own father never pardoned him when he was the king of our people." King Lava was being cautious, after all his standing in their world would be voted on after he leaves office.

"I'm sure that an injustice has been committed upon this person. I was there and I was the only witness to this terrible mistake. I think thirty-five years in jail for a mistake that a youthful blind male made is more than he should have been made to endure."

"What do you think Mr. Murphy?" I asked hoping for and expecting support from Mr. Murphy.

"I think that if they want me to help them out with their cattle feedlot they'll let Mr. Gemstone out and make him my assistant along with his brother." Mr. Murphy came through for me big.

"So be it." Was all King Lava said as he turned and walked up to a small podium and began to write out an executive order to release the prisoner.

"You're going to be freed soon Mr. Gemstone, what are you going to do first?" I asked thinking that he would go and spend time with his family as a free individual.

"I think I would like to go to church and pray for Berry and his family first."

"Then I would like to go and visit my mother and father's grave." Mr. Gemstone was still surprising me. This was not the beast that I had thought about for years and years.

"King Lava is this going to be a problem with the United States government for you and your people?" I didn't want to get anyone in trouble but something had to be done to fix the injustice and cruelty that had been committed here.

"I don't think so Mr. Black your government has had cameras down here monitoring Mr. Gemstone for years. I'm sure that they are watching and listening to us right now." King Lava revealed that the United States government still didn't trust the Sandstone people even though they have had a treaty with them for years. I don't know why that would surprise me the government doesn't trust their own people either.

King Lava picked up a telephone and started talking to someone on the other end. My guess is that it was a direct line to the ones in charge of keeping Mr. Gemstone in jail.

Mr. Murphy and I sat down in the open cell discussing our day together while Mr. Gemstone and his brother stood by each other with bars between them for the last time.

King Lava was busy writing at the podium and talking on the telephone, putting into motion the release of Mr. Gemstone. Things moved fast down here apparently there's not a lot of red tape.

Before long there were several Sandstone people coming down the arched hallway towards us. Two of them were rolling a large cutting torch with them.

I hadn't noticed before but there was no door in the bars. Once Mr. Gemstone was put in he was expected to be there until he died.

The workers cut three bars out using the cutting torch they had brought with them. Mr. Gemstone stepped through the bars a free individual for the first time in almost thirty-five years. Mr. Boulder grabbed his brother and hugged him.

Mr. Murphy and I sat and watched as the other Sandstone people congratulated Mr. Gemstone. It was time for us to go and leave these people to enjoy the moment.

"Are you about ready to go home Mr. Murphy?" I asked in a soft voice as I put my hand on his shoulder and gave him a little squeeze.

"You go ahead Butch. I think that I'm going to stay and help these people with their problems they have with raising cattle. Besides that I have my own assistants now." Mr. Murphy told me as he sat there with a big grin on his face. I believe that he has that feeling of being needed again. Something he hasn't felt since Mrs. Murphy passed away.

"I think you're going to like it down here teaching the Sandstone people how to raise their own cattle Mr. Murphy." I said to Mr. Murphy as I shook hands with him and gave him a hug goodbye. These creatures needed all the help they could get with trying to raise cattle.

"It's time for me to go now Mr. Gemstone, I would like to shake hands with you if I may." I asked as everyone stopped what they were doing and stared at the two us.

Not realizing what I wanted to do Mr. Gemstone stuck both hands out. I grabbed his right hand with my right hand and began to slowly shake it up and down. Mr. Gemstone put his other hand with our two hands and gently squeezed.

We were friends now.

King Lava, Mr. Granite, and Mr. Magma walked with me to the staging area where this tour all began for me; Mr. Webster was waiting for us.

"I hope you have found what you were searching for Mr. Black. I would like to thank you for your kindness and understanding." King Lava said as he departed leaving me there alone with Mr. Webster and my two escorts.

"Are you ready to go back up to the surface now, Mr. Black? Or do you have any questions that didn't get answered?" Mr. Webster asked in a smug and patronizing way.

"Mater of fact Mr. Webster I do."

"Why didn't you or the government just tell me about Mr. Gemstone from the beginning?" I was more then a bit angry with my own government. All these years and they knew and didn't say anything.

"Let's face it Mr. Black you would have never believed us to begin with."

"Besides that we felt that you finally deserved to know the whole story about your friend's death. We just never guessed that you would have agreed to release Mr. Gemstone." Mr. Webster was right I wouldn't have believed the government.

"I want to thank Mr. Granite and Mr. Magma for their help. Without their help I wouldn't have been able to understand their world as easy as I did. They are a true asset to their people and should be commended." I said to Mr. Webster as I turned to shake hands with the two of them.

I started walking back up the stairs that I had walked down with Mr. Murphy and Mr. Webster hours earlier.

My two escorts were right behind me. I could see some light at the top of the stairs, it was almost sunrise.

I noticed that Mr. Granite and Mr. Magma hung back a few steps as we got closer to the top. As I stepped up and out of the hole that lead down to the Sandstone people's world, one of my escorts pulled the big rock back over the hole. It happened so quickly I didn't even see which one did it.

"Are you alright Butch?" Sheriff Wells hollered out as he came running up to me.

"I'm alright and Mr. Murphy is alright too, he has decided to stay behind and teach the Sandstone people." I told the sheriff as everyone else came walking up to us.

"Hey brother, you doing ok?" My brother Leon asked.

"I'm doing just fine."

"Why are all of you here anyway?" I asked as I looked around at all my friends and brothers.

"You can thank this tin star here." My brother Roger said as he pointed at Pete.

"I want to thank everybody for coming out on my behalf, but I'm ok and you all can go home now. Thanks I owe you one"

I was a little embarrassed that all these people had been called out on my account.

As everybody started walking away I told them that I would explain everything to them when I had a chance.

I told my brothers that I was tired and I needed some sleep. We hugged and they let it go for now, knowing that I had some explaining to do later.

"Come on Butch Mrs. Decker is waiting for you in Deputy Wallace's patrol cruiser."

"I think that she would like to see and talk to you before you go anywhere." Sheriff Wells explained as we started walking through the pasture towards the patrol cruiser with Deputy Wallace following behind us.

"I hate to be the one to tell you Pete, but that's not Mrs. Decker." I said to the sheriff as we walked closer to the car and I could see Special Agent Cook sitting in the front seat.

"Deputy Wallace." Pete said as Frank walked faster to catch up with us and take a look at who was sitting in his patrol cruiser. Frank was obviously just as surprised as we were to see Special Agent Cook sitting in his patrol cruiser.

"I don't know what happened to Mrs. Decker, Sheriff when I left my patrol cruiser she was sitting on the passenger side with the doors locked." Deputy Wallace explained to Pete just as Special Agent Cook was stepping out of Deputy Wallace's patrol cruiser.

"Good morning gentlemen."

"Did you find everything that you were looking for Mr. Black?" Special Agent Cook asked knowing very well what happened down in the Sandstone people's world.

"Where is Mrs. Decker? What have you done with her?" Pete asked Special Agent Cook as we stopped in front of the patrol cruiser. Pete reached behind his back and pulled out a pair of handcuffs from a small pouch on his belt.

"Relax, she's just fine."

"We felt that since Mr. Black was going to get the whole story about what happened to his friend Berry, and to what happened to him. It was only fair that Mrs. Decker should get to hear what happened to her son herself."

"So we asked if she would like to watch and listen on a monitor that we had set up in one of our remote locations. She took us up on our offer, and we treated her with the utmost respect."

"When Mr. Black was confronting his monster from the past, Mrs. Decker was watching and listening to everything he said and did." Special Agent Cook explained to us just as he turned towards a black S.U.V. coming down the dirt road.

"Well gentlemen have a nice life; I'll be leaving Hicksville now, here comes my ride."

"By the way Sheriff, about that little stunt you pulled out in the pasture with all those hillbilly's. You and I aren't through with that one yet." Special Agent Cook wasn't going to forget about being made a fool of.

"Hillbilly's?"

"What hillbilly's?" I asked as Special Agent Cook stepped into his government issued S.U.V. and road away.

"He's talking about your brother's and your friends." Sheriff Wells said with a big grin.

"Well that just goes to show you how much he knows. They're not hillbilly's there rednecks."

"Do you see any hills around here? This is Kansas, we're as flat as flat can be. On a good day you can see all the way to your home town of Chicago." I said to Pete as we watched the government's S.U.V. with Special Agent Cook in it drive out of sight.

"Deputy Wallace you can call it quits and go home now. By the way, you did an outstanding job last night I was proud of you."

"Go ahead and take tonight off Deputy Wallace you deserve it." Sheriff Wells told Frank and then stuck his hand out to shake hands with him.

"Thanks Sheriff I appreciate that very much."

"You can always count on me Sheriff." Frank told Pete as they were shaking hands. Frank wasn't use to the sheriff complimenting him, but he deserved it tonight.

"Thanks Frank I appreciated your help too, I couldn't have done it tonight without you." I said to Deputy Wallace as I shook hands with him.

"I guess I'll see you in a couple of days Sheriff." Frank said and then got into his patrol cruiser; hi-hatted me, backed out of the driveway and slowly drove away.

"That was nice of you to give Frank the night off tonight. He can be a handful from time to time but he means well." I was telling Pete as we got into his patrol cruiser.

"That was nothing. Tonight is Deputy Wallace's night off anyway." Pet said as we both started laughing.

Pete backed out of the driveway and started heading towards my house. I was tired, very tired and I wanted to go home and see my family, but there was something I had to do first. Something I had to do before I did anything else.

"Pete could you drive me to the cemetery please?"

"There's something I need to say to a friend there, and I need to take care of it this morning before I go home." I was tired and I needed rest, but Berry had to come first. I needed to explain myself and my actions to my best friend.

"Are you sure you want to do this now? Can't it wait until tomorrow?" Pete asked knowing that I was exhausted and needed to sleep.

"I need to take care of this now Pete it's important to me." I just felt the overwhelming need to go to Berry's grave and explain things to him. I tried to not let him down, I really did try I hope he will forgive me.

"Ok Butch you win I'll take you to the cemetery." Pete knew deep down in his heart that this needed to be taken care of first. It was a matter of respect and of friendship. I'm afraid that I might have let Berry down.

When we pulled into the cemetery I instructed Pete where to go, and I asked him to wait for me in the car while I talk to my friend.

Pete slowly came to a stop about thirty yards from Berry's grave. I got out of his patrol cruiser and walked over to Berry's grave. I took my hat off and knelt down beside his grave.

I really didn't know where to start. Should I start with Mr. Murphy's dead cow from yesterday? Maybe I should start with Special Agent Cook and his attempts to stop me. No I think the best place to start would be when Mr. Murphy and I went down into the Sandstone people's world.

It took me about twenty minutes or so to explain what happened and for me to ask for forgiveness.

"I'm sorry old friend if I've disappointed you." I whispered and then stood up and put my hat back on.

I could see someone in the distance walking across the cemetery towards me.

As they got closer and closer I could see it was an elderly woman. She walked to within about twenty yards and stopped. She raised a veil that she had hanging down from her hat.

It was Mrs. Decker.

I couldn't hear what she said but I could read her lips.

"Thank you."

I stood there in the morning light and watched her turn and walk away as a tear rolled down my right cheek.